MOTHERS and Daughters

MINNA HOWARD has had
an exciting career in fashion
journalism and now writes
full time, whilst enjoying
time with her grandsons and
working as an occasional
Film and TV extra. She lives
in London and is herself a
glamorous Granny.

Also by Minna Howard

A Winter Affair
Second Chances

MOTHERS and Daughters

Minna HOWARD

First published as an ebook in 2016 by Aria,
an imprint of Head of Zeus, Ltd.

First published in print in the UK in 2017 by Aria.

9 7 5 3 1 2 4 6 8

A catalogue record for this book is available from
the British Library.

ISBN (PB): 9781788541015
ISBN (E): 9781784975852

Typeset by Divaddict Publishing Solutions Ltd.

Printed and bound by CPI Group (UK) Ltd,
Croydon, CR0 4YY

Head of Zeus Ltd
First Floor East
5–8 Hardwick Street
London EC1R 4RG

WWW.HEADOFZEUS.COM

For my daughter Lydia with much love.
(It's not about you!)

Chapter 1

'No... Evie, you're pregnant?' Alice sank down on the sofa, staring in dismay at her younger daughter. This was a bad joke, it couldn't be happening, not just now. 'You... you never said you were seeing anyone,' she said weakly, imagining some careless young man barely out of uni, the same age as Evie, with little hope of giving the child a decent start in life.

'But you're going to be a granny, Mum,' Evie said, as if awarding her a prize.

'I don't want to be a granny, nana... whatever... like this Evie, and just when you've got that wonderful commission for your drawings.' Alice was near to tears now, tears of panic at having to deal with this without the support of her beloved husband.

'You'll be such a glamorous granny, a glammy granny.' Evie, who'd tossed out her bombshell almost as an after-thought as she was leaving the room, appeared to mistake her mother's reaction as the fear of being thought old, jumping too soon into the world of cardies and slippers. She frowned, her mouth set in that sulky way she had when thwarted. 'It's no big deal today, people do have sex before marriage you know, Mum, and sex makes babies.'

'Not if you're careful,' Alice snapped, annoyed by Evie's apparent lack of responsibility in this serious situation that had poleaxed her. 'So... how old is the father, has he a job, is he going to stand by you, by the child you are both expecting together?'

Evie now appeared troubled, her eyes, a moment ago so defiant, now stared at the floor. She chewed her thumbnail, a habit she had when stressed, her body sagged, all her cocky energy gone. 'It's Nick's,' she whispered.

'Oh Evie... you don't... you can't mean Nick Ebury?' That was surely the worst. Nick Ebury, the village roué and a married man. 'That *is* wrong.' Alice struggled to curb the fury that threatened to splash out like acid over both of them, causing even more damage to their fragile state. How could Evie have been so stupid, so careless? Now she wished that it had been a young man, someone who loved her, would do his best to support her and their child. Not Nick...

Alice believed in fidelity in marriage – though she accepted she'd been lucky in hers, and besides, she liked Freya, Nick's long-suffering wife, and counted her as a friend.

'You're so old-fashioned.' Evie fired up again. 'It's how life is today,' she went on with a flounce. She was good at flouncing, having perfected the art of it. She was pretty too, but none of that was an excuse for becoming so intimate with Nick, the bon viveur and serial seducer, suspected father of goodness knows how many other children scattered round the district.

'But that doesn't make it right, Evie, think how much its going to hurt Freya and their children. You should have thought of them before you jumped into bed with Nick. It's not as if you're a gauche teenager, you're twenty-two, old enough to know better.' It was a struggle to curb her anger, it was just as well Nick wasn't here or she'd be put away for murder, or for assault for castration at least.

If only Julian, her beloved husband and Evie's father, were here. The now familiar clamp of grief squeezed hard. He'd have dealt with this crisis, he wouldn't have approved of it either, but he'd be there beside her, solid and wise. He'd been eighteen years older than her and he couldn't help dying, he'd done everything he could to stay well, but he'd inherited his heart condition from his father and grandfather before him and even modern medicine couldn't save him in the end. It was almost two years now since they'd lost him and she'd never stopped missing him with a pain that was sometimes physical in its intensity, though to her surprise and relief, her grief had become easier recently... until now, with the arrival of this catastrophe.

Her grief at losing Julian clung to her, clawing at her like a monstrous insect. It seemed that in about seven months time she'd be granny to a child with multiple half-brothers and sisters. Oh Julian, she cried inwardly, however will I cope without you? She wanted a wedding with Evie beautiful in a white dress and a loving man waiting for her at the altar, was that too much to ask?

It seemed that it was. Evie, now in a sulk, had returned to their 'weekend' cottage in Suffolk. Julian bought it when the girls were little and they'd spent many happy times there, and now Evie was living there on her own. She'd come to London to see her editor and drop in to the house in Fulham to see her mother to break her devastating news.

Alice had been so proud of Evie. She'd recently got a commission from a top publisher to illustrate a series of children's books and she'd announced a few months ago that she wanted to make her home in Suffolk, in their weekend cottage, as she found the open space and peace of the countryside more inspiring to work in.

Alice thought she'd understood her decision at the time, suspecting that Evie couldn't handle her mother's grief as well as her own, and in fact at first Alice found she preferred to be left alone to come to terms with Julian's death and not have to try and 'be happy' for both her daughters' sakes. Now she was beginning to enjoy having the house to herself, though she was rarely alone for long as friends and the girls often visited. But she wished now that Evie had stayed in London instead of escaping to the country and being seduced by an amorous and irresponsible Nick on the prowl.

Evie had left her in a furious mood, some of it no doubt fear of the mess she'd got herself into. She'd flounced out before either of them could calm down and discuss the pregnancy rationally. Alice closed her mind to images of her daughter lying mangled in the wreck of a car crash on the motorway on her way back to Suffolk. Evie did what she wanted, always had. She remembered the angelic child grabbing toys from Laura, her older sister, chanting, 'mine, mine'. Had she told Laura she was soon to be an aunt to this unexpected child? Alice hadn't time to ring her now and anyway Laura wouldn't want to be disturbed at work. She'd ring her this evening; better to talk than to text.

It was a relief she was seeing Julian's Aunt Cecily today, you could talk about anything with her, she was unshockable, and although old and infirm, her mind was as sharp as ever and the closest older person Alice had in her life now that her own parents were gone.

Alice left her house in the early afternoon. She'd lived here, in a small street of white-painted Victorian Houses, off the New King's Road, all her married life. The house had belonged to Julian's mother who had given it to them – or rather swapped it with Julian's flat – as a wedding present, as she wanted to downsize and, by selling his flat, found something that suited her better.

Alice passed the coffee bar on the corner, waved to Gail, who was clearing the tables, and walked up past the Green. A group of small children from the local nursery were running round laughing, being chased by their carers. Barring accidents, next year there would be Evie's child. The thought sat heavily in her, and yet, as she saw the children's simple joy in life and their eager faces, her heart stirred. But who would have the time to give this coming child the love and care it deserved?

She passed the Tube station and went on up to the Fulham Road to take the 414 bus to Marble Arch and Cecily's flat. When the bus came she sat upstairs. She'd bought a suspense novel with her that she'd been longing to finish, but now, with her mind so agitated, she couldn't concentrate, and instead of reading she stared out of the window at the passing streets. It was the tail end of March and her glimpse into the enclosed gardens from her high perch, showed them stirring after the long winter with splashes of golden daffodils and the intense blue, soft pink or gleaming white of hyacinths.

Cecily still lived in the flat that once belonged to her parents. She'd never married; her two fiancés, both fighter pilots, had been killed in the war and she'd never found anyone she loved more.

'Safety in numbers,' she told Alice soon after she'd first met her as a young bride deliriously in love with Julian. 'I have a collection of lovers in various parts of the world to choose from, so I'm never disappointed or bored.'

Alice, much to Cecily's delight, had struggled to hide her shock. Surely, she'd thought then, with the arrogance of youth, no one over about forty – she didn't count Julian in this – had a sex life? But Alice had soon come to love Julian's irrepressible aunt.

As the bus trundled up the Fulham Road, past the cinema and the Brompton Hospital where they'd tried so hard to save Julian, she thought of him. She'd got used to the pain of missing him, it sat there like a tight garment sometimes barely felt, at others almost suffocating her. She often chatted to him in her mind, saving up things to make him laugh as she had when he was alive. If only one knew if the dead were still somewhere, hovering about between worlds, able to catch the thoughts of those they'd left behind. She wanted there to be a 'Heaven' to meet up again with all those she'd loved, her parents, grandparents, friends and Julian. Julian used to tease her when she said this, 'What about the people you don't like. How will you avoid them?'

'What shall I do about Evie?' she asked him silently now as the bus swung down Sumner Place towards South Kensington Tube station. 'Should I confront Nick, and whatever can I say to Freya? As you know he's years older than Evie and married, to such a special wife. What could be worse, except perhaps a serial killer? Please, darling, wherever you are, tell me what to do?'

She scrabbled for her handkerchief and blew her nose, yearning for the solid, comforting bulk of him, the way he held her close, both arms tight round her, making her feel secure, able to face anything with him by her side. For a few months after his death she'd still felt him there, could recall every feature of him, even the scent of him, but gradually he'd slipped further and further away until even the sound of his voice no longer echoed in her mind.

He'd been a cautious man, which sometimes irritated her. But he was a courageous man in many ways and a wonderful, amusing companion, enjoying the arts and travelling and being with friends. He was a stalwart prop in the dramas of life but had never seen the need to throw himself off a mountaintop attached to a kite, or dive deep to the bottom of the sea. Skiing on a well-kept piste, sailing in safe waters and riding a sleepy old horse was as daring as he got, but, as friends remarked, if that was his only fault she was lucky indeed.

Alice got off the bus at Marble Arch and crossed the few streets to Cecily's flat. It was in a large, solid building, close to the Edgware Road. Each room was spacious with high ceilings and deemed 'unmodernised' by developers who often ripped out all the good features and charged a fortune for a series of characterless boxes squeezed into elegant, old buildings. She walked up to the first floor and rang the bell. The door opened and Kalinda, an Asian woman of indeterminable age, welcomed her.

'She is looking forward to seeing you,' she said, taking Alice's coat.

Kalinda had been here for as long as Alice had known Cecily. She knew little about her except that Cecily rescued her from a violent marriage, finding her terrified in some refuge in the North of England. She'd given her a home and a life and, in exchange, Kalinda loved her and, now Cecily was old and frail, cared for her devotedly.

'My dear, how good to see you.' Cecily greeted her as she went into the living room. Alice bent over to kiss her soft, powdered cheek. 'I hope you've some amusing gossip to tell me, I'm so bored of myself.' She laughed, she was never one to be gloomy and Alice felt guilty that she had nothing amusing to say, only to tell her of Evie's dreadful dilemma.

'Not really.' Alice sat down on the sofa beside her. The

room was crammed with pictures and antique furniture that was once in a beautiful Queen Anne house in the country where Cecily had been brought up, but had long since been sold. There were phalanxes of photographs on almost every surface, men in uniform with the glamour of film stars, some of Cecily as a young woman getting out of a Spitfire and one of a huge bomber with Cecily, having just landed it, laughing beside it, pictures of people and places long gone. It was difficult to imagine those times now, to imagine that this old, still elegant lady, her hands clawed by arthritis, her hair pure white, was once that bright young woman who'd ferried Spitfires and bombers across Britain, often without instruments, in fog and sometimes under fire, with the ease of driving a bus.

'There must be something, how are the girls?' Cecily examined Alice gravely with her faded eyes.

Alice felt the tremble of tears. She swallowed; Cecily did not care for weakness in herself or anyone else. 'I saw Evie today, she…' she paused.

'She's either pregnant or run off or about to with some man you don't like, and probably belonging to someone else,' Cecily filled in the gap.

Despite her concern, Alice laughed. 'You're right, how did you know?' Had Evie already told her? Both her daughters loved visiting Cecily and listening to her war memories, and indeed stories of her romances.

'I guessed, she's such a pretty girl and a little reckless, just like you might have been if you hadn't married dear, dependable Julian.' Cecily smiled. 'I loved my nephew very much and am still annoyed that he died so young, though at least he had a life, not like my two loves.' Her eyes glazed over a moment as she remembered her young pilots who would be forever young while she had grown so old. 'So,' she shook off the memories, 'what has she done?'

'There's a man in Suffolk, I don't think you met him when you used to come and stay, but you know the sort who never grow up and possess more charm and sexual allure than they deserve. He's got a lovely wife, she's a potter and turns a blind eye to his sexual shenanigans, he's a joke really, but Evie's fallen for him and now she's having his baby, to add to the others strewn around the district.'

'Oh dear, and she *is* having it?' Cecily looked concerned.

'Yes, she's vague about dates. The affair's been going on for some time, since she moved in there, and well, termination doesn't seem right somehow.'

'No, not if the child's wanted and will be loved, for you will love it, you know you will, Alice. And it is a life...' She glanced again at her photographs of people whose lives had been cut short. 'But I'm sorry for his wife having a sexually incontinent husband, but it sounds like she puts up with it. Sometimes it's better to ignore it if the rest of the marriage is workable than go through an expensive divorce and family break-up.'

'So far, Freya's put up with it. She's chucked him out a few times but she always takes him back. They have children together and amazingly they're a close family. But I feel so bad that *my* daughter has got involved with him and is having his child.'

'Very careless of her, but you know, my dear, she's probably missing her father, and if this man is older, kinder than some of the young men she's met, she may have been attracted to him, though foolish to end up with a baby, but there it is. Perhaps she should come back to London, bring the child up away from the gossip and his wife and children's feelings.'

'I don't know what to do about it. Julian would have been

9

such a support over this, though he wouldn't approve of Nick as the father of his grandchild.' It was hard enough to accept that they were going to be grandparents let alone that she was left to shoulder the burden alone.

Alice went on. 'Nick runs a garden centre and Julian used to say all those budding, shooting plants must have turned up the switch to his fertility. He's a joke, people tease him about which plant food he's on to make him so randy.'

'No,' Cecily said, 'Julian would not be happy about a man like this Nick fathering his beloved daughter's child.' She sighed, took a sip of tea, before saying, 'so just as Evie got this wonderful commission for her drawing, she gets pregnant. She'll be alone with this child and maybe expect too much from you, so don't fall for that, Alice.' She wagged one of her knotted fingers at her. 'Don't allow yourself to be locked away in the nursery again. It may be tempting, but you have your own life to lead and I sense there's a lot of things you want to do while you still can.'

'You're right. I'm sure I'll love the child when it's born, but it's Evie's child and she must bear the brunt of it.' Alice felt a dart of sympathy for Evie who, no doubt, imagined this baby would lie happily in the sun while she illustrated her books and would be no trouble at all. She'd probably felt the same when she was expecting Laura. She was twenty-one then, a year younger than Evie was now. But not until someone had their first child did they know how much they dominated their lives and how much commitment was needed. That was why two loving parents were better than one, but it was no good telling Evie that. Perhaps she hoped Nick would play a part in the child's upbringing, even leave Freya and move into the cottage with her. If she thought that, she'd be disappointed.

'So what is Laura's reaction to this?' Cecily asked her. 'What does she think of being propelled into being an aunt?'

'I don't know. I haven't discussed it with her yet. I'm going to ring her tonight when she's home. I don't know if Evie has told her. They are fond of each other but they can grate on each other too, having such different temperaments. Laura is more like Julian, sensible and solid.' Alice smiled, 'That makes her sound dull and I don't mean to because she's not, but you can rely on her, and that's not because she's two years older than Evie, you always could rely on her like you could on Julian.'

Cecily smiled, patted her hand, 'Yes, you could rely on him and I've always thought Laura took after him. But even though your girls are in their early twenties, they are still quite young and have lost their beloved father so it's bound to have an effect on them, though perhaps Evie's reaction is a bit extreme. It will work out somehow, you'll see.'

Alice left Cecily feeling happier, more positive. She had that effect on her, her love of life still burning bright. She'd lived through a war, with many of her young friends and the two men she'd loved killed or severely injured, and yet she'd gone on and lived a good, an exciting life, as a photographer. She'd travelled the world until now, in her nineties, her body was slowing down, though she kept her mind active playing bridge, reading and listening to intelligent programmes.

Alice scolded herself, she was only in her mid-forties, and hopefully had plenty of life left in her yet, but it was high time that instead of thinking about everyone else, she got on with some of the things she wanted to do that Julian disapproved of, or perhaps disapproved was the wrong word, rather *not encouraged* her to do.

'I wish you were here, darling, but as you're not, you're not to mind if I do some exciting things – paragliding, overnight skiing experiences, sleeping in the mountains – be more like Cecily really, though I'll never be as brave as she was.'

She walked down Park Lane; a haze of late sun lingered in the air. She loved the elegant houses there and wondered how many were still lived in in their entirety and had not been turned into offices or flats. Perhaps, because she and Cecily had talked about Julian she felt him close to her now as if he'd be at home with her this evening, and she'd cook dinner and he'd open a bottle of wine, and they'd laugh together about Cecily's stories of her life and her lovers.

She passed the war memorial to the animals that had given their lives in the war, and went on down Park Lane still holding Julian's memory to her. She reached a car showroom, the cars gleaming like huge beasts behind the glass. She stopped and stared at them, feeling Julian slipping away from her, but instead of the familiar, bleak emptiness, she had a sudden memory of being in such a glamorous car as that dark blue sports car, speeding down the road, the wind whipping back her hair and a feeling of exhilaration surging through her. Who had she been with? Julian would never have driven so fast!

Then she remembered it was Frank. Frank Trevelyan.

Though a few years younger than Julian, he was one of his closest friends and what her mother called 'wild'. Always off somewhere, skiing the valleys, sailing in round-the-world boat races, piloting a plane to obscure islands. Soon after her marriage he'd gone to live in France and she didn't see much of him, though he kept in touch with Julian and was Laura's godfather. He hadn't come to the funeral, being the other side of the world and unable to get back in time, but he'd written her a wonderful letter that made her cry just thinking of it.

She studied the cars in the showroom still thinking of that drive with Frank, the throb of the engine charging forward like a powerful animal and that sense of freedom. She laughed, ah, youth and the tricks the mind played. You couldn't drive at those speeds on the roads today without breaking the law.

A Lexus convertible the colour of cranberries stood seductively before her. She imagined the power coiled taut within its shining skin, poised to spring into life. A sleek young man, his face leaden with arrogant boredom stared at her through the window, she felt suddenly reckless and before she knew it she'd pushed open the heavy glass door and gone inside.

'Can I help you, Madame?' The man glided across the floor like an old-fashioned matinee idol. For a second she sensed Julian urging caution but she ignored it, something stronger got hold of her, pushing her on.

'I'm thinking of buying a Lexus convertible,' she heard herself saying, almost giggling at the foolishness of it.

A look of surprise flitted across the matinee idol's face, as well it might, but she pressed on.

'It's between this and a Bristol,' she said, remembering that that was the car she'd been in with Frank. She peered inside the Lexus and then smiling directly at the sales man, she said, 'I wonder, is it possible to have a test drive?'

The minute she said it she cursed herself for being such a fool, she may look younger than forty-six, but not that much younger. She imagined the matinee idol sitting her down in a quiet place with a cup of sweet tea while explaining such a thing was not possible; it was surely against health and safety. But to her amazement he agreed, showing her to a comfortable leather chair while he made arrangements and she sat there among all that glittering metal wondering what on earth had possessed her.

A short while ago she'd felt anxious and depressed at Evie's thoughtless predicament, which, like it or not, would involve her, make her the granny she wasn't yet ready to be – not in such circumstances – but the sight of these cars and thinking of Frank had turned her into this madwoman, filling her with energy, her lost youth bubbling in her like champagne.

The matinee idol, whose name was Nigel, brought the car onto the road and opened the passenger door for her to get in. He then got into the driver's seat and eased the car out into the traffic. Alice guessed he'd agreed to a test drive so that he could have a spin in it himself. As the engine sprang into life and he sped down the road 'to go somewhere less busy', her spirits soared as they had all those years ago with Frank. In fact, she'd have been perfectly happy to let Nigel drive her where he would, but the moment came when they were 'somewhere less busy' and he offered her the wheel.

The power of the engine thrilled her, reminding her of an excitable horse raring to go, but she kept it in check. They could hardly go very fast with all the traffic, but Alice felt so vibrant, as if she'd been swimming through pea soup all these months, getting nowhere.

They drove down some streets off the Bayswater Road and when the time came to return to the showroom she drove past Marble Arch, wishing Cecily could see her from her window, then on down Park Lane. The traffic snarled up here and whilst they were sat idling just outside the

Dorchester she heard someone call out her name.

'Alice, is that really you? Whatever are you doing in that car?' And there were her two friends, Margot Benson and Petra Lindsay, staring at her with amazed envy.

She smiled and waved to them both before roaring up the road as the space suddenly opened up before her.

When they reached the showroom; she parked the car carefully and turned off the engine, feeling rather flat.

'Have you ever done paragliding?' she asked Nigel, as he opened the door for her.

He gave her a strange look. 'No, I haven't, have you?'

'I'm going to do it soon.' She wondered what he'd think if he knew she was also soon to be a granny. Perhaps he'd think she should be sitting cosy somewhere, baking scones or knitting.

She got out of the car reluctantly. 'Thank you so much, I really enjoyed that.' She smiled at him and before he could launch into his selling spiel, she walked away, leaving him by the car and jumped into a taxi that had just unloaded a passenger.

'Just drop me by the bus stop at Hyde Park Corner, please,' she said, not looking back at the car showroom.

The bus came almost at once after the taxi had dropped her, and she got on and she'd just settled herself in her seat, when her mobile rang. It was Margot.

'Alice, whatever were you doing in that car with that gorgeous young man?'

She laughed and explained, though she didn't mention Frank, remembering now how all her girl friends lusted after him. She wanted to tell Margot about Evie, how she was going to be a *grandmother* – it sounded so old and staid – but Margot had to go and Alice was left feeling overwhelmed with the problem of welcoming and caring for a child born in such circumstances.

A few moments ago she'd been filled with such energy, eager to do more daring and exciting things in her life. She was not ready to be a granny yet.

Chapter 2

Alice was relieved when Evie rang to say she'd arrived home safely. It was something she'd taken to doing more frequently, a clutch of the security blanket of a family now fragmented by Julian's demise. She had wondered if Evie would contact her this time after her fury over her reaction to the mess she'd got herself into by succumbing to the notorious Nick.

'Will you be up again soon, darling?' Alice asked lightly, treating Evie like a hand grenade primed to go off at any moment. Evie was used to being bathed in praise for her beautiful artwork, her looks and her generally sunny nature – provided she got her own way – how was she going to cope with the condemnation of having Nick's baby, let alone looking after it and keeping up with her work?

'Not for about a month, got all these drawings to do, but you might come down.' She heard the need in Evie's voice and her heart went out to her, but she must remember Cecily's advice and not allow herself to be lured into taking on the bulk of the childcare.

'I will if I can, but I've got a lot on,' she said, knowing that she hadn't, at least not anything she couldn't change or postpone, but she was angry and disappointed with Evie and fearful of saying something about the situation that might fragment their relationship. Evie was too streetwise to have been seduced unknowingly by Nick. She wasn't short of admirers either, being often surrounded by charming young men who were not already committed to somebody else.

'Like what?' Evie exclaimed. 'I mean it's not as if you have a full-time job or anything now your decorating thing with Margot has folded.'

'It hasn't exactly folded; orders are just quite sparse at the moment. I have a life, Evie, I want to see my friends and…' She didn't add anything about taking up new challenges.

'I just feel so sick and…'

'I know, darling, pregnancy is difficult for a while, but you made the choice to have…' She was going to say 'have sex' but it sounded so basic, like going to the loo, she went on, 'To go to bed with Nick without taking proper precautions, not that you should have been in bed with him anyway.'

'You don't understand, Mum, I couldn't help it, he is so attractive and persuasive, and he loves me.'

Why did each generation think that they'd been the ones to discover the all-consuming sexual desire for someone, often confusing it for love?

'What does Freya, *his wife*, think?' she said briskly.

'She doesn't know yet. Nick says it's best to wait three months to make sure the pregnancy sticks. He didn't want me to tell you until then, but as I was with you and might not see you for another few weeks I thought I should tell you.' Evie sounded near tears.

It was not surprising that Nick was such a coward, perhaps this time Freya really would chuck him out for good, but Alice didn't want him as a son-in-law. He was like an incontinent rabbit, though admittedly a very attractive one.

'Does she know you're having an affair with him? News

like that usually travels fast, especially in the country,' Alice said.

'No, we're very careful. He loves me,' Evie said again.

'That's not a good enough reason to sleep with another woman's husband, and anyway, I would say the only person Nick truly loves is himself,' Alice said, exasperated by it all.

'I'll ring off now as I'm tired and I expect you are after your busy day and long drive… Take care of yourself, darling, love you.' She slumped back on the sofa closing her eyes, overcome by a wave of panic.

The telephone rang again and for a nanosecond she thought it was Julian ringing between meetings, or from a hotel while on a business trip, until remembering wherever he was he was beyond communication. It was probably Evie again, needing reassurance. She picked it up, her heart heavy, hoping it was one of her friends who'd cheer her up. It was Laura, her elder daughter.

'Hi Mum, would it be OK if I bring someone over for Sunday lunch?'

Laura had a special way of asking for something if she knew her parents might not like it. Alice scolded herself for jumping to conclusions. Laura's main fault – if fault it was – was 'feeling sorry for people', a kind trait in itself but one which had caused her problems over the years. She'd much rather have Laura to herself for lunch so she could discuss Evie's predicament with her, but she said as cheerfully as she could 'I'd love to see you, darling and who are you bringing?'

Laura went on as if she hadn't heard her. 'Evie's gone back hasn't she? She's told me about the baby, pretty stupid of her to sleep with Nick anyway, let alone get pregnant,' Laura said, as if her sister's predicament was no worse than dying her hair the wrong colour or having a tattoo she'd live to regret.

'So,' she went on before Alice could respond, 'Evie won't be here, so you can really concentrate on *my* news.'

'News?' Alice's heart dipped, her intuition was right. This lunch guest was obviously not one of Laura's usual friends. She didn't want any more challenges – emotional ones anyway – how could she get out of having this 'someone' to lunch? Why did she always say yes when she meant no?

Laura ignored her question, 'So Sunday's OK, or Saturday if you'd rather.'

As if Laura could see her, Alice picked up her diary and opened it at the weekend; both days were blank. For a few months after Julian's death she had been inundated with invitations and, kindly meant though they were, she found it so hard sitting there on her own while others, still in couples, talked of the plans they'd made together. She was now getting used to making plans on her own.

She'd vaguely thought she'd ring a couple of friends and go to a film and supper this weekend but she hadn't got round to it yet. There were three more days to go after all, but now she wouldn't do it, she'd have Laura and her *friend* to lunch instead.

'Sunday's fine, are you bringing someone special?' It was a minefield asking Laura such a question. Unlike her younger sister, she'd never had many boyfriends, and why should this be a boyfriend? It could be a woman... It could be... no, she wasn't gay, was she? Not that it would matter, it just hadn't crossed her mind. But why hadn't Laura said this person's name? 'Someone' sounded... sinister? Oh, it was so much easier to question friends about their lives than her daughters, especially Laura with her tendency to read things into them that were not intended. 'So who is your friend?'

'Douglas Greenwood,' Laura said.

Alice tried to think of the names of all Laura's friends that had trooped through the house since her childhood; she couldn't remember a Douglas.

'I've had a difficult day with Evie breaking her news, so I feel a bit senile, darling. I can't remember if I've met him before,' she said blithely, thinking it better to admit to it now than cause embarrassment when he arrived.

'You haven't and he's asked me to marry him,' Laura finished in a rush.

'Marry? But...' What a day for shocks. Perhaps Laura was winding her up, pretending to outdo Evie. Laura usually went on endlessly about the few men she fancied. Her father used to wonder if she really was having a relationship with them or was just 'worshipping them from afar', as he put it, but she'd never mentioned Douglas.

'Some people do still marry these days, Mum,' Laura said acidly. 'I thought you'd be pleased, especially after Evie telling you she's having a baby with an old man who can't take his own marriage seriously.'

Alice disregarded this jibe. The two girls did care for each other, had been a wonderful support these last months, but they also grated on each other's nerves and juggled with petty jealousies. Evie, always popular with men, had messed up big time now, but if Laura had found the man of her dreams, Alice should be relieved and pleased for her, even if she hadn't heard of him before.

'I just didn't know you were with anyone serious, darling. I'd love to meet him. We'll have something special.' She'd splash out and get a good joint of beef, then, knowing the food fads of many of the young, she said, 'He's not a vegetarian is he, darling?'

'No, why should he be?' Laura sounded offended as if Alice had suggested he was a cannibal.

'Just checking. I don't want to offer anything that might cause offence. I look forward to seeing you both then, about one.'

'Thanks Mum, and could we have your dark chocolate and orange mousse for pudding, please?'

'Of course.' That was a small, safe request after the bombshell of a coming wedding. Please God *she* wasn't pregnant too.

'And Mum, Margot says she saw you driving a sports car with a young man – that's not like you? Who was he?'

'How do you know it's not like me?' Alice retorted. Not like her? It *was* like her, a person she'd carefully wrapped up and put on one side to please Julian. Now with him gone that person had resurfaced again. If she had to be a granny she'd be a granny who'd do exactly what she felt like.

'I was test-driving a car. He was... the salesman or whatever.'

'Test-driving? Are you going to buy a sports car? I mean... Dad would...'

'Dad's not here any more, darling, and no, I can't afford a new car, especially one like that, but I just felt like driving one.'

'Well we'll see you Sunday, Mum.' There was a small silence before Laura rang off and Alice half expected her eldest daughter to tell her to behave as her children expected her to behave, but Laura said no more.

It would be comforting to talk to Cecily about Laura's surprising news but the old lady would be in bed by now, though she said she barely slept these days. But perhaps Cecily had been right, Evie and now Laura had been so missing their father they'd got involved with unsuitable men, not that she knew if Douglas was unsuitable. But it was odd that this was the first time she'd heard of him.

Laura lived in a bedsit in Battersea and was a legal secretary in a large, well known chambers. She often dropped round for supper and sometimes stayed the night, back in her old bedroom. She'd last stayed three weeks ago, strange she hadn't mentioned Douglas at all, or had she tried and Alice had not picked it up? Well she'd soon meet Douglas; only four more days to go.

*

The table was laid and the lunch almost cooked on Sunday. Alice planned her cooking meticulously, allowing time for Alice and Douglas to be late and have a drink before lunch so the beef should be perfect and have its 'rest' before being carved. She'd roasted potatoes, parsnips and carrots with it and also cooked French beans and made Yorkshire pudding. The dark chocolate mousse flavoured with grated orange rind and Cointreau stood on the side and beside it a green fruit salad, grapes, kiwi, apples and melon. There was also cheese.

She wished they weren't coming now, or rather she wished Laura was coming alone – and Evie, both her girls without this baggage they'd laden on themselves and, by default, her.

She heard the front door open, rasping over the too thick

doormat, and Laura's voice telling Douglas to come in and, pinning a smile on to her face, Alice went into the narrow hall to greet them.

Douglas Greenwood was so nondescript that Alice feared she might fail to recognise him again. She continued to smile, welcoming him in, knowing that Laura was watching her intently to pick up every nuance of her behaviour and would catch any sign of disapproval.

Surreptitiously, Alice studied him for some distinguishing mark that would single him out in a crowd. He was taller than Laura, with broad shoulders and mousy brown hair, grey, green eyes and a square, easily forgettable face. He shook her hand – at least his hand was cool and smooth, she hated wet, limp handshakes. He addressed her as Mrs Garnet; he was well spoken, though his voice had a deadening quality about it that even if he'd cried out 'fire! fire!' or 'murder! murder!' she doubted his tone would generate enough excitement for anyone to take action. However, would they get through a whole lunch together?

Where was that spark that came with love, or at least lust? He was five years older than Laura and seemed so sensible. She knew – from the dysfunctional men some of her friends' daughters had chosen, some, middle aged adolescents who seemed incapable of settling down, or another Nick – that she should be grateful for that.

'I don't know if Laura has told you, Mrs Garnet, but we've known each other quite a time.'

'Do please call me Alice,' she said for the umpteenth time. 'I must say I didn't know that.' Then, seeing him throw Laura a fretful glance, she added quickly, 'I've been a bit scatty since I lost my husband.'

He blinked at her like a wise old owl. 'I'm so sorry about

that, I would have liked to have known him.'

There was a lump in her throat but she ploughed on. 'So, where did you meet?'

'We met through work,' Douglas said.

Laura broke in impatiently. 'Mum, it is not important where we met, we know each other now.'

'But for how long have you known each other, darling?' Alice attempted to throw out a silent warning that as Laura was only in her early twenties, she didn't need to rush into marriage, especially with someone they didn't know. She'd feel differently if she'd chosen the son of one of their friends, someone they'd known since childhood.

Laura ignored her flashing eye signals and said, 'We've known each other on and off for over a year and...'

Douglas then stirred himself. 'I feel very sorry that I can't ask Laura's late father for her hand in marriage,' he said formally, 'but I shall ask for yours instead. I have a good job and a house and...'

'Do you love her? Love each other?' Alice interjected. He reminded her of the Prince of Wales when asked the same question at his engagement saying 'whatever in love means'. She would not have been at all surprised if Douglas had mimicked him.

'Mum...' Laura blazed as if she'd asked something more intimate.

'That goes without saying,' Douglas cut in. 'We are very happy together and my children love her.'

'Children!' Alice burst out in dismay. 'What children?' She turned accusingly to Laura. 'You never said that there were children involved.'

'Mum... I was... going to explain, but you didn't give me... us... a chance.' Laura's jaw was set in the rigid way

25

she had when she was trying to justify herself.

'Mrs Garnet,' Douglas began cautiously, as if fearful that she might erupt and deluge him with molten lava. 'I'll explain about myself and my circumstances.' He paused, sat back in his chair, folding his hands carefully on his lap as if he were about to embark upon a fairy tale.

Alice poured out more wine, gulping at it while thinking of Cecily's advice. Perhaps she'd take a gap year. She'd recently read an article about 'empty nesters' setting off by themselves to explore the world. What if she set off on one of those trips and left her daughters to sort themselves out?

'My marriage went wrong very early on,' Douglas started. 'I hung on for my children's sakes, but now it is over and I have custody of them.'

'How old are they?' Alice could see the picture now. Douglas needed a wife and mother for his children – this was a job offer and, for whatever reason, Laura was about to accept it.

'Eight and six,' Douglas said, 'and they love Laura already. And for you,' he smiled the warmest smile she'd seen from him so far, 'you will have two instant grandchildren and I knew the minute I met you that they will love you.'

But will I love them? Alice thought, poleaxed at the thought of having acquired three surprise grandchildren, in less than a week.

Chapter 3

It must be all that digging and pruning in the open air that made Nick look so good for his age. Alice tried not to look at him as he sprawled elegantly in the cane chair in the garden, basking in the pale spring sun, a slight glaze of sweat on his face from his gardening activities, or perhaps... no, better not to go there. He wore a much worn, but once expensive pink and blue striped shirt, the sleeves rolled up, showing off his tanned arms; his legs too were on show from the knee down in his well-cut shorts. She didn't want him to know she was covetously watching him, but he probably did, he probably expected it.

Alice felt a squeeze of resentment at him being here even though she'd insisted on seeing him while she was in Suffolk. It was Nick's attitude that annoyed her most. He was not the slightest bit contrite for impregnating her daughter and his smug arrogance made her feel that somehow *she* was the one at fault for being so judgemental.

His presence, combined with her anxiety for Evie and the coming child, had spoilt her usual sense of tranquillity at being here in the peace of the countryside after the bustle of London. She loved it here. The house was a typical Suffolk cottage; its thick walls painted a soft yellow, though a tiled roof had long since replaced the thatch. The small garden

27

was mostly given over to flower beds filled with easy-to-care-for plants and a few trees dotted the lawn. She and Julian had planned it carefully so it did not need the likes of Nick to maintain it when no one was here.

Alice hadn't wanted to go to Suffolk so soon after Evie's news, though she did want to discuss Laura's impending marriage with her, and as she was in Suffolk on business it would be churlish not to visit her.

When the girls started full time school, Alice and Margot Benson, an old friend, began a small interior decorating business. It had done quite well at the beginning, before people had the confidence to choose their own colour schemes, but life, changing fashions and various hiccups had slowed it down to half what it used to be. Two unmarried sisters, Edith and Amy, who were both wonderful needlewomen, made the curtains, cushions and bedheads here in Suffolk. She had an order from someone whose house they'd done up before and was now downsizing, so here she was, having arrived with rolls of fabric to pass on to the sisters and staying the night with Evie.

And here was Nick glowing with energy, his blond hair greying beautifully as if the grey streaks were expensive highlights – which perhaps they were. He was long and rangy, his nose rather misshapen – he said from an accident on the 'rugger field' while at school, while others joked that it was from punches from jealous husbands – either could be true. His main attraction was his love of women.

Alice understood this. Many English men she knew – other people's husbands – didn't seem to bother giving their own long-term wives much warm attention, though they often stirred themselves with other people's. It was as if once they'd got a wife they felt they could sink down into cosy apathy with them and seek their fun elsewhere.

Nick overdid it; she'd watched him across the years affecting women like a ray of sunshine, making them glow. They'd gravitate towards him, stand a little taller, put on interesting, even seductive expressions. Even though Julian had been warm and loving to her, Alice too had felt Nick's charm, though she'd ignored it. But this gift of his – or perhaps curse – did not bode well for any woman who expected his undivided attention and commitment, and it made her fear for Evie and the baby.

Nick had arrived in his gardening van on his way back from a new client, who wanted the overgrown garden in the house he'd recently bought turned into an instant paradise.

'They've come from London and bought a country house with his huge bonus, and have no idea how long a garden takes to establish,' Nick said, as if to steer the conversation onto a safe subject.

Evie drifted out into the garden and snuggled into his arms just as she used to with her father, touching Alice's heart as she remembered how close Evie and Julian were. She looked away, finding the sight of Evie in Nick's arms slightly obscene. Cecily was probably right; Evie missed her father but that was no excuse to get so involved with Nick.

'So, Alice, how are you really?' Nick smiled fondly at her. 'Julian was such a charming man and you must miss him dreadfully.'

'I do.' Nick was so direct, but she'd rather that than a sinister silence as if no one wanted to mention the departed and cause pain, when the one left behind could not help but think of them every waking moment.

Nick's voice was soft and smooth, soothing the pain inside her. She tried to ignore it, gear herself up to say what she wanted to say. Julian would have done it perfectly, man to man. She swallowed, took a deep breath. 'You know why I asked to see you. I'm very unhappy about your relationship with Evie and…'

'Mum,' Evie whimpered.

'Alice…' Nick said softly, smiling at her as if she'd somehow missed the joke.

'No, listen.' Her voice sounded sharper than she intended. 'You have a wonderful wife and I can't bear to think how hurt and betrayed she will be over this. If you were my husband I'd have chucked you out long ago.'

'But, Alice, I'm not your husband,' he said gently. 'Freya and I go way back and we have an understanding. She knows I'll never leave her, or stop loving her.'

'You have a very odd way of showing it, seducing other women and worse, having children with them. How do they deal with it? Do they know you are their father and what about your and Freya's children? It must be dreadfully upsetting for them?'

He shrugged as if none of this was his fault. 'But you'll be a granny, and I know you'll be a wonderful one.'

How crass he was, thinking he could flatter her into accepting his selfish behaviour.

'I don't want to be a grandmother this way,' she retorted, ignoring Evie's murderous expression. 'I'd hoped Evie would be married – but not to you – to a loving, decent man her own age who'd put her first, love and care for her and their children, instead of having a sort of timeshare with a man who can't keep his trousers on,' she finished, surprised at her own vehemence.

'I'm sorry you feel like that, Alice,' Nick said defensively, glancing at Evie who'd grabbed his hand, holding tight to it, tethering him down as if her mother's outspokenness would scare him away. 'I won't let her or our child down. We didn't plan it this way but...'

Evie, her expression like a sulky child, snapped, 'Why are you so mean, Mum?'

It was so hard and lonely sitting here taking the brunt of their guilt, but this is how it was going to be, Alice alone dealing with the family dramas, and she'd have to toughen up, get on with it.

'I'm just telling the truth, just as your father would have done, Evie,' she said, as Evie flounced indoors saying she was tired of listening to them and had her drawing to do.

'Have you told Freya?' she challenged Nick when she had gone.

'Not yet, I mean babies don't always stay put do they? Lots of women miscarry before three months.'

'And lots don't, and that's a pretty thoughtless remark to make, Nick, and I hope you haven't said it in front of Evie,' Alice retorted. 'She must be at least three months pregnant now and you must tell Freya straight away. I like her very much and I feel really sorry for her.' Alice was ashamed that *her* daughter was partly responsible for Freya's pain.

She could see it clearly now she was here. Pretty Evie living here alone in their weekend cottage. There were other houses and cottages dotted along the lane, close enough for comfort but not so close as to be spied upon, a perfect place for an illicit love affair. She would have seen Nick about, maybe told him she was here alone while she created her magical illustrations, and he'd come to call and no doubt taken advantage of her grief at losing her father, and worked his considerable charm on her. Alice understood it, might even have fallen for it herself in some lonely moment now Julian had gone.

Nick said defiantly, 'I am going to tell her; I know I behave badly, but I don't desert the women and children I love. Because I do love them,' he said, as if he were confessing to a religious conversion, 'but I love Freya the most and she and the others,' he smiled at Evie, who'd come back into the garden and he held out his hand to her, 'know that.'

Evie bowed her head, hiding her feelings, but she went to him and stood by his side clutching his hand. Alice guessed that she hoped Nick would love her more than anyone else, and perhaps even move in when their baby was born. Cecily's idea of Evie moving back to London with the child, where she wouldn't be tormented by waiting for Nick to call, seemed a good one, but now was not the time to discuss it.

'There's so much psychobabble about raising children these days,' Nick went on. 'Children need love, masses of it. My old dad wasn't one for sitting around at home and I was lucky enough to have a succession of beautiful women spoiling me, hoping that by doing so they'd get closer to Dad.'

'Where was your mother in all this?' Alice asked. Perhaps she'd died and so there might be some slim excuse for Nick's behaviour.

'They realised their marriage was a mistake at once. My mother and I lived happily together in the country when I wasn't at boarding school, and I saw my father often. I didn't know any different. In fact,' he smiled disarmingly, 'the other boys at school envied me. They just had two dull old parents struggling to pay the fees and being strict and difficult.'

Alice was about to remark that he was lucky not to feel abandoned, when she glimpsed a flash of pain under his bravado and guessed that he too had suffered, which perhaps had a lot to do with him not being able to settle down with one woman, however loving she was. She said lamely, exhausted by it all, 'I don't want my daughter and grandchild hurt.'

'No one is going to hurt your daughter. I certainly am not.' Nick unlaced his hand from Evie's and got up, saying he was late for his next appointment, but Alice was not to worry, he'd never let Evie and the baby down.

'Make sure you tell Freya today,' Alice said, moving away when he tried to kiss her goodbye.

Evie was grumpy when he'd left. 'Why did you have to be so rude, Mum? I wouldn't blame him if he never wanted to see you again.'

'He needs to face up to his responsibilities; Dad would have been the same, worse even. I know you and Laura miss him terribly but I wish you hadn't got mixed up with such... well, *unsuitable* men.'

'So you didn't like Douglas, then?' Evie sat down in the place Nick had just left as if clinging to the last traces of him.

'I didn't mean that,' Alice was afraid her displeasure would get back to Laura and cause trouble. 'I just feel that a divorced man with two young, possibly traumatised children and an ex-wife is a lot for anyone to take on and Laura is still young and has no experience with children.'

'I think she's mad taking on someone else's kids,' Evie said, relieved that her older sister – who'd always been so sensible – was now in trouble too. 'Do you think he's only marrying her because she'll be cheaper than a nanny?' she added, watching Alice for her reaction.

The same thought had crossed Alice's mind but she wasn't going to say that to Evie. She worried that perhaps Laura, feeling so lost without her father, was relieved to fall into the arms of such a dependable man as Douglas.

'They seem very fond of each other,' she said lamely.

'Have you met them – the children I mean – I haven't, being stuck here and having all my work to do.'

'No. I've only met Douglas once, at that lunch. He seems…' She racked her brains for some flattering description of him.

'He's deadly dull,' Evie said. 'I've met him a couple of times, but he'll look after her.' Her mouth tightened and Alice thought she might add, 'At least he's marrying her,' but she didn't.

Dull though she thought Douglas was, she felt he could be relied upon and that's what Laura seemed to need now her father had gone, but later, when the pain of his death became easier, would she become bored, wished she'd waited for someone more exciting?

'I wonder what the children are like,' Evie went on. 'I think the older one is all right, but apparently there's something wrong with the younger one, the boy.'

'Something wrong?' Alice's heart dived. So-called 'normal' children, especially someone else's, were hard enough to accommodate in a relationship, but surely so much worse if they had something wrong with them.

After a glass or two of wine, Douglas had opened up a bit more. His ex-wife, Thea, had fallen pregnant with Zara, their daughter, they'd married and tried to make a go of it, even having another baby – which led to a temporary reprieve though it didn't last. They limped along until Thea had been offered a high-powered job with her firm in Hong Kong; she'd taken it, leaving the children with their father and grandparents and seeing them when she could.

'What exactly is wrong with the little boy?' Alice asked

again, wondering why neither Douglas nor Laura had mentioned it.

Evie shrugged, 'Oh, introverted, slow, something like that.'

Her words crushed her, how was she going to cope with all these dramas without Julian's comfort and good sense?

Chapter 4

'So, have you test-driven any more glamorous cars complete with sexy men?' Margot greeted Alice and Petra when they met at a restaurant in Covent Garden for lunch.

Alice was getting bored of the jokes and innuendo aimed her way after her test drive had become common knowledge. 'No, but I might do it again. It gave me such a lift.' She pulled out a chair and sat down next to Margot at one of the tables that were set up in the square on this sunny day in early May. Petra piled her shopping on one chair and sat down on another, complaining of the heat and how she wished she hadn't put on a jumper, fanning her flushed face with her hand.

The three of them had known each other since school. They'd been through marriage, childbirth, divorce in Petra's case, and widowhood in hers, and despite their teasing and occasional rows, they were firm allies against the world.

'Take me with you, next time,' Margot said.' It's not like you, I couldn't believe it when I saw you speeding by.'

Alice laughed, 'You sound like Laura, but it is like me. It's just that Julian didn't like risky sports and things. Perhaps it was an age thing.'

'We've no idea what he was like before we knew him,' Petra said, 'for all we know he could have lived the most daredevil, rackety life before you met him, then when he fell in love with you, he calmed down.'

'True.' Anxiety sunk its teeth into her. Her mother had said the same thing and she'd briefly wondered about it, but she'd never seen that side of him. He was first and foremost a family man and he wanted to keep them safe. She needed him now, calm and reassuring, soothing away the bouts of anxiety that plagued her with Evie's unfortunate pregnancy and Laura's engagement. She went on quickly before either of them could throw up anything else unsettling, 'I don't know what came over me that day of the test drive. I'd just left Cecily and I was wishing Julian were here to be a support with Evie... I didn't know about Laura's engagement then.'

She took a mouthful of the wine Margot had ordered while they studied the menu. 'Then as I passed the car showroom I suddenly remembered Frank Trevelyan and driving in his Bristol, ages and ages ago. Goodness knows why I thought of Frank then. I haven't seen him for years.'

'Ah, Frank.' Petra went all misty-eyed. 'Sad he left the country to live abroad, wasn't long after your wedding, was it? I wonder what he's up to now.'

'I can't remember. All I could think of at that time was Julian.'

Petra sighed, put her hand over hers. 'And now he's gone, and far too soon, he really was the perfect husband. The rest of us who'd married lesser mortals were deadly jealous. But, love, time's marching on and you're still young and very attractive, you ought to start dating again.'

'Oh no,' Alice gave a horrified laugh. 'I don't know how dating works today and I can't image ever going to bed with anyone else, showing my body to someone new, especially now it's not so young and slender any more.'

'Dim the lights and lie down, the wobbly bits sort of disperse then,' Petra giggled. Since her divorce, and perhaps before it, she'd had lots of lovers, none that stayed long and usually men discarded by their wives because of some unfortunate trait – drink or trouble with finance or a mental condition, all things Alice felt were hardly fair exchange for a steamy interlude.

'You'll change your mind if you meet someone you fancy,' Petra said knowingly. 'But don't use Evie's baby as an excuse to stay hiding at home.'

'Cecily said the same thing… about the baby. Don't worry, I won't do that, and I've got Laura's wedding to think about.' Anxiety clawed at her again. 'I only hope she's doing the right thing.'

'Who's to know?' Margot poured more wine. 'We all started off with such hopes, didn't we? You had a happy marriage though, which makes it worse that it was cut short too soon. I'm sure you'll find new things to do now with your life. It's a kind of freedom, it has its compensations.'

Alice said nothing. Margot and her husband, Glen, seemed happy enough, but she never said much about her marriage so none of them really knew.

A troupe of colourful acrobats leapt and cartwheeled on the square before them.

'I'd like to try paragliding,' Alice said to change the subject. 'I always wanted to do it when we went skiing and people jumped from the mountains. Julian went on about the statistics of accidents and I knew if I did it, it would put him through unnecessary torment. But now he's gone, I could try it, what do you think?' She regarded her friends; they'd weathered well since they'd met as shy little girls starting school for the first time.

'But you still have children and soon grandchildren, you don't want to put yourself in any danger. Imagine if you paralyse yourself or something,' Margot said.

'You sound just like Julian,' Alice laughed. Margot hated sport – 'makes me feel sick' she used to say at school, though now she had a personal trainer and did Pilates – and perhaps more exciting things – with him on her living room carpet.

Petra said, 'As you know, I love travelling, perhaps we could go on some weekend breaks together?'

'Yes, that would be fun.' Alice was not sure she wanted Petra as a travelling companion; her interests were usually confined to checking out the local male talent.

They watched two of the acrobats holding on to each other and rolling along the ground like a wheel.

'Since driving that car I feel like doing more exciting things: spending the night in a mountain hut before getting up at dawn to ski, travelling to places I've never been to, having my own gap year.' Alice laughed, feeling a little foolish. 'I can't explain it really. Put it down to middle-aged madness.'

Petra smiled, 'Most people I know – and I've read articles about the over sixties – not that we are nearly there yet,' she added hastily, 'want to jazz up their sex lives. Look at those books on bondage that are selling in shedloads.'

'Yes, but how many cookery programmes are watched on television and cookery books sold, yet no one seems to cook these days,' Alice said. 'Perhaps those books are a substitute for the real thing, but Julian is all I want in that department.'

'Never say never,' Petra said. 'There's no rule to say you can't love someone else, it doesn't cancel out your love for Julian.' She flinched as an acrobat twirled beside her, his leg extended, skimming her head, his goblin face smiling wickedly at her.

Alice shrugged; falling in love again herself was the very last thing on her mind. Her daughters' affairs occupied that space, and look at the problems they were causing.

'But Frank. It's funny how you suddenly thought of him like that outside the car showroom. None of us have heard of him for ages.' Margot glanced at Petra, who often kept tabs on the most attractive men.

'Don't look at me,' Petra said, 'I haven't seen or heard a whisper of him either. It seems he's disappeared into thin air. Probably married with lots of children.'

'Perhaps Julian was sending you a sign to prove that you do have the strength to cope without him, Alice,' Margot joked to ease the atmosphere.

Alice remembered that she had asked Julian for strength as she passed the showroom, but it was romantic madness to imagine he'd sent her a message reminding her of driving with Frank in his glamorous car, especially as she'd barely thought of him for years.

Chapter 5

'You don't much like Douglas, do you, Mum?' Laura accused her almost as soon as she came into the house and the front door was shut behind her. She dropped her bag on the hall table, pulled a packet out of it and thrust it at her. 'Bought you a scarf, there were masses in the market, but it's pretty, I'll have it if you don't like it.'

'I'm sure I'll love it, you have such good taste.' Alice unwrapped it; wishing Laura didn't run herself down so much. She'd become so much worse since her father was no longer here to bolster her up.

Alice hadn't seen her since that infamous lunch over three weeks ago when she'd first met Douglas. Douglas and Laura had taken advantage of the children being with their mother on one of her brief visits and snatched a quick holiday together. She'd chatted with Laura on the phone, though both were obviously careful not to antagonise the other.

'It's perfect, thank you, darling. It will go with so many of my things.' Alice held the scarf up against her blue shirt, before knotting it round her neck and tucking the ends into the front. It was made of a rose pink material, edged in matching lace and looked very pretty. She kissed her daughter and, hoping Laura would forget her question about liking

Douglas, went on, 'So how was the holiday? Did you have a good time? I'm longing to hear all about it.'

Laura flung herself down on the sofa, 'Yes, it was quite hot but we swam a lot and...' She paused, fixed Alice with a determined look. 'But tell me what you think about Douglas. I just feel you... well you weren't your usual welcoming self when he came here to meet you for lunch.'

'I'm sorry you feel that, darling, but I was quite stressed about Evie's news. I don't think she realises that a child is a lifelong commitment and having one with a man who is so irresponsible, not to mention being another woman's husband is a serious undertaking.' She struggled to explain. 'And you did rather spring your news on to me, but I like him, not that I know him very well... after only one meeting.' She hoped she sounded sincere; it was difficult to enthuse over the man she'd thought dull, and her worry that in time Laura would think so too.

It wasn't as if she didn't want her daughters to find love and have families of their own, just not with the people they'd chosen. But she could not say any of this, especially to Laura, without causing an emotional crisis.

'I missed your father being there, both of us meeting your future husband together,' Alice said.

'Well, he's not,' Laura said. 'I want him here too, but we'll have to get on without him.' She studied her nails intently, her eyes glazed with tears.

'We will, but... tell me about your holiday. You look wonderful, all tanned and rested,' she went on, changing the subject before Laura could come up with more ways her mother had let her down when meeting her fiancé.

'We spent most of the time on the beach. I told you all about it when I rang.' Laura sounded impatient as if she didn't want to be sidetracked from the matter she'd come to discuss.

Alice sat down beside her on the sofa and said gently, 'You must admit, darling, that the news of your engagement came as quite a shock. It's not at all like you to produce your fiancé without even hinting about him beforehand. You used to bring the men home you were interested in. Why haven't we... I seen him before?'

'I... I know this sounds weird, but I too wanted Dad to be there... so I kept putting it off, and also Douglas wanted his children to get used to the idea. We both agreed if they hated the idea we'd put it off for a while. Anyway...' Laura gave a tiny shrug of hopelessness that clutched at Alice's heart. 'Douglas was there for me when I most needed him, you and Evie were so unhappy, as I was, and Douglas was not involved, he was outside it all. Do you understand, Mum?' She turned to her in anguish.

'Yes, I do.' Alice hugged her. The three of them had been so locked up in their own grief and anxiety over Julian's sudden deterioration and death it was difficult to reach through the deluge of their own pain to comfort each other. Douglas may well have been just the person Laura needed then and Alice was glad he'd been there for her, but did she really want to be with him for life and take on his children, one of whom was meant to have 'something wrong' with him?

'Now we're back you must see him again and meet the children,' Laura went on.

'Of course, let's make a date, but... I... I am a little worried about him having children. That's quite a lot to take on at your age, you are only twenty-four, darling, and really you have no experience with children.'

'You don't say that about Evie, and she's two years younger than me and having Nick's child who'll have dozens of half-brothers and sisters scattered about the place.'

'I'm not comparing you, I...'

'Your generation are never happy about your children. Half of your friends moan that they'll never become grandparents as their daughters seem so set on their careers and their sons don't want to commit, and here you are with three grandchildren already, or you will have when Evie's baby's born, and you're not happy either,' Laura grumbled.

Alice gave up. There was some truth in Laura's remark and it was wishful thinking to expect one's children to marry a lovely person who gelled well with the whole family and have angelic, perfect children and everyone live happily ever after. Only princesses in fairy stories did that, and anyway their stories finished on the wedding day so no one knew if their marriages worked out or not. With social values so different today, family set-ups came in all sorts of shapes and sizes, and if Alice didn't accept it she could lose her children and that was the last thing she wanted.

'I only want you to be happy, darling,' Alice said weakly.

'You must get to know the children.' Laura got up and paced the room. 'Douglas could bring them here, my flat's too small and his... well, it would be better here, they need to get to know here. Tea's best, they have so many allergies that a cooked meal could be difficult.'

Her heart sank, but this is how it was going to be and she must accept it if she wanted to keep her daughter in her life.

'Whatever you think best, the supermarkets are stuffed with more kinds of foods than we had when I was a child, but most of it appears to be poisonous – threatening obesity, cancer, heart problems and all. If you tell me what they're

44

allergic to, I'll try and avoid it, though you know I'll bake most of it myself,' Alice said.

Her children and, as far as she could remember, their friends were never plagued with food allergies. She'd read the occasional article about it and it seemed that the lives of today's children were in constant danger from nuts, eggs, honey and all sorts of food that her generation and Laura's ate without a care.

'I didn't know about it before. Douglas's mother, Elspeth, drilled it into me as if I had to pass an exam.' Laura sighed. 'There's quite a list.' She picked up a photograph on the table beside her and studied it. Julian had it taken by a roving photographer of them all on holiday a few years ago, happy and content together, blissfully unaware of the tragedy about to shatter their lives.

'That's another person to meet.' Alice didn't like the sound of her fellow grandparent, the *real* grandmother who'd probably not welcome a step-grandmother with her lackadaisical methods of childcare. 'What's happened to Douglas's father?'

'Oh, he's been dead for ages. Couldn't wait, I'd have thought. Douglas's mother's so difficult, not like you with lots of friends, going out and things. She's miles older than you are anyway, and her house is so clean and tidy you don't like to ask for a coffee, or even sit down and dent the cushions, not like our house.' Laura waved her hand at an untidy pile of newspapers and magazines waiting for Alice to go through them before she chucked them out.

'Dull women have immaculate houses,' Alice quoted from one of the magnets scattered over the front of her fridge, though looking round the cluttered room she thought she'd better have at least a small tidy up before Douglas came again.

'Exactly,' Laura giggled and things were easy between them again. Their conversation switched to clothes and possible wedding dates and whether they should wait for Evie's baby to be born.

'I think we should,' Laura said, 'or knowing her she'll have it on the day and ruin it for everyone.'

Alice ignored her remark; there'd always been rivalry between the two girls.

'So do you want to be married in London or Suffolk?' Alice steered onto more neutral waters.

'It would be lovely to have the reception in the garden in Suffolk, if the weather's good, so that means a summer wedding, perhaps next summer as it's almost June already and the baby's not due until near Christmas,' Laura said.

Next summer, Alice felt a dash of relief, perhaps in a year's time Laura would have changed her mind over this union.

'There's no guarantee of good weather so we'd have to have a marquee and…' With prices rising by the minute and the savings Julian left now dwindling, such expenses for a wedding added to her anxiety. 'We'll have to make sure the garden looks nice though in case the weather is lovely.' Laura paused and looked away and Alice guessed they were both thinking of Nick. Nick, who in other circumstances, would be just the person to transform their garden into a wonderful, romantic setting.

'Nick…' Laura said, her voice slightly wistful, bleakness in her eyes. Alice suddenly saw the truth as if it were flashed in neon lights across her face. *Laura* was in love with Nick, and Evie had nabbed him.

The three of them had spent some time in the cottage after Julian's death as he'd been buried in Suffolk. Their friends came round to offer comfort, as did Nick and Freya, but, now as she thought of it, she remembered that Nick came round more frequently, as Freya was busy with their children and her work. Alice had been too deep in the abyss of her own grief then to take much notice, but had Nick flirted with both the girls, played one off against the other until she and Laura had returned to London leaving Evie alone in Suffolk?

Laura loved Nick, or more likely, had become infatuated with him. Had he seduced her too and then thrown her over her for Evie? No, surely that was too far-fetched even for Nick? He had probably waited until she and Laura had gone and pounced and Evie, broken without her father, was an easy victim.

Had Laura become involved with Douglas because she couldn't have Nick or because he was a substitute for her father? Or even to spite Nick or her sister?

How could she voice all this to Laura? However she put it she'd take it the wrong way.

It was all so complicated.

Chapter 6

There was no way she could put it off. It worried her in the night, chewing at her like a puppy at a bone. Like it or not, Laura was going to be stepmother to Douglas's children and she their grandmother, *step*-grandmother, Alice kept reminding herself, as if that somehow excused her from having much to do with them, not that she'd met them yet, but she would soon, for they were coming to tea at the weekend.

The children lived – except for occasional weeks with their mother when she found the time from her high-powered job – with their father, so that meant that Laura would be their main carer. Douglas earned more money than she did and, in his own way, was climbing high in his profession. Up until now, Elspeth, his mother, this exceptionally tidy, organised woman and nutritional expert, and the maternal grandparents, of whom Alice knew nothing except that they lived in Surrey, and various babysitters helped out while he was at work. The arrangements sounded complicated and were no doubt expensive, so it was hardly surprising that when they married, Laura would be expected to take over, though Douglas's mother would surely want to keep her beady eye on them in case her new daughter-in-law inadvertently poisoned them or brought too much excitement into their lives.

Laura enjoyed her legal job, but she was not a high-flyer, happy to coast along while the more ambitious people scrabbled past her on their way to the top. She would still want to work and, no doubt, wanted her own money, so, as various friends had pointed out, if she were not careful, Alice – living near by – would be landed with the children, perhaps share their care with the *real* grandmother, who, by the sound of her, would disapprove of her. She'd better quickly find herself something more time-consuming to do than ferrying occasional bales of fabric to Suffolk to be transformed into curtains and cushions.

Alice made a shopping list of the ingredients she needed for the tea party with Douglas's children. She'd cook with the normal flour, eggs and butter she always used. After a quick read of Laura's list of things the children were allergic to – strange additives she'd never heard of, which reminded her of chemistry lessons at school with all those initials and numbers she'd never got the hang of, she saw they were clear of those. She enjoyed making cakes, she hadn't made any for ages and she looked forward to spending the afternoon surround by the warm, comforting smell of baking.

Alice learnt to bake long before she left home. 'Bought' cakes and scones tasted stale and bland, and her mother thought it a sign of laziness to buy them. Julian used to tease with one of his twinkling smiles, saying he only married her for her baking skills.

Concentrating on cooking for her first meeting with her future step-grandchildren helped to soothe her nerves. She made fruit scones, cupcakes topped with whirls of pale coloured icing, shortbread biscuits and some chocolate crispies, which were Laura's favourite. These were a sort of superior chocolate-covered cornflakes, with added butter and coconut and good, dark chocolate. She cut them into squares and put a thick layer of chocolate buttercream on top, she also made some cheese and ham sandwiches.

She laid the table, tensing herself for this meeting, worried about the children now and how they would feel meeting her and what if *she* didn't like them? That could be worse than them not liking her.

There was a bustle of arrival and she heard Laura say, 'Come on, come into the house,' as if she were luring the children into a witch's cottage. She went to greet them, wondering what she was going to see.

Zara – who was forbidden Coca Cola and various other concoctions, as it made her hyper – was a pretty child with sparkling blue eyes and blonde hair and seemed very together. She probably took after her mother, Alice thought as, at her father's request, Zara stuck her hand out in her direction for her to shake. Douglas, hovering in front of her, darted his head forward in a semblance of a kiss, somewhere in the air by her left ear, his arm propelling a small boy towards her.

'Say hello, Johnny,' he said.

Alice smiled down at him; he was the child that Evie had implied had some sort of difficulties. At first sight, whatever it was didn't show up. He was small, skinny like a sparrow, brown hair like his father and enormous dark eyes that gazed fearfully upon the world. He tentatively shook her hand with his left hand, while holding on to his father with his right.

Zara walked straight into the living room and sat down on the biggest chair, glancing round as if she were looking for something to amuse her. Johnny scuttled in beside his father, dodging to keep in his shadow, using his bulk as protection, as if he were afraid of snipers. Douglas told him not to be silly in a weary way, as if he said it often.

'Hi Mum.' Laura kissed her. Alice recognised her expression. Her 'I forbid you to make any remarks, or dislike these people I've chosen,' message flashing in her eyes.

Julian would have told a joke, welcomed them in as if they were old friends, making it easy. No wonder Laura found it hard to bring her new family home, knowing her mother was prone to pointing out the complications of a situation that loomed like hazard lights before her.

'It's lovely to see you... all, darling.' She hugged her, feeling detached from them as if she were in a play.

'And you, Mum.' Laura snuggled close a moment and Alice realised this was an ordeal for her too. If only they were alone, she'd try and explain that the void left by her beloved father could not be easily filled and surely taking on a divorced man and his two children was going too far in trying to achieve it.

Douglas, as if he guessed her thoughts, said jovially, 'We've almost decided on the wedding day. Venues for the summer, as you know, are always booked up way in advance, and anyway it's nearly summer already, so what about Christmas? You can never rely on the weather in this country, so we might as well choose somewhere indoors from the start.'

'This Christmas?' Alice exclaimed. Hadn't Laura said the wedding was to be *next* summer? Over a year away and by then she might have second thoughts.

'Yes,' Douglas said, 'it's over six months away and surely Evie's baby will be born by then. Would that suit you?'

Laura seemed rather quiet, standing by the table and idly flicking through a magazine that Alice had put down when she'd heard them arriving.

'Is that all right with you, Laura?' Alice said. She felt

trapped, as if Douglas had spoken and no one would dare to argue with him.

'Yes... if that's... all right with you, Mum.' Her voice was firm and she went on quickly, eyeing Douglas as if she needed his support. 'We haven't chosen where to have it, I thought Suffolk, but as Douglas said it will be difficult for people to get to. We're not having a big thing and most of his friends, and his mother, live in London, as do you, and Evie can come up and...'

'I'm going to be bridesmaid and have a pink, floaty dress,' Zara piped up.

Johnny crept even closer to his father, his eyes wide with horror as if he too might be pushed into some outlandish outfit.

Douglas, perhaps guessing Alice's feelings, said quietly, 'We don't want a big affair. I think too much is made from some of these do's, so much planning and themes and expense and then people are left feeling rather flat after them. It is after all the marriage that is important, not the scale of the wedding day? Don't you agree, Alice?'

Alice, who'd had this conversation with friends, nodded. Some of the weddings she'd been too had been so elaborate it was hardly surprising that the couple couldn't settle down to an ordinary life together when they returned from an equally over-the-top honeymoon and usually in serious debt. But she wanted Laura to have a day she could look back on with pleasure, but that didn't mean it would have to be expensive.

'I do, but it should be special,' she said.

Douglas went on talking about venues and numbers and she stopped listening, his voice droning on like a bee caught in a window. There was a huge question looming in the room and no one seemed to pick it up. With Julian gone and no brothers, who would give Laura away?

Before she could think how best to mention this, Zara announced she was hungry and they all trooped into the kitchen/dining room for tea.

It was Douglas who was the most appreciative. His eyes lit up when he saw the laden table. 'I haven't had a proper home-made tea in ages,' he declared, smiling at Alice as though delighted, and perhaps surprised, she had this talent. Alice suspected that Elspeth would never do such a thing; she'd noticed that really tidy people didn't cook much as cooking made so much mess and no doubt she'd think it dangerous to unleash so many additives into her space. Douglas turned to Laura. 'How lucky you are to have a mother who bakes.'

'Yes, I am. Thanks, Mum.' She smiled at Alice and glanced at the children to see what they made of it.

'Great cakes, I want that pink one with silver balls.' Zara stretched for it and put it on her plate before sitting down.

Douglas told her to wait until everyone else was sitting down and to have a sandwich first, but she took no notice of him and bit into the cake, wriggling on her chair and talking at the same time.

'My friend Becky had cakes like this at her party. They were all piled up on a plate, oh, there were hundreds of them.'

'Goodness,' Alice said, 'and did she have a birthday cake as well?'

'Yes, of course, it was like a pink handbag with things inside,' Zara went on, then catching her father's expression she said, 'but these cakes are very nice.'

'I'm glad you like them,' Alice said, not overly keen on this child but perhaps she was finding it difficult to cope with this new situation in her life, her mother gone, a new step mother and now a new step granny.

Alice went over to the kettle to make the tea, urging Douglas, who hovered like an awkward heron, to sit down. While the kettle boiled she watched Johnny, who sat next to his father, regarding the cakes and biscuits warily as if one might jump off the plate and bite him. She ached to hug that fearful little boy, try and soothe away his fears. Couldn't his parents have stayed married long enough for him to grow up a confident person? If two adults found they couldn't live together that was one thing, but once you had children surely it was your duty in all but exceptional circumstances to make a secure home for them. As far as she could see Johnny's only problem was not knowing how to deal with the drastic changes in his family.

Laura came over to help her make the tea and pour out milk for the children.

'Happy for me now?' Laura said, her eyes hesitant, reminding Alice of when she was a child, yearning for approval, though why she craved it so much she never knew, as both of them, but especially Julian, was always praising 'his girls'.

'As long as you're happy, I'm happy,' Alice said, glancing across at the others at the table. Zara was holding forth about something and Douglas was listening dutifully to her.

'They won't be your real grandchildren, not like Evie's baby.' Laura's voice was flat.

They would not be the same, though she would try her best to care for them. Johnny had already touched her heart with his insecurity. She felt closer to him than she did to Zara, who seemed very together, but then this was only their first meeting.

'Grandmothers come in all shapes and sizes and have different names depending on their culture, we are just a part

– I hope an important one, as your grandparents were to you and Evie – to bring more love to the children. We'll all get used to each other,' she said, hoping that in time they would.

'Mum has plates like this,' Zara said, running her finger round the rim of her plate. 'Only they are green not blue. I think I like green best.'

'OK, Zara, now eat your sandwich,' Douglas glanced at Alice with embarrassment. 'They are very pretty plates whatever colour they are.

'I haven't seen them in green or I might have chosen it,' Alice said quickly to soothe his reaction.

'They have them in pink too,' Zara went on. 'I like pink best but Mum didn't.'

Laura glanced at Douglas as if she hoped he'd put a stop to this. Zara was only a child and her mother is part of her life so it was natural she'd talk of her sometimes, Alice thought, and Laura would have to get on with it, difficult though it might be.

Douglas cleared his throat and said, 'Now Mrs... um... Alice, what should the children call you? I thought Granny Alice, if that suits you, or would you prefer Nana or Grandma?' He smiled at her.

She hadn't thought about that, it was all becoming too intimate, but she smiled and said, 'Granny Alice, or just Alice...' – Granny still felt so old – 'would be fine.'

'Granny Alice, it is then,' Douglas said firmly. 'Now, what's this I hear, Alice, about you test-driving a sports car? Are you thinking of buying one?'

'Oh no, I...' Glancing at him, she felt that he didn't approve, no doubt his mother would never do such a thing. 'It was just spur of the moment.' She smiled at Laura. 'It was wonderful, reminded me of Frank, your godfather. He, your father and I used to have such fun together.'

Laura looked a little alarmed, 'You're not going back to your youth like poor Gina's mother, she's gone all peculiar since her divorce, so much Botox she looks petrified all the time and wearing skimpy clothes, you know...' She stopped, glanced at the children, 'Clothes that...'

'Are not suitable for older people,' Alice finished wearily. 'But the thing is I... don't feel old. Remember, I'm some years younger than your father, and I've some years to go yet.'

'You were acting out of character, Mum,' Laura said kindly, though there was a touch of steel under her tone as if she was warning her not to do so again.

Alice understood her insecurity. Her beloved father was dead and now it seemed that her mother was in danger of making a fool of herself and, as a consequence, her, in the eyes of her new man whose own mother was so sensible and so house-proud, constipated with convention, as Alice thought it. But one thing Julian's death had taught her and, Cecily had encouraged, was to live the life you wanted as near as possible without hurting anyone else.

'It is a part of my character, a part you didn't see, as you didn't know me when I was young.'

She turned impatiently to Douglas, struggling to hide her irritation with them both. They were young for goodness sake, yet where was their excitement, a splash of daring to step out of their comfort zone? 'My husband was a wonderful man but he was also quite a cautious man and I didn't want to upset him, but I like to drive in sports cars, not that I'll ever be able to afford one and... to paraglide,' she added for good measure.

'I'd like to paraglide,' Johnny, who'd been watching them anxiously, announced.

'Would you, Johnny? Then perhaps we could do it to-gether?' Alice said, feeling elated that inadvertently she'd got through to him.

'Mum,' Laura said impatiently, glancing at Douglas, his face now tinged rosy pink, as if she'd said something indecent. He threw her a pained look.

'Yes. I'd like to paraglide,' Johnny said, looking animated for the first time since he'd arrived.

'Now Johnny, Granny Alice was only joking,' Douglas said hurriedly.

'Were you?' Johnny's small face creased with disappoint-ment.

Alice couldn't bear it. She *did* want to do it. It annoyed her that Douglas and Laura thought her too old or it was not suitable, whatever... for a grandmother to do. Her remark had perked up Johnny and she wouldn't let him down by making him think she was only joking.

'No,' she said firmly, 'I wasn't teasing about paragliding and maybe...' she avoided Laura's eyes, 'we'll find a way to arrange something to do with paragliding when Laura and your father are there. We could watch it anyway. There's no harm in that is there, Douglas?' she confronted him.

'Perhaps *watching* is all right,' Douglas said doubtfully and Johnny's smile made Alice feel she'd won a tiny victory, with Johnny anyway, Zara would take a little longer to get close to, she thought, but hopefully they'd get there in the end.

Chapter 7

'I'm glad now that I didn't have children,' Cecily said when she'd heard Alice's description of the tea party. 'I had twinges of regret after the war. But from my experience, listening to my friends with children, they sometimes do seem to be such a headache.'

Alice understood. Though she did not regret for one minute having her children, there had been a few – minor seeming now – gut-wrenching dramas at school and uni, but nothing so life changing as the muddles her daughters had got themselves involved in now.

'You were a wonderful aunt though, Julian adored you, more than his own mother even.'

'Ah, poor Sybil, she liked living such an ordered life, with her beautiful house and garden – an extension of the doll's house she had as a child, where everything stayed just where she'd arranged it.' Cecily's eyes twinkled mischievously in her wrinkled face as she remembered her childhood. 'Sometimes I used to get up in the middle of the night and cause havoc in that house. I was jealous of it, you see, but I hadn't the patience to arrange it like she had.'

'Cecily, how naughty, what happened?' Alice laughed, remembering the difficult times she'd had with Julian's mother. When she was first married and determined to do the right things, she'd suffered nights of anxiety about having the house spotless and tidy before her mother-in-law came. Julian would tease her, saying he'd always hated living in a museum, and it was her home and she must have it as she wanted it, as long as it was clean. He hated grubbiness and changed his clothes if ever there was a mark on them, but she didn't mind that and felt she'd got off lightly, after all he could have taken after his mother and demanded a pristine house at all times.

'I pretended I knew nothing about it and that it must have been the dolls or Beatrix Potter's two bad mice. But I was fond of Sybil, she was wonderful when both my fiancés were killed, and I adored her children, especially Julian. And now I have you and your girls, I'm very lucky.' Cecily smiled, 'I have the luxury of children without the aggro.'

'I suppose you do,' Alice said, 'and soon you'll be a great-aunt.'

'Heaven's, I suppose I will.' Cecily turned to Kalinda who'd just come into the room. 'I shall have to stay alive a little longer to meet all these great-grandchildren, Kalinda, and hopefully go to Laura's wedding, though what we'll do about Evie, I don't know.'

'You'll outlive us all,' Kalinda said. 'So you are to be a grandmother,' she smiled at Alice.

'Yes, in rather strange circumstances,' Alice said. Kalinda took life as it came and never made uncomfortable remarks, but Alice had found it difficult to explain to some of her friends, especially the ones whose children had married in the conventional way to conventional people, that Evie would be a single mother and that the father was married and had various offspring scattered round East Anglia, and possibly further afield.

'A child is a blessing however it comes,' Kalinda said.

'So true, and we'll all love it,' Cecily said. 'And as they say, Alice, there's nothing new under the sun. During the war there were many babies fathered by men no one knew at all, sometimes not even their names. Girls drinking too much – remember we were much more innocent then about alcohol and the facts of life, and it was a disgrace if you were caught out, even if you were ignorant of such things. People married quickly but often regretted it later. And the men who came back after the war often had become strangers from the dashing, amorous men those girls had fallen in love with.' She sighed. 'Each generation has its own problems.'

'I know,' Alice agreed, wishing she'd been spared these ones.

Seeing her expression, Cecily patted her hand. 'You'll cope. I know you will.'

Alice felt ashamed of her weakness. Cecily had lost the two men she loved before they'd barely lived, while she had been lucky having a life and children with Julian.

'So, are you going to test-drive a car on your way home today?' Cecily asked with a mischievous gleam in her eyes, and seeing Kalinda's quizzical expression explained what Alice had done last time on her way home from visiting them.

'No, not today, I'd better take the bus or walk down through the park in case the salesman sees me and tries to pressurise me into buying one.'

Cecily laughed, 'You do amuse me, Alice. Now tell us about Laura's wedding, who will give her away?'

It was so like Cecily to ask the question no one else had so far voiced. Who indeed? Julian had an older sister, Selena who had a son, Christian, who worked in some highly important job in Washington, and there were a few male cousins dotted about, none of whom they knew well.

'You could do it,' Cecily said. 'I've been to a few weddings where a woman, usually the mother, gave the bride away. Unconventional, I know, but why not?'

Alice frowned, 'I'd feel awkward somehow. I expect we'll find someone, one of Julian's friends or… someone. Anyway it's up to Laura to choose.' She didn't want to think about it, which was stupid really as Julian wouldn't come back to step in on the day, but somehow she didn't want to accept that he would not be there to lead his daughter down the aisle.

'Has Laura any ideas?' Cecily asked.

'It's something we have to discuss,' she said.

Cecily took her hand and squeezed it. 'Julian will be much missed, but he'd expect you to find someone he approved of, I'm sure he's got many good friends who'd be proud to take his place. I know… what about Frank Trevelyan, isn't he Laura's godfather? What would she think of asking him?'

'Yes, he is her godfather but I don't know where to find him. I think he still lives in France. I suppose I might have his address somewhere. He wrote me a letter when Julian died, but the address was of a hotel as he was away working.' Alice felt reluctant to track him down but if Laura wanted him, she'd do her best to find him, although whoever took Julian's place would not be the person they longed for.

Cecily said, 'He's such a nice man, he always sends me Christmas cards. If you like, I can look out his address and write to him, just to find him and inform him of the wedding, and then if we do make contact, leave it to Laura to ask him if that's what she wants.'

'That would be great, Cecily, thank you. I'll tell Laura, so she can make up her mind what she wants.'

The next day when she met up with Petra and Margot, Alice told them about Cecily writing to Frank. 'Just to make contact with him as we are not sure of his whereabouts as he travels so much,' Alice explained.

'Much quicker if I go and find him,' Petra said eagerly. 'I've been thinking of going to Saint Tropez, and I'm certain he's got a house around there, Port Grimaud, I think. He told me about it once; it belonged to his grandmother and he inherited it. He even invited me to stay,' she giggled, 'but I never got to go. But I'll go and find him for you,' she finished with a bad attempt of nonchalance as if she were offering to look up someone's elderly uncle.

'Oh really. Petra,' Margot protested, 'we're in the time of computers, instant texts, emails and all. You don't have to set out on long journeys, like some medieval traveller going on a pilgrimage. Anyway it's almost August, the French go away then – *le grande depart*.'

'Then he'll be there,' Petra sounded triumphant. 'I'm only trying to be helpful. 'I'm going to be in his part of France, so it's only common sense to go and knock on his door.'

'And bring him back as a trophy, I suppose,' Margot said sourly.

'What a fuss you two are making over him,' Alice broke in; wishing she hadn't mentioned Frank at all if he was going to cause such upset between them. 'I told you, Cecily's going to write to him, he sends her cards at Christmas and she has an address for him and she offered, so I'm leaving it to her, thanks all the same, Petra,' Alice said impatiently, annoyed with Petra for wanting to go and find Frank, remembering how attractive he was. No doubt she'd grab him as she had once grabbed their toys – and later some of the boys they were interested in – when they were younger.

How complicated everything was. Just thinking of it all exhausted her.

Chapter 8

The plane from Singapore landed with a bump and a rush of engine noise at Charles de Gaulle airport, jolting Frank Trevelyan awake. He was cramped and stiff, his mouth dry, his eyes scratchy and he longed for a shower. These flights were so wearing and he felt stale and unkempt, still wearing the same clothes he'd worn for almost twenty-four hours.

He'd take a few weeks off, he promised himself, France all but closed down in August when most people went on holiday. He thought longingly of his boat, he hadn't had time to get it ready this year, he been swamped by work, but this case was done and he could relax a bit now. He'd go to his house in Port Grimaud and sail, let the sea breeze freshen him up. He was exhausted, he'd been working too hard these last months and it was time to let up, he could afford to take a break.

He pushed up the blind in the window beside him and looked out, it was raining, not heavily but enough, the sky pearly grey, thick like a blanket over the earth, quite different from the humidity, the hard light of the sun and the swarming bustle of Singapore. Strange, how you could completely change your environment in just a night, flying across the world. It must have been far more fascinating in the past when travellers had to physically make the journey, crossing

64

land, countries and seas, and able to become accustomed to other races, different scenery and customs by being among them.

Hervey, his driver and assistant, was waiting for him at arrivals.

'Bonjour, c'est bien passé? Everything good?' Hervey was bilingual, as was Frank, and they communicated in both languages, sometimes not even knowing they had changed from one to the other.

'Oui, merci, but glad to be back.'

While they crawled into Paris in the morning rush hour, Hervey filled him in with one or two business affairs, nothing that important, there were still a few loose ends to tie up on a couple of his legal cases which he must see to before the start of August, which was a few days away. He'd finished and filed the article he'd gone to write about an important takeover in Singapore, so after a few days in the office here to see everything was in order he'd escape down to the South.

'You're in demand anyway,' Hervey said. 'You had a call from an English lady with immaculate but quite old-fashioned French. Cecily Barnes, she was trying to contact you, make sure she had your correct address so you could be sent a wedding invitation.' He eyed him in the driving mirror, his pugnacious features split with a grin. 'It's in London at Christmas time.'

Alice, the thought hit him, she'd been a widow almost two years now, was she getting married again? He felt a jolt of pain. But why shouldn't she find love with someone else? She was far too young to remain alone for the rest of her life; naturally, a woman like her would not remain alone for long.

Hervey, seeing his expression, said, 'It's your goddaughter, she's the one getting married.'

'Oh...' He felt a rush of relief, went on, 'I only have one goddaughter, the rest are boys. It's Laura, Julian's daughter.' Frank sat in silence, staring out at the crawl of cars beside him. He still missed him, missed his calls, their meetings when Julian came over on business or he was in London himself. He owed him so much; he'd been such a good friend. A friend he could always rely on to do the best he could in any situation as honestly as possible.

He thought of Cecily, Julian's aunt. What a woman, they didn't make them like her any more, a woman who'd given so much to her country that had snatched away even the men she'd loved, though, Julian had told him, she'd never been short of lovers, which didn't surprise him.

'Cecily sent you a letter,' Hervey continued, 'but she hadn't heard from you and wondered if she'd got the right address so she telephoned the house in Port Grimaud. I was there, as you know, to check on the dubious plumbing. As yet no letter from her has arrived, I think she must have used your old address, from when you were married, but at least she's tracked you down. She wants you to ring her or Alice, about this wedding.'

'Did she leave Alice's number?' Frank asked carelessly, trying to ignore a surge of excitement. He wasn't sure he had Julian's home number in London; they had always contacted each other through the office or his mobile.

'Yes, she didn't know if you had it or not.'

'I'll ring her tomorrow,' Frank said, leaning back in his seat and closing his eyes a moment. They felt itchy and tired. He'd had the house at Port Grimaud for years now, with its ancient telephone and dodgy plumbing. Julian had come a few times, passing through from somewhere, but Alice never had. Now Laura, his goddaughter, was getting married and he must do his best to be there, anyway give her something nice for a wedding present. If he went to it, it would mean seeing Alice again.

He'd missed Julian's funeral, been bogged down with a complicated assignment in India which he couldn't leave. He'd been relieved, he thought guiltily. Julian's death was hard to take after what they'd been through, he'd been the only person who knew the truth about it, and then there was Ned and Sarah.

'So when did you say this wedding is?' he asked Hervey.

'Around Christmas time, the date hasn't actually been decided, or hadn't when Cecily rang. It will be in London so at least that's easier than being deep in the country. You can stay in the flat.'

Somewhere, he had a letter from Alice when she'd written to him thanking him for his letter after Julian's death. He'd found her grief so painful, he wished he could be with her to comfort her but was afraid to intrude as he had not seen her for so long.

Hervey filled him in with some of the news from his office here, small tiresome things to see to and he was relieved when they arrived at his Paris apartment. It was tiny, tucked into the middle floor of a beautiful house once occupied by one family, in the sixteenth arrondissement. Now he was alone he didn't need anything bigger, it was compact and chic, full of the books and music he loved; if he wanted to entertain friends he went out, there were plenty of good places nearby to choose from.

He gave Hervey the rest of the day off knowing he probably wanted to get ready for his holiday, trekking somewhere in South America. They'd meet up tomorrow in the office to go through things, then as soon as he could he'd head off for his house near Port Grimaud, and relax and sail.

He showered and then, feeling restless after being cooped up in a plane for so long, he went out into the bustling streets and walked up the hill to the Maison de Balzac. His mind was focused on Alice now. He remembered when he'd first seen her when Julian brought her to a party, having told him he'd met the girl he wanted to marry, only she was so much younger than he was.

'Love is love,' he'd said, amused that Julian had been so smitten, until he had met her. There was more to Alice than her looks, a sort of joy in life that captivated him. Her face had a pure beauty of which she seemed totally unaware, she was slight and slender and utterly in love with Julian.

He was pleased for his friend, of course he was, he should be anyway, he deserved so much, and yet Frank couldn't help being drawn to Alice himself. There were so many reasons why he could not be with her. Besides, kind and friendly though she was to him, she only had eyes for Julian. He'd kept away all these years, seen Julian when he could, but he'd rarely seen her.

The years had passed now and she must have changed, grief anyway would have altered her. And he was different too, he'd been married and had grown-up children, knew how the problems of life often eroded love. It was easy to love from afar, when the object of one's affections was rarely seen and then through gilded eyes and while on their best behaviour, letting the love grow unchecked by the foibles of character and life's problems.

He was too experienced now to be seduced by feelings he'd experienced so long ago, tempted back into a youth that would not return. He'd contact Laura, congratulate her about her engagement and ask if there was anything she or her mother needed him to do, but there would be no mention of him once, long ago, being in love with Alice. He would keep a respectable distance; there were too many reasons, even now, all these years on, why they could never become close.

Chapter 9

'I do wish you hadn't made those ridiculous remarks about paragliding to Johnny.' Laura greeted Alice some days after the tea party. 'He won't stop saying you are going to take him to do it and Elspeth, Douglas's mother, is having a hissy fit and of course...' her face was anguished, 'she's taking it out on me.'

Alice sighed, tension squeezing at her and irritated with this woman for upsetting her daughter. 'I'm sorry, darling, but...'

'I've just come from seeing her, she really pisses me off, she always has a go at me, first it was about Evie having a baby she shouldn't be – little digs like "it's so selfish to have children as possessions and with another woman's husband," now she's criticising you for saying you're going to paraglide and take Johnny with you.' Laura glowered at her.

Alice dreaded meeting Elspeth, just the sound of her made her feel rebellious, provoking a determination to shock that she hadn't experienced since her school days. Julian may not have been keen on the more adventurous side of life, but he was fun, had a wicked sense of humour, and although he would not have approved of Evie and Nick's situation, he would not have been judgemental.

'I don't know why it's upset *her*,' Alice was indignant. 'I'm not suggesting *she* does it.'

'And nor can you, Mum. It's for young, fit people. Johnny's got it into his head that you have done it or will do it and take him with you. He's a very imaginative child and now you've said this to him he believes you and is upset that you've let him down.' Laura dumped her bag on the kitchen table and slumped down on a chair, her face creased with frown marks, making her look quite disagreeable. Alice hoped she didn't show such a face to Douglas, but then, she thought darkly, perhaps if she did he'd call the wedding off.

'*I've* let Johnny down. I have not,' she retaliated. 'I've always wanted to try it and Dad would never have let me. No that's not true, he would have let me but he'd have been so anxious I wouldn't have enjoyed it, and I may seem old from where you are, but I don't feel it and Dad's death has made me feel that I must do things I've always wanted to do now while I'm fit, before it's too late.'

'But his other granny...' Laura wailed.

'That's up to her,' Alice said childishly, annoyed that Laura had not stood up for her. In a more rational moment she might have realised that Laura must keep in with Douglas's family, but it rankled that they expected her to be just like Douglas's mother, the other granny. 'I thought that everyone was worried about Johnny being so withdrawn and if the thought of paragliding has brought him out of himself, surely that's a good thing, darling?' She tried to keep her voice calm.

'He's overexcited about it now.'

'Oh Laura, at least that shows he's got some spirit. The psychobabble talked about children today is utter madness;

whatever they do they are "labelled" with some weird condition. I read recently that many of these so-called conditions are made up, perhaps by doctors coining in money from anxious parents. Things like high spirits, mischievousness, all normal childhood behaviour, are turned into a disability.'

It was exasperating that Laura was being sucked into this new family. Alice imagined Elspeth, who was some years older than she was, as a sour, dried-up old woman jealous of the young or perhaps of anyone having a good time, though Elspeth, like her, was a widow, living with the terror of loneliness. Her son's first marriage had broken up and she must feel afraid that it could happen again, or that Laura, his new wife, might spirit away her grandchildren. She should feel empathy towards her instead of irritation.

Laura got up and paced the room. 'You don't understand, Mum. His other grandparents, on his mother's side, are to some extent; set in their ways too, though they don't interfere like Elspeth does, and at least they are predictable. You used to be like that when Dad was alive. I knew you were at home or working with Margot, or at your art course, calm and mostly in a good mood, but now you've changed, got all these mad ideas, test-driving a car you're never going to buy, talking of paragliding, extreme skiing and goodness knows what else. You're going to be a grandmother and...'

'But I'm still young, even if you think I'm not, Laura.' Evie's description, 'glammy granny' echoed in her head. She hated the fact that these people were judging her before they'd even met her, though she was guilty of doing the same thing herself.

'I expect Zara and Johnny's grandparents are at least in their sixties, not that that is old today, Laura, but our life has changed forever now that Dad's gone. I love you, we are still a family, but I want my independence to do things *I* want to do without everyone getting upset.' She stretched out her hand to Laura but she didn't seem to notice, so she went into the kitchen, Laura following her.

'I don't feel I can rely on you any more,' Laura muttered, piercing Alice's heart.

'Of course you can, darling, but now I won't be sitting here with Dad, nor am I going back into the nursery with Evie's baby. I'll help out, of course I will, but I've things I want to do and you and Evie must respect that and, to a certain extent, fit into my life. I want to travel,' she said a little wildly, wishing she had someone to travel with, feeling that her children and Douglas's mother were determinedly spinning a web to trap her and tie her tightly to them.

'You've got to meet the other grandparents, Mum,' Laura said, watching Alice load up the dishwasher. 'Douglas's ex in-laws live in Surrey. Naturally they want to keep in touch with the children, they promised their daughter they would and they are quite nice to me. It's almost as if they're afraid I won't let them see the children if they're not, though of course I will,' she laughed awkwardly. 'It would give me a break sometimes to send them there and they have a nice house and garden for them to play in,' she added as if reassuring Alice that that was the main reason she encouraged these visits. 'But Elspeth,' she went on, 'lives in Richmond and she thinks as you will be their step-grandmother you ought to get together and agree on the rules and things for the children.'

Alice bit back her despair, the feeling of entrapment. She remembered Sybil, her own mother-in-law, so different to Cecily who'd lived such a colourful life. Sybil had married a politician and her life had been taken up with entertaining all sorts of people important to his career. Her husband had died before Alice had a chance to meet him but Sybil devoted the rest of her life to her house and garden, bridge parties and good works and she disapproved of Julian choosing such a young and scatter brained bride. But she and Laura, like countless other women, had to learn to tolerate their mothers-in-law, and now, the thought hit her, she herself was to be a mother-in-law to Douglas and perhaps he was not ecstatic with the idea either. Would she have to conform to these new duties pressed upon her? 'Wear beige and shut up,' a friend had once described it, having just become one herself.

'Getting married is always a fraught time.' Alice remembered her own wedding, her mother geared up into overdrive about flowers, champagne and wedding venues, when all she wanted was to slip away with Julian, just the two of them, alone with their love.

'But it's going to be hard, without Dad. Who is going to lead me up the aisle?' Laura's eyes filled with tears.

Alice reached out and hugged her daughter, feeling her quivering in her arms, it was on the tip of her tongue to ask if she shouldn't postpone the wedding a little longer, make sure she really *was* doing the right thing, but before she could think how to put it, Laura said, 'Douglas suggested one of my godfathers but James is usually drunk, so it has to be Frank. Do you know where he is, we haven't seen him for ages?'

'I didn't want to say too much about who to have instead of Dad, as it's so painful to think he won't be there, but Cecily brought it up and suggested Frank too – though of course it's entirely your decision, darling, who you want to lead you up the aisle. She wrote to him, just trying to make contact with him and asking him to get in touch with you,' she added quickly in case Laura was annoyed she hadn't been consulted first. 'We must ask him to the wedding anyway and if you want him to give you away you can ask him yourself, or have you someone else in mind?'

'I do want him, I was thinking about it, there's no one else I want, but what shall I do if Cecily can't find him?'

'If there really is no one else then perhaps I could do it. Times have changed now, darling, haven't they? And I've heard of mothers taking the father's place.'

'Yes, but it would be good to find Frank, no offence Mum, but I would like him to do it. Do you think he would?' Laura said.

'I'm sure if you asked him,' Alice said, thinking of the last time she'd seen Frank. He'd been a few years younger than Julian; he could be in his fifties now. She tried to imagine him with greying hair, wrinkles and perhaps a beer belly, but all she could see was that image of him in a photograph taken many years ago. A tall young man with laughing eyes and an irrepressible smile, who thought life was to be snatched up in handfuls and enjoyed.

She hoped he hadn't changed and lost that enthusiasm for life. She could do with someone on her side, someone who could show her family and Douglas's that there was much more to her than just being a grandmother.

Chapter 10

'I know I was so lucky having such a happy marriage to such a special man,' Alice said to Margot as they sat over coffee in the garden of the V and A, watching the children splashing in the pool in the courtyard. 'So I probably can't understand why Laura should just settle for Douglas, not to mention having to be judged by his mother and the other grandparents, his ex in-laws.'

'I suppose it's hard to accept that one of your children is going to make their life with someone else, I know I'll find it hard to accept it with my boys,' Margot said, 'but most people's marriages aren't perfect, so she'll be just like everyone else, muddling along.' Margot looked away, not wanting Alice to see the disquiet in her eyes.

'You're right, but all the same I feel she'd have more chance of real happiness if she married someone without all these ties. After all she's only twenty-four and I can't help feeling she's so lost without her father, she's settled on Douglas. He's a nice man, kind, but there doesn't seem to be much excitement between them, the sort of "can't keep their hands off each other" that both of us knew.' Alice remembered that sensation now, the constant urge to touch Julian, be close to him. 'Don't you remember?' she said, regarding Margot intently, wanting to open up the conversation, dissect these new roles for her of being a mother-in-law and a granny, both thrust upon her without warning.

Margot was staring into space, making Alice wonder if she'd inadvertently hit a sore spot in her. Margot and Glen always seemed happy enough, though no one knew what went on in other people's marriages and what one person put up with another could not. Glancing at her friend, she sensed that all was not right but she knew better than to pry. If Margot wanted to confide in her she would.

As if she guessed she was being watched, Margot seemed to pull herself back to the conversation. 'It's all a toss-up; well, all life is really, isn't it? Who knows who is going to get ill, lose all their money, love the wrong person, we just have to do our best to get on with what life throws at us.'

'True, but I just think Laura could find someone who has not already been through a marriage and has children to bring up. I'm probably being unfair to Douglas, after all, Nick would be even more of a disaster as a husband and Evie will have to bring up his baby on her own.' Alice would have liked to confide her fears that she wondered if Laura was also in love, or more likely lust, with Nick too, but she decided against it. She trusted Margot not to spread it around, but it was best not give more life to the subject.

'Douglas is dependable and has a good job, loves his children and in his own, perhaps low-key, way loves Laura,' she went on.

'You can't ask for much more than that,' Margot said, 'though I know you think he snapped her up to keep house. You don't think she jumped into it because Evie is having a baby, do you?'

Alice frowned, 'I don't know. There's always been a sort of rivalry between them and Nick... the father of Evie's baby is... terribly attractive... and...' Again she hesitated, wondering whether to tell Margot about Laura's feelings for him.

'But Laura is more like Julian, sensible, not the sort to fall for that sort of man. I'd say Laura's just settling for safety and security, and you say he is a kind person,' Margot said.

'He is, and I think he does love her – more slow burn than raging fire that might last longer – I just wish she'd wait a little longer.'

Alice had not taken her own advice. The moment she'd met Julian she'd known he was *the one*. It was hard to explain, she'd had a couple of lukewarm boyfriends her own age and then she'd met him at her cousin Beth's wedding. Perhaps it was the romance of the occasion: a wedding held in a castle beside a beach in Scotland, the sea gleaming like black satin under the light of the moon, the way Julian danced, holding her close and yet not too tight or leering over her as some of the older men did. They'd spent the evening together and met up again the following day. She'd been twenty, younger than Evie and yet she'd known he was the one.

'No one can ever know if they've made the right decision if things change,' Margot pushed away her empty cup. 'You did wonder sometimes, didn't you, what sort of life Julian had before you knew him, after all he'd had many years of independent life before he married you, and you'd barely left uni and hadn't lived much.'

Alice frowned, she'd forgotten that, but surely her curiosity was just the possessive anxiety of a young woman feeling a little insecure with the situation? The boys of her own age hadn't done much – left school, gone to uni, bummed round the world on gap years. Julian had done all that and moved on to a serious job with serious responsibilities, and, she'd assumed – accepted – had many more love affairs than a man around her own age.

'I was a bit jealous then, but looking back I think that in a complex way all his experience in life was what drew me to him, made him more interesting and he was so attractive and he loved me and…' Her mouth wobbled, 'I do miss him so much.' She fumbled for her handkerchief and blew her nose.

Margot patted her arm, 'Of course you do and it was bloody bad luck he had to die so soon. But apart from being dull, there's nothing weird about Douglas is there?'

'No, I don't think so, you just never know today, do you?' Alice said in a worried voice, seeking reassurance.

'No,' Margot said gravely, her eyes troubled. 'You never know, life is full of surprises, and not all of them good ones.'

Alice had expected a joke, even a bawdy putdown, and this remark surprised her. 'Odd remark, Marge, have you had any strange surprises recently?' She kept her voice light, though watching her friend's face she saw the tight lines pull round Margot's mouth and a sad, faraway look glaze her eyes. Had something happened in her family, her marriage? She sometimes felt they all walked on tightropes, half waiting to fall.

'God no,' Margot's mouth smiled but it didn't reach her eyes. 'Don't mean to sound deep, but we all took chances when we married, didn't we? No one knows how things will turn out. I bet you never thought you'd be a widow so soon,' she said gently.

'No, I never thought of death at all, well, not until we were really old,' Alice said. 'I certainly never imagined Julian wouldn't be here for his daughter's wedding. Laura is hoping we find Frank so she can ask him to lead her up the aisle.'

'If you can't find him, *you* could do it. It would make

quite a splash, two beautiful women coming down the aisle together.' Margot giggled, 'As long as the vicar doesn't marry you off to Douglas by mistake?'

'Don't say that,' Alice looked horrified.

'I'm sure Frank can be tracked down. You said Cecily has left messages. We've just got to wait for him to come home and find them.' Margot seemed to be her old self again, throwing out reminiscences of him and reminding Alice of some of their female friends who'd known Frank well and could still be in touch. Alice, caught up with thinking of him and wondering if he would be found, thought no more of Margot's remark about the difficulties of marriage or the pain in her eyes.

Chapter 11

Finding Frank to give Laura away on her wedding day became even more imperative when Nick, hearing of the problem, suggested cheerfully that, if needed, he would oblige and step in for Julian.

'He means well, Mum,' Evie scolded Alice when she complained at his arrogance and his cheek. 'After all, like it or not, he is now part of the family.'

'But not a part we want, or need,' Alice responded, annoyed with Nick for seducing her daughter and fearful for Evie being left in the lurch with a baby to care for. These new family combinations disturbed her. She'd barely got used to life without Julian and now her girls were changing the balance of the family even further with their surprise couplings and instant grandchildren.

'It's too late now, Mum, and he's only trying to help.' Evie went on, her voice, far away at the end of the phone, crisp with impatience.

'He should have thought of that before he went to bed with you and got you pregnant,' Alice said, before cursing herself for her remarks as, true to form, Evie got all huffy and rang off.

Later, when she'd cooled down, Alice felt sorry she'd spoken so harshly to Evie, though she couldn't help feeling upset with her for getting herself caught in this way. If she had to sleep with Nick, she should have taken precautions, but with Evie alone in the cottage going through a pregnancy that was not welcomed by the rest of the family and would bring more pain to Nick's, she should have bitten her tongue to keep the balance on the tricky tightrope between parent and adult child. She explained it all to Cecily when she went to visit her that afternoon on her way back from looking at fabrics for her downsizing client. She'd have to return to Suffolk soon to fetch the curtains Edith and Amy had almost finished. She didn't like doing the trip in a day, preferring to break it with a night at the cottage and to see Evie, though now, with this set of affairs, she dreaded facing Evie's angst and probably Nick strutting about, so pleased with himself.

'No need to martyr yourself over Evie,' Cecily said firmly, her pearl grey eyes like steel as they regarded her. 'She's old enough to make her own decisions, and, unlike my generation and possibly yours, able to get reliable contraception without being married or preached at. I suppose with all this sperm donation and everyone sleeping with whomever they fancy we'll all be related to each other by blood eventually, and I must say I'm glad I won't be around to see it.' She moved restlessly amongst her many cushions on the sofa.

'I've said I'd give Laura away if needed and she agrees, though I know she'd rather have Frank. I wish he'd get in touch to make her happy, and Nick would stop stirring everyone up by offering to give her away himself.' Alice got up from her chair to rearrange the cushions behind Cecily as she struggled to get comfortable.

'Thanks, dear, I ache so much today, another bother of old age,' she smiled ruefully. 'I'm sure Frank will contact us when he gets back to France, though now it's August everyone in France disappears on holiday. I told you I spoke to a very nice sounding man when I got through to the old number I have. He said Frank was on his way back from Singapore and he'd pass on my message.'

'I hardly remember Frank,' Alice said, though she had certainly felt his presence when she'd test-driven that car. The energy of him, his careless good looks and his laughter came back to her now, though to describe a man as always laughing sounded wrong, as if he were some sort of giggling schoolboy. Frank wasn't at all like that, just someone who found human foibles amusing and didn't seem to take anything seriously. Was that true too, or just a figment of her imagination?

'What does Frank do, I can't remember?' she asked Cecily.

'He writes for legal magazines about financial matters, His articles are very well written and very informative. He travels all over the place interviewing banks and other similar companies. I used to see him from time to time, when Julian brought him here, or we'd go out to lunch sometimes.'

'Oh... did you? I haven't seen him for ages,' Alice said in surprise. She knew that Julian made frequent visits to his aunt but he'd never said that Frank had been there too – in fact, if she thought about it, she hadn't heard him mention Frank for years.

'I knew him well when they were young men, Julian had many friends as you know, and one of his best friends was Frank's older brother, Henry... oh, before your time,' Cecily said, seeing the query on her face. 'I expect he told you about him, they were great friends, went to school and Cambridge together. Then Henry had a riding accident, left him virtually paralysed and he eventually died, it was a mercy really.'

Alice was shocked, 'I didn't know. Julian once said he'd

lost a friend in an accident and perhaps that's why he was so cautious about us doing anything he thought dangerous, but he didn't want to talk about it so I didn't push it.'

Alice remembered the scene now. Someone in their office had been knocked off their bike and been severely injured and, telling her about it, Julian had gone on to speak about his friend but he hadn't enlarged on it, not even said their name, and it obviously upset him to talk about it. It was fairly early on in their relationship and she didn't know how to cope with it so she hadn't questioned him further, fearful of causing him more distress, and somehow the subject had never come up again and she'd forgotten it.

Watching her, Cecily said, 'He hated talking about it and I understood, after all my generation were used to the untimely death and dreadful injuries of our young friends in the war. Some put it from their minds and never mentioned it again, others, but not so many, did talk about it. After Henry's accident and death there was a sort of bond between Frank and Julian, even though there was some years difference in age. Frank will turn up when he gets the message.' Cecily smiled, 'I'm sure he'd love to walk Laura down the aisle in Julian's place if he can.'

Alice took the bus home. It arrived at the stop just as she reached it at the beginning of Park Lane, so she got on it instead of walking part of the way home as she often did, telling herself she was avoiding the car showroom but knowing really that she wanted to sit quiet and think, and anyway it had begun to rain.

Cecily's news about Henry unnerved her. She didn't remember Frank talking about his family, he might have said something in passing but he'd never touched on anything as momentous as losing a brother.

Henry's death had happened before she knew Julian. How long before, months, years? He'd often talked of his days at Cambridge, places he'd been to on holidays, even an old love affair, yet Julian had never mentioned Henry apart from that fleeting reference to losing a friend in an accident – who, come to think of it, could have been someone else.

She sat upstairs at the front of the bus; there were not many people up here and she stared out of the window watching the raindrops run unchecked down the glass as the bus started on its way. Thinking about Henry, Julian's great friend he'd never talked about, she remembered something her mother said when she'd told her she was in love with him.

They'd been in the garden in their house in Sussex, picking apples before the wasps got at them.

'There are so many years between you,' her mother said, flinging away an apple that was home to a wasp, and Alice recalled her sudden movement and her concern that she'd been stung though she hadn't. 'He will have done so much more, known so many more people than you have, might that not make you feel a little unsettled, darling? Excluded, not knowing about so much of his life experiences?'

She'd laughed then, thought her mother mad, being so sure of Julian's love and the wonderful life they'd lead together. Evie and Laura would think the same as she did then if she made such a remark about the men in their lives. But now she understood it. She'd been so young, so madly in love with Julian, none of his previous life seemed to matter. Of course he'd had girlfriends, if that's what her mother meant, but he only loved her now – from all of them he'd chosen her. But there had been times, she admitted, when she'd felt out of her depth, when they'd been with his friends and one had brought up something they'd done years ago while she was still at school.

When she met him, Julian worked in a large financial company, not, unfortunately, earning the mega bucks some such people were reported to be earning today, with huge bonuses and shares on top. He travelled to Europe quite often and occasionally the States, though he was always back within the week, but once or twice over the years he'd rung her to say there were some difficulties and he'd have to stay over a few more days. She'd been annoyed the first time just after their honeymoon. It had meant them missing two social occasions – a wedding and a large dance. He'd apologised, told her to go alone. 'Not that you'll stay alone for long, my darling, all the men will want to dance with you,' he'd said with a laugh, before saying he'd make it up to her. Later on she'd been busy with the children, juggling them with her interior decorating job, and these things happened and she learnt to behave more maturely, but now, infuriatingly, they niggled at her.

That was one of the worst things about people being dead: you couldn't ask them any questions.

Chapter 12

It was hardly surprising, as it was his wedding and he'd done it once before, that Douglas took charge of it, or at least tried to steer it in the right direction.

He invited Alice to join them for dinner in an Italian restaurant close to her house, and after plying her with a delicious white wine, and shooting a quick glance at Laura, which reminded Alice of a stern parent, started. 'I'm sure you'll agree... Alice...' he still had trouble calling her by her first name, 'that we must settle on a date after Evie's baby is born which will be in about...' He regarded her intently as though she were on *Mastermind*.

'In about three months,' Alice felt decidedly shaky at the thought, 'and we ought to give her a month to recover, and then it's Christmas.' She went on hoping perhaps to postpone it, give Laura more time to consider it. She glanced at her, was she really sure about this union? If not, now was the time to walk away.

Laura just smiled, said a little breathlessly, 'We'll have it before Christmas. We thought that easier for people travelling and things, and we thought London, if that's all right, Mum. A small wedding but,' she frowned, went on urgently, 'we still haven't heard from Frank. Has Cecily heard anything yet?'

'No, but she did get through to someone who works with him and said he'd tell him. France is apt to shut down in August, so he could be on holiday and not have got the message yet. I'm sure we'll hear soon,' she said with more certainty than she felt.

'Petra said she knew he had a house in the South of France and could go and find him if I wanted,' Laura said.

'That would be a last resort,' Alice said, remembering the scene with Margot and Petra and how Petra had gone all fluttery and silly when there'd been mention of Frank. Remembering how attractive he was, he'd probably got a string of women in his life, glamorous, foreign women who somehow had a shine about them, possessed a sexy sophistication that many British women did not have. Though they must not forget that time had passed and Frank, like the rest of them, had got older. He could be bent over with arthritis, or florid and paunchy, no longer the glamorous man they remembered. But none of this was important, Laura had set her heart on having him walk her up the aisle in her beloved father's place.

Now in this restaurant with Douglas and Laura, she felt panicky again. Whatever her feelings over this union it was obvious that it was going ahead and she must accept it. But there was so much to organise and often the most popular venues were booked up months in advance. But it was up to them to make the decisions and she must be a help to them not a hindrance.

'W... where do you want to get married?' She hoped she sounded carefree, not wanting Laura to catch the undercurrents of panic and become difficult, imagining it was because she disliked the whole idea – which she did – but couldn't admit to it.

'There's a nice house in Putney you can rent, overlooking the river, with a small garden,' Douglas said.

'But if it's in the winter won't it be dark and...' she was about to say gloomy, but seeing Laura's petulant look, stopped herself. She didn't know this house, it might be beautiful, and with clever lighting, some sort of candlelight, it could be romantic. If this wedding was going ahead, she must forget her own feelings and support Laura in what she wanted. She was worried about the cost of it. The bride's family used to pay for most of it, but that was when people got married younger, before they had careers of their own and, anyway nowadays, she thought, both sets of parents shared it. She took a deep breath.

'There are so many reasons that I wish my hus— Julian was here, but as he's not I will...' She paused, then went on in a rush, 'I'm not sure, Douglas, about the cost of things and who pays what.' She smiled at him. 'I do know you've only got to ask for a white dress and white flowers for the price to rocket, and though I want Laura... both of you to have a lovely day I...'

'I... we... don't believe in spending ridiculous money on our wedding day,' Douglas said firmly. 'Some people go mad, think only of planning the day and then find the rest of their life rather dull in contrast.'

'I've heard that too.' Alice wondered if his first wedding day had been like that, an expensive extravaganza. 'But I would like it to be a special day.'

'It will be,' Douglas said, taking Laura's hand as it picked restlessly at the tablecloth, 'it just won't be over the top, and we'll go into the cost very carefully.' He smiled at her, 'And discuss everything with you – price wise. I think families share the costs more today.'

'I think they do, but I'll pay for Laura's dress, perhaps the reception, things like that,' Alice said. She'd ask some of her friends whose daughters had married what the form was.

'So any date in December... before Christmas will suit you?' Douglas went on.

'Yes...' Alice tried to look excited. 'I'll check my diary but I'm sure it's fine.'

The next big occasion was Evie's baby, due near the end of October. She'd promised to go and stay with her for the week before her due date and a little time after, until she was settled. Evie had joined some sort of birth group and signed in with a midwife and it sounded more personal and comforting than being one of many, in a large London hospital.

'I just want to find Frank,' Laura said. She looked young and vulnerable and Alice knew she was missing her father. It was him she wanted on her special day but she'd convinced herself that Frank would be a good substitute, and now, without him, the day would not be a success.

'We'll make it a lovely day, darling. I'm sure we'll find him,' Alice smiled at her. A wedding day should be a special day and she'd do everything she could to make it so. There were so many reasons people chose to be together and Douglas was a good man and Laura was happy with him. How much worse it would have been if Evie were marrying Nick, even though she was carrying his child.

She must stop stressing about it and accept Laura's choice. There was no magic formula for a happy life together. Laura must take her chance like everyone else.

Chapter 13

Frank telephoned that weekend. Laura, who seemed to be spending more time at her old home than she used to, making Alice wonder if she was feeling more insecure than before and was perhaps having second thoughts about the wedding, answered the telephone.

'Hi... Frank!' Her face lit up, she shot Alice an excited look. 'I'm so glad we've found you. It's Laura, can you come... be there to walk me up the aisle instead of...' her voice wobbled, 'Dad?'

Alice, on her way to the kitchen, came back into the living room and perched on the arm of a chair, waiting for Laura to hand her the phone. She watched Laura's face; she couldn't hear what Frank was saying but it became obvious from the dawning joy and relief in Laura's expression that he would come to the wedding.

She waited in a slight flutter of apprehension, expecting to speak to him, but Laura went on about dates and Evie's coming baby, chattering on as if she'd known Frank forever, when in reality she hadn't as he hadn't been here for ages.

Laura curled up on the sofa, the receiver tucked close to her ear as she did when having a good gossip with her girl friends, while Alice waited for Frank to ask to speak to her.

It occurred to her that they'd all been remembering him as

he'd been when they'd last seen him – a carefree spirit with a sense of adventure – but surely, by now, after all these years, he must have a wife and children and they must be invited to the wedding too. But perhaps he had a 'partner', you never knew these days, but whomever he was with must be invited.

Surely soon Laura would pass the telephone to her and she must ask him who he wanted to bring with him. Should she say 'wife' or 'partner'? Better to say 'someone' or did that sound too causal, almost impolite, as if he couldn't come alone, or had some random person in his life. But Laura solved the problem by saying straight out: 'Frank, we don't know if you're married, got a partner or whatever, you can bring them of course and any children, if you want.'

Alice couldn't hear his answer, but she heard his laughter and she felt a sudden buzz of... what was it exactly, joy, relief? She was as bad as Petra with her schoolgirl delight that any half attractive man induced in her. Then Laura said goodbye and put down the receiver, leaving Alice with an ache of disappointment that he had not asked to speak to her, or that Laura had not offered her the phone.

'So, he's been found at last,' she said with relief, sitting down on the chair opposite Laura.

'Yes, he apologised for taking so long to answer but he was exhausted after a difficult trip and went down to his house in the south of France and forgot to take our number with him, or Cecily's. His assistant had also gone away on holiday and couldn't be contacted and no one else he knew in Paris was there to send it on.'

'But at least he's rung you now.' Alice was relieved for Laura's sake.

'He's coming on his own; he'll be here in a couple of weeks. He lives in Paris but he's got a flat in London that his nephew stays in when he's studying, working or whatever here. He's left now, so Frank will stay there, he's got some work to do in London and will stay until Christmas, so we must settle on a date and let him know.' Laura's face was more radiant than Alice had seen it for a long time. She went on, 'He wants to take us... you, me and Evie, if she's around, out to dinner to catch up. He's so looking forward to seeing us.'

'Good, did he give a date for this dinner?' Alice felt let down by him, though why on earth should she? She should be glad he'd been found, he was coming to London for some weeks, and he had a flat to live in. Had he often come to London in the past and never told them though? Had Julian known, and if he had, why hadn't he said anything, invited him round, included her in doing things with him?

And why hadn't he asked Julian and her to keep an eye on this nephew, invite him round to meet her girls so they could show him London, if he didn't know it? But even if he did, why had they never met him? The questions buzzed round in her head like bees.

'Did you know his nephew?' she asked Laura now.

'No, I didn't know he had one,' Laura said, before rushing on to what she was more interested in. 'So he'll be here in a couple of weeks, so we better tell Evie, get her up here, then we can go out to dinner and take it from there.'

'Is Douglas included in this invitation?' Perversely, Alice felt unsettled now. She'd longed for Frank to be found for Laura's sake and now he had she felt it had thrown up more problems than it had solved, but she was being silly. Though if he had a flat here, why hadn't she seen more of him?

But the important thing was Frank was coming for Laura for her wedding day.

'Frank will meet Douglas another time,' Laura said. 'He

just wants to see us as he hasn't seen us for ages. I don't remember when I last saw him, after I left uni I think, I went with Dad and we had lunch together, don't know where you were?' she frowned at her mother. 'Anyway he'll be here soon and he said he'll help all he can.' She got up and almost danced into the hall to find her mobile to ring Douglas and check the list of possible dates for the wedding.

'That will be nice,' Alice said weakly. She couldn't remember about the lunch Julian and Laura had had with Frank but there was nothing sinister about that. There had been other occasions, even further back, when she had something of her own to do and she didn't live in Julian's pocket – she had work, friends and interests of her own and Julian encouraged it.

'You're so refreshing to be with,' he'd said once, 'having interests away from home, having other things to talk about, not hanging about waiting to be entertained, like some of my poor friends' wives do.'

She'd laughed at that, felt a warm glow of pleasure at his remark, remembering discussions they'd had about history, art, music and politics. She'd had her job with the decorating business, and joined book clubs and attended lectures, so she did have more to talk about than just the house and the children.

She felt a stab of insecurity now, it must be just having to cope without Julian beside her. She couldn't remember the last time she'd seen Frank and how strange it was that she'd suddenly thought of him when she'd passed that car show room, though it was probably because as she looked at those gleaming sports cars she'd recalled that drive with Frank in his Bristol. She wondered if he still had it.

The telephone rang again and this time Alice answered

it, certain it must be Frank having forgotten something he meant to say or wanting to speak to her. It was Petra.

'I wondered if you'd heard from Frank yet? I thought I'd give a little party, ask all his old friends.'

'Not yet, I'll let you know.' She found herself lying; she couldn't bear the thought of all her girl friends mobbing him like a frenzied bunch of adolescent girls around some celebrity.

Frank's reappearance in her life had unsettled her, Julian's dearest friend whom she had not seen for so long, although it appeared that he had a base in London and Paris was hardly far away. She felt as if he held a key to secrets she didn't know about, but that was foolish, why ever should he? She was just dreading seeing him without Julian, the two had been such friends it would be hard to see him without her husband at his side, like stripping off a scab on a healing wound. But her emotions were so muddled at the moment with all that had happened to their family, she mustn't overreact or make too much of it.

Chapter 14

He hadn't seen Laura for about five years. She'd come to lunch with Julian and he'd found her rather shy and gauche, but after speaking to her on the telephone just now, she seemed happy, more sure of herself and about to be married.

He was touched that she wanted him to stand in for Julian and give her away, it was something he hadn't thought about, and if he had, he'd have imagined there'd be a relation or some other friend closer to her. He'd just assumed they wanted to tell him about his goddaughter's wedding. They might not have even have invited him; weddings cost so much today and often the couple would rather have their own friends there instead of their parents' friends or relatives they barely knew.

But now she wanted him to take Julian's place, he must go, for Julian's sake as well as Laura's. Ned had left the flat now, having, rather reluctantly, gone back to the US, so Frank could stay there in peace. There was plenty of work to do in London, so much financial news to report on, and more than once he'd been asked if he could advise on certain legal cases, so it might be sensible to be based there for a while, though he could just as well stay here, at home, and commute to London for a few days here and there.

But he was kidding himself, he wanted to see Alice, make

sure she was all right without Julian. He'd died nearly two years ago now and he should have gone back to see her sooner, but somehow he'd always put it off, though it was true he was heavily involved with various complicated cases the other side of the world. But now Laura was getting married and she wanted him to give her away, he must go, for whatever his feelings were about the past, he owed it to Julian.

The wedding would be at the end of the year. Though the date had not been fixed, it all hinged on when her sister Evie's baby was born. He didn't know Evie, though Julian had been proud of her, she was a talented artist apparently, but now she was having a baby and there was no mention of a husband, but he'd find it all out when he saw them.

Maybe Alice had found someone else; there'd be no shortage of men wanting to take Julian's place. He pushed away a twinge of jealousy; she must be in her mid-forties, still young, and surely she wouldn't stay alone for the rest of her life. He hoped she wasn't one of those women who thought she was being unfaithful to her dead husband if she loved again, tied herself to a long life alone; Julian would have hated that. Perhaps she'd be like Cecily, losing both her fiancés and deciding not to marry but having lovers instead, though the little he knew of Alice he felt sure she'd rather have one lover, one person to spend the rest of her life with. She'd struck him as being a one-man girl, unlike Cecily, though Cecily had lived through the war when life was snuffed out in a moment and nothing and no one could be relied upon.

He was making too much of it; all these years had passed since he'd seen her. She would have changed from that bright, young woman she'd been then, kept buried deep in his thoughts. Time and circumstance would have changed her as they had him, and with luck they could be friends now, comfortable together without the tumult of passion – his passion, not hers. He'd held on to his feelings for her too long, it was high time he let them go, they could only ever be friends. It was not possible in the circumstances for them to be anything more than that.

Chapter 15

Alice couldn't keep Frank's arrival from Petra and Margot forever so she told them a week before he was expected that he was coming, and both women – with the excitement of adolescent groupies – set about planning parties for him. Alice was relieved to escape to Suffolk with work for her sewing ladies, making new curtains for Cecily who'd been mortified to find holes in the ancient curtains in her guest room.

'I don't often go in there but I did the other day, in bright sunlight, which was a mistake,' she laughed, 'as it showed up all sorts of horrors, and they've rotted. I think my mother bought them before the war, so they've had a good innings, not like things you buy today that fade and wear out so soon.' She'd been on an expedition with Kalinda to buy some material and the roll of pale blue and cream fabric stood to attention by the front door ready for Alice to pick up.

'It will look very pretty, it goes perfectly with the room,' Alice was pleased to do it for Cecily, though she wished her pleasure at going to Suffolk was not overshadowed by Evie's dramas with Nick and poor Freya, who naturally, as Evie's pregnancy was quite advanced, now knew about it, as did everyone else in the county.

'You must think how difficult this is for her and their children,' Alice scolded when Evie moaned about it.

Evie was coming to London for Frank's dinner and as Alice was going to Suffolk with Cecily's material she suggested that she bring her back to London. It crossed her mind that Evie might move back permanently. Bunk down at home in her old bedroom until the baby was born and then stay on. How would she feel about this? She was struck with guilt and anxiety. She loved Evie, was anxious for her future, bringing up a child without a father, and she knew she'd love the baby – this grandchild – whatever its parentage, but she knew too how time-consuming and disruptive babies were. She'd done it twice and gladly, but then she had Julian to share childcare with, and she didn't want to take it on full-time again.

Alice confided her fears to Cecily who said, 'Of course you want to help out, but you've also got Laura and her stepchildren and perhaps one day, a child of her own. If Evie wants to live in London and there's no money to help her out perhaps you should think of selling the cottage. I know you love it but... well.' She smiled to soften her words, 'Perhaps it could be better all round if Evie moved away, so this wretched man's wife and children didn't have this latest fruit of his loins growing up on their doorstep.'

It wasn't advice she wanted to hear, but Cecily had a point. She loved the cottage, Julian had been thrilled to find it quite by chance through a work colleague whose mother had died and wanted to sell it. They'd gone without a lot to be able to buy it and they'd had many happy occasions there and made good friends. But Evie, under Nick's influence, had disrupted the happy vibes, she admitted, and why should Freya be made to suffer more than she must be already?

'I'll see when I get there,' she said lamely, 'and get the wedding over.'

'The birth will come first,' Cecily reminded her.

'It will, I keep forgetting, well hardly forgetting, but as I'm not with Evie and Laura's here talking about her wedding all the time… it occasionally slips my mind. Oh,' she sighed, the complications exhausting her, 'Evie's all booked in down there for the birth, got her own midwife and all, I suppose she's too late to sort that out in London, I don't know how they do it here.'

'My poor girl,' Cecily took her hand, 'facing this without Julian, but at least Frank has contacted you, I'm sure he'll be a tower of strength.'

'I do hope so, I haven't spoken to him yet, Laura's sorted things out with him, but you'd think George Clooney or someone like that was coming by the fuss my girl friends are making over him.' Alice laughed, though she wondered how much time Frank would have left for Laura and the wedding with all the events her friends were planning for him.

'He was a very attractive man, probably still is if he hasn't gone to seed. Perhaps you didn't notice as you were so besotted with Julian.' Cecily smiled a rather maddening secret smile, Alice thought, though she didn't remark upon it.

*

Alice left London just after 6 a.m. and arrived at the cottage at breakfast time to find Evie slumped on the sofa in the little sitting room, in tears.

'Nick says I must go back to London with you, stay until after the baby's born as it will be better for me,' she sobbed. 'I agreed to go with you for a few days, but he thinks it better I stay away for a bit, until it's born and everything.'

Alice bit back a retort; Evie's news did not surprise her. Now the pregnancy and Nick's part in it was common knowledge, Freya had confined him to barracks as it were, or perhaps without the added excitement of a secret affair he was tired of Evie and now that she was large with his child perhaps not so sexy or carefree as she used to be. This was the trouble with affairs; they often only worked when they were illicit and exciting, something apart from everyday life, a gilded treat that falls to pieces when the sparkle wears off.

'Darling, it was always going to be hard.' She held her close, biting back her views on being seduced by a married man, and she felt the movement of the child within, filling her with a sudden joy. She sat back, put her hand on Evie's stomach. 'I felt it, it's... well, it's a person, a person we have to love, look after.'

'Of course it's a person, Mum, not an elephant, though I feel so fat it might as well be,' Evie snapped, her face tear-spattered and grumpy. 'Nick said he'd help. Was longing for it to be born, but now, because Freya is so upset, he thinks it best if I come home with you and he'll visit me. He said he would anyway,' she added in a small, lost voice that smote Alice's heart.

Alice struggled with her fury with Nick. The selfish bastard, impregnating her daughter and then leaving her to cope with the consequences, but Evie was not an innocent child, surely she could have rebuffed his advances, or at the very least taken precautions? She'd never said he'd forced her or got her drunk or anything, and they'd obviously slept together more than once. Evie was just like countless other women, some far older and more experienced in life than she was, who'd been seduced by Nick's charm.

'Come back home with me tomorrow and let's see what happens,' she said gently. 'We must think of Freya and his other children, but Nick must face up to his responsibilities and provide for his child. I suspect he's feeling bad now that everyone knows about it, but somehow things will work out.' She wondered if Evie had really believed that Nick would leave his wife and their children and set up home with her and their baby. Freya might chuck him out, and Alice wouldn't blame her if she did. She hadn't thought seriously enough about the situation herself either, not faced it in a constructive way. What with that and missing Julian, and Laura springing her marriage to Douglas on her and her concerns about that, she hadn't thought through what the birth of the baby would actually mean. For a start this poor child needed a bed, clothes and a buggy. Had Evie thought of buying or borrowing those? Later she would have to make a lot of important decisions on her own, for she doubted if Nick would bother. She would need childcare while she worked, it would be tragic if Evie had to give up her work, then schooling, money for clothes and such, and all as a single mother.

'If only Dad were here, he'd know what to do,' Evie said.

'He wouldn't have approved and he's not here, so we'll have to cope with it ourselves. Get packed and we'll leave for London first thing in the morning, and perhaps we ought to go and buy a few things for the baby,' she said, leaning close to kiss her daughter before leaving the room, fearful of Evie's future.

Alice drove over to her sewing ladies, Amy and Edith, who lived in a thatched cottage in a small village close to Bury St Edmunds.

After leaving the material with them for the curtains and Cecily's carefully written-out instructions and measurements, she drove on to Bury to buy food for the day. A quick look round Evie's kitchen had revealed that, apart from fruit and biscuits, there didn't seem to be much of anything.

Having bought a chicken and some vegetables and feeling faint from her early start from London, Alice decided she'd have a coffee before going back to Evie. As she crossed the square, she saw Freya and a small girl coming towards her. She stopped, wishing frantically she could disappear, but before she could escape up a side street they'd seen her and there was no way she could get away.

'Alice,' Freya stopped in the middle of the pavement confronting her. She was a voluptuous woman, who obviously cared little about trying to be a size zero. She wore a beautiful turquoise garment that flowed around her and a silk scarf in cobalt and jade, tied bandeau style round her head to secure her thick, dark hair. She was like a bird of glorious plumage standing out against the rest of the dull sparrows.

'Freya, how are you? Good to see you.' Her words felt trite and mechanical, but however was she supposed to greet her?

Freya sighed. 'Not happy, as you can imagine, Alice – that bloody old goat, it's time he was neutered, I'm...' She paused and Alice wondered if the child should be listening to this, but she seemed happy enough peering into the shop window beside them. 'I'm spitting, and I don't suppose you're very pleased about it either.'

'No... I don't know what to say... it must be so hurtful for you for...' she glanced at the little girl who was now pulling on her mother's hand as if impatient to be off. 'For everyone,' she finished lamely.

'It's not the first time,' Freya said. 'Look, I've a few minutes; could we have a coffee, just talk about it. I... I'd like to know if Evie's going to stay in Suffolk or go back to London.'

'I was just going to have a coffee. I left London at dawn this morning... I had some material to take to Amy and Edith... I'm... we're going back tomorrow,' Alice said. 'But what about...' she smiled at the child, not knowing her name. 'Won't she be bored?'

'Oh, Lexie won't be bored if there are chocolate biscuits,' Freya said.

'But we'll be late for my friend, she's got chickens,' Lexie addressed her. 'But chocolate biscuits...' She danced up and down beside her mother. She was a beautiful child with wispy blonde hair and merry blue eyes, just like her father's, and Alice wondered if Evie's baby would look the same. Feeling it move this morning made her wake up to the fact that here was a little person who in a few weeks would arrive in their lives clamouring to be cared for.

'We didn't make a definite time, just before lunch,' Freya said to Lexie. 'We have time for a quick one.' She gestured to the café on the corner of the street and Alice followed them in.

'I don't remember seeing you before, do you live here?' Lexie asked Alice when they'd sat down and ordered coffee and chocolate biscuits.

'I only live here sometimes; I really live in London,' Alice said, watching as the child unpacked a pink cloth bag of treasures that she laid out on the table in front of her. She was soon engrossed in these – tiny dolls and animals, a couple of marbles, a notebook and pencil and various pieces of plastic jewellery – so Freya and Alice could talk quietly together.

'I don't know what to say,' Alice started. 'Julian's death unhinged us all and perhaps Evie was looking for... well hardly a father figure, but still it's not right.'

'It's not the first time, but it better be the last,' Freya said grimly. 'They usually look like him, so there's no need for a paternity test,' she added darkly.

'I'm... just so sorry,' Alice said weakly.

'It's hardly your fault that Nick can't keep his trousers up. I knew it before I married him, but I love him and love is a foolish thing, like quick sand sucking you in and not letting go.' Freya took a savage gulp of her cappuccino. 'I've thought of leaving him many times, even have a couple of times, but quite honestly there is no one else I'd rather be with. When he's at home with us he's great, and the children adore him. I've wondered if he's jealous of my work, as you can imagine he likes... needs... to be the centre of attention, but I don't see why I should stop working, especially as I've just got a big commission from the V and A for their shop.'

'Freya, that's wonderful, congratulations.' Alice was impressed; Freya was a potter, and her work was sublime.

Freya shrugged, 'Perhaps he chases after other women to punish me.'

Alice laid her hand on Freya's arm, her eyes wide with horror, 'He wouldn't do that,' she said, thinking that he probably would.

'It's complicated.' Freya began. 'He... didn't make it in the art world and I have... though he's great with gardens. He needs an awful lot of attention.' She sighed, 'It's the old story, crap parents, put themselves first, kept abandoning him. There was something sort of lost about him when I met him at Art school, and I imagined, foolishly,' she smiled sadly, 'that I could save him, love him enough, but in truth no one can replace the love a mother is supposed to give her children. One of the reasons,' Freya glanced at Lexie who, seemingly oblivious to their discussion, was quietly bossing about her toys, 'I'm determined our children will have as secure an upbringing as possible.'

'But don't they know. I mean, don't they hear the gossip?' Alice asked, knowing there were older children in the family but not sure of their ages.

'Yes, but as long as we are together at home, which we are, it doesn't seem to affect them, not yet anyway,' Freya said.

There was a moment's silence between them, both waiting for the other to speak. Alice felt enormous sympathy for Freya, a good woman in love with a hopeless man, struggling to keep her career and home life on track while Nick sabotaged it, playing the little boy who couldn't help himself, causing mayhem. And now *her* daughter was caught up in it, bringing yet another child into his dysfunctional world.

Seeing her expression, Freya said, 'He won't leave me, you know, even though he professes to love these women at the time, it never lasts. He won't leave me and the children.'

'No, I don't expect he will,' Alice said quickly, not wanting Freya to think she hoped for that, she didn't. Who'd want their daughter to set up home with a man who so obviously didn't agree in remaining, or even trying to remain, faithful to his wife and children?

'And now, after all these years of hard graft, I've got this commission from the V and A and I won't give that up. I accept I'll have to make some sacrifices – mostly putting up with Nick's love life, but I've told him no more children. The women can look after themselves, but these children can't.' Freya regarded Alice intently. 'I'm so sorry Julian is gone and you're on your own, Alice, but I'm sure you'll look after Evie and the child, so that might be one less mucked-up kid in the world. Nick will visit it, pay something towards it, but he won't see it enough to be a proper father. I'm afraid Evie will have to find a father figure elsewhere.'

'I understand,' Alice said, having sussed that out for herself already. She didn't want Nick in Evie's life, but what about the child? Surely it had a right to know its father, even if he was a dysfunctional Casanova.

Chapter 16

Despite Evie's frantic text messages – her mood becoming ever more the tragic heroine – Nick did not come to the cottage to say goodbye to her. Alice said little, her heart aching for Evie's distress but burning with anger too at Nick's treachery with her daughter and his own family.

She had not yet told Evie about her meeting with Freya the day before and that she'd been left in no doubt at all over Nick's idea of commitment for Evie and his coming child. He'd sown his oats and was not going to hang about to nurture his offspring, though, she supposed, he would appear from time to time with presents and a brief onslaught of love, mainly because he was proud of his virility and the beautiful babies he fathered.

But even if he wanted to do more he'd have to choose between Evie and Freya, and there was no doubt that he'd choose to stay with Freya and their children, Freya was convinced of it anyway and that's how it had been with his other affairs, and though she was furious with his cavalier attitude to her daughter, Alice accepted that staying with Freya and their children was the right thing to do.

'Let the dust settle, darling,' Alice said. 'We must set off or we'll never get home. You must think of your own health and the baby's, and it's probably a good thing to have a rest from all this. Have you got all your paints and stuff for your illustrations?'

'Once I've gone he'll forget me,' Evie said dramatically as she checked the old vanity case she'd snitched from her grandmother where she kept all her painting equipment.

'No one could ever forget you, darling,' Alice said gently, 'it's just that he had no right to seduce you when he has a wife and family already.'

'We fell in love, and I still love him,' Evie retorted as though that explained everything, and perhaps it did, for love broke all rules and, more often than not, brought suffering with it.

Evie slept most of the way back to London and Alice, glancing at her from time to time, her face so childlike in repose, was suffused with love and fear. What would really happen once the baby was born? It wouldn't stay a baby for long, decisions over school and home and childcare would have to be made and, like it or not, Evie would have to give up a lot of her freedom to raise it. Alice must now, before it was born, make it quite clear that though she'd help out, she would not take over.

Laura turned up at the house that evening, almost as if she was staking her claim to being part of the household too, and Alice was glad of it. Perhaps Evie could unload some of her feelings of injustice onto Laura, confide things to her that she felt her mother would not understand. Perhaps Laura could make her see sense, give up Nick and somehow get on with her own life and meet someone better who'd take on the child too.

But watching the two sisters together Alice became even more convinced that Laura thought herself in love with Nick as well, and although shocked at her sister's predicament, part of her was envious. Evie saw Laura as the lucky one, getting married, though she wouldn't want someone she thought as worthy as Douglas for her husband.

'You should have known Nick never commits,' Laura said as they sat over supper. 'I don't suppose he loves anyone but himself.'

'That's not true, you don't know anything about it, about him,' Evie retorted and Alice saw the quick dart of pain in Laura's eyes, the tightening of her mouth.

'Let's forget him for this evening and talk about Frank instead,' Alice said firmly. 'He'll be here in two days then he's taking us all out to dinner. It will be fun to see him again; it's been so long. Do either of you remember him?'

'No, I don't,' Evie said. 'Have you got some photos of him, Mum?'

'I suppose I have, I never thought of that.' Alice got up from the table and went into what she still thought of as Julian's study. It was a small, cosy room snitched off another larger one, with lots of book-laden shelves and cupboards.

Alice saw that Evie had taken the room over with her art things. She'd cleared the desk by the window and laid out the illustration she was working on and the paints and pencils around it. It would please Julian to know that his daughter was creating her beautiful drawings here, but guiltily she worried that it was a sign that Evie was moving back in.

Julian enjoyed taking photographs and had made up yearly albums. She took a couple of relevant albums out of the cupboard; these were taken before most people stored their photographs on a computer and she preferred them this old way, in a book, browsing happily through them.

She hadn't seen the pictures for years. After Julian's death they'd been too painful to look at, but now the three of them, her in the middle and a daughter each side, sat close together on the sofa looking through the book.

'But you're so young, and look at your figure, Mum, in that bikini, so thin,' Evie exclaimed. 'And Dad, so fab looking,' she added wistfully.

Alice made herself look at them. There was a bright-faced Margot in skimpy shorts showing off her long legs, and Petra with Hugh, whom she'd married and later divorced, and Julian, the most attractive, gorgeous man in the group, his arm round her, and how happy she looked, dazzling because she was in love for the first, the only time in her life and, she remembered, with a stab of loss, they had just started sleeping together.

'Is that Frank?' Laura asked, pointing to a dark-haired young man who was laughing at something Petra had said, or anyway, looking her way.

'Yes.' Alice studied him; he was in some of the other photographs too. He was tanned, his face expressive with full lips creased in a smile, his thick dark hair, worn slightly long, his large eyes dark too, 'like liquid chocolate' someone had teased him and he'd retaliated saying one of his ancestors was Italian, possibly a pirate, he'd added mischievously.

She remembered him now, as he was then, a man of adventure, completely the opposite of Julian who was more cautious, but then Julian was older.

What was Frank like now? They'd soon find out, he'd be here in a matter of days and she hoped she'd be able to prise him away from her girl friends long enough to discuss the wedding arrangements with him, although they were still almost three months away from it, and Douglas and Laura seemed to have it under control.

Alice left the plan of meeting up with Frank to Laura;

they were now texting or emailing each other frequently. She wasn't going to ask what they discussed; if he wanted to talk to Alice he easily could and she felt a little miffed that he had not.

All she knew was that Frank would be taking the three of them out to dinner on Saturday night. She did not sleep well the night before the outing; somehow Frank coming and making concrete arrangements for the wedding confirmed that it was going ahead, that he was taking Julian's place because he was not here, would never be here again.

Her life had been devastated by Julian's death and in the matter of a few months it would be changed again by one daughter becoming a mother and the other a married woman and stepmother, and her a granny, not, as Evie teased her, so much a glammy one as a reluctant one.

She spent much of Saturday outside pruning her shrubs. There seemed to have been a growth spurt in the small garden and the plants were struggling for space with each other. Evie asked to be left undisturbed while she worked in Julian's study on her illustrations and Laura sorted through her clothes, discarding the ones she no longer wanted to wear.

When life got complicated Alice liked to prune the plants. It soothed her mind, cutting off branches, perhaps cutting off problems. The escallonia had got too big again and she began to cut it back, climbing up into the thick branches, stretching to pull them down with their shiny green leaves and few remaining white flowers. She lost track of time, enjoying the task, the smell of the sap and the leaves, the easy way her secateurs cut through the wood and a better shape to the shrub began to emerge.

'Mum, there you are, I thought you'd gone out, or were

sleeping,' Laura called her from the kitchen step. 'What are you doing massacring that tree? You look such a mess and Frank is here. He rang and I told him to come straight over.'

'Frank?' Oh, no, not already, it couldn't be dinnertime yet. She tried to see him through the branches, feeling hot and bothered, her hair was all over the place and scattered with leaves, and her face was surely dirty. She felt as ungainly as an elephant as she began her descent. He was supposed to be coming over this evening when she'd showered and brushed up and put on something pretty.

'Alice.' His voice was deep and warm. He came out into the garden. 'Just like you to be up a tree.' She heard the laughter in his voice, and it echoed with something far away in her distant memory. He came over and stood under the shrub.

'I didn't expect you so soon,' Alice said lamely, struggling to get down. She bent, scrabbling at the trunk, trying to find a place to put her foot.

'Let me help you.' She felt his hand on her back, guiding her down, she slipped and fell the last bit but he caught her and for a second she lay against him and the feel of him and his masculine scent reminded her so painfully of Julian she almost wept. She'd forgotten how good it felt to be in a man's arms and reluctantly, and rather embarrassed, she moved away from him.

'Frank, how good to see you. Sorry I'm such a mess, I had a sudden urge to tame this tree.' There was a slight look of defiance on her face, knowing how hideous and grubby she must look.

'I'd say you've overdone it, one side's thicker than the other,' he smiled at her, his eyes appraising her. He was older now, of course, his dark hair feathered with grey, his face lined, but somehow that gave it a nobility; he'd certainly give George Clooney a run for his money.

'You have made a mess of it, Mum,' Laura scolded her. 'Well, Frank, it's good you're here, she's been test-driving sports cars and told my stepson she's going to go paragliding and he won't stop talking about it, wanting to go with her. Now you're here I hope you'll be a calming influence.'

'I doubt it,' Frank said, and the look he gave Alice made her heart flip, or more likely it was just protesting at her climbing trees.

Alice pulled herself together, 'Let's have a drink out here, what would you like Frank, it's lovely and sunny so we can sit outside and catch up on everything. Laura will see to it while I go and spruce myself up. I'm longing to hear what you've been up to all these years.'

'You look fine as you are,' Frank said. 'Let's drink the champagne I've brought with me to celebrate us being together again. I've been cooped up travelling most of the day and I'd like to sit outside.'

Alice and Frank sat on a bench in the corner of the garden; Evie sat on a chair and Laura on a cushion on the ground. It was Laura who asked the question Alice longed to know but wondered how to put.

'Are you married, Frank, and do you have children?

'Yes, to both questions,' Frank said, and Alice was engulfed in a wave of loneliness. She was getting used to it now, the feeling hit sometimes when she was with couples, reminding her she was now on her own.

Chapter 17

Laura blossomed as she talked to Frank, her face glowing, her eyes shining, her hands swooping like graceful birds while she spun him stories of her life. Alice had not seen her so animated since her father's death. It was as if she'd been starved of the attention only a father could give her and she needed to offload all her achievements and fears, craving his approval and support. Did she shine like this when she was alone with Douglas? She had a feeling she did not. Frank seemed to bring light and life to them, while Douglas, kind though he seemed, held his emotions in check as if they were wrapped tightly in cling film, and he was afraid to unleash them.

Now and again Alice wondered if she should butt in and tactfully curb Laura's deluge. She kept expecting Evie, who hated to be in her sister's shadow, to interrupt, but she did not; she looked tired, drained of her usual bright energy, though she watched Frank with fascination.

Alice caught Frank's eye and, as if he read her intention to curb Laura's verbal outpouring, he responded with a tiny shake of his head, so she sat beside him, still and quiet, studying him surreptitiously.

He was toned as if he played a lot of sport, his skin lightly tanned. He wore well-cut grey trousers and a mid-blue shirt open at the neck, and a navy jacket, surely Italian chic. He sat slightly sideways on the bench, one arm was elegantly draped over the back of it, the other held a glass of the champagne he had brought – ready chilled – to toast their meeting after so long. On his ring finger glinted a wedding ring. Where, and indeed who, was his wife?

'So,' Laura finished at last, 'I'm marrying Douglas but I find his family, or anyway his mother, Elspeth, such a pain. How can I cope with that?'

'In-laws can be a curse to a happy marriage.' Frank turned to Alice, 'Remember Sybil?'

Alice grimaced, 'I'll never forget her.' Julian's mother was highly organised, too organised. She remembered Cecily's description of how it annoyed her and how she'd crept downstairs at night to mess up her immaculately kept doll's house. Sybil was always bossing Alice to do far more than stay at home, 'playing', as she termed it, with her interior decorating business, and looking after her family. She had died soon after Evie was born so neither girl had known her.

'His mother was a frustrated director of a huge company if ever I saw one,' Frank said. 'She could have run anything, the treasury or even the country. She was on every sort of committee, studied another language while she cooked the supper, and ran her family like a boot camp.' He laughed, turning to Alice, his eyes tender. 'One of the things that fascinated Julian about you was your untidiness. He found it a breath of fresh air after Sybil.'

'Mum, you're always on at us to tidy up,' Evie complained.

Alice ignored Evie's comment, mortified by Frank's remark about Julian being drawn to her by her untidiness. 'Oh, Frank. Did it really? That's hardly very romantic,' Alice said. Early on in the marriage she remembered Julian asking her quietly if a pile of clean laundry perching on the back of a chair waiting to be put away was to be a permanent fixture of the living room as it had been there some time. Her own mother had always been too busy doing other more amusing things to worry about keeping the house in pristine order.

'But why didn't she get a high-powered job if she was so good at running things?' Laura asked.

Frank shrugged, 'I think she tried, but it was harder in those days for women to get decent jobs in the more male-orientated companies, and she was quite difficult, being much cleverer than most of the men and she showed it too. A story went round that she was in the office of some chairman of a huge company and she ridiculed the firm's figures, pointed out mistakes and told him in no uncertain terms how he could improve the efficiency of the company.'

'Sounds just like her,' Alice said. 'And she was probably right too.'

'Poor Julian,' Frank looked thoughtful. 'I wish I'd seen him more often these last years. We kept in touch though; through emails and phone calls, and then he got so ill and died quite suddenly it seemed. I... well, I was going through a bit of a tough time myself and I was working in India and I couldn't get back for the funeral and I'm really sorry about that, Alice.' He faced her, his eyes touched with pain. He put his hand on her shoulder a moment. 'He was always afraid he'd die young like his father did, though he had regular check-ups, didn't he?'

Alice nodded; lowering her head so he wouldn't see the sudden rush of tears, but he guessed, for she felt his hand again, firm on her shoulder. There was a cold, empty space between them where Julian should have been, sitting there with a glass of champagne in his hand while he and Frank mercilessly teased each other.

'I'm so glad we found you, Frank,' Laura broke in. 'I wish Dad were here but you are the next best thing.'

Frank flushed, his eyes suspiciously bright at her praise, but Laura didn't seem to notice. 'You'll save me from having my other godfather giving me away, half-drunk and making pathetic, sexist remarks. So nothing like that from you, I hope, Frank. Promise no jokes about seeing me naked in the bath as a baby, or boyfriends I might have had. Nothing like that, promise?'

'I promise. I don't know any stories about you like that anyway.' He smiled mischievously at Alice. 'I know quite a few about your mother.'

'No, you don't,' Alice protested, racking her brains as to anything she might have done in her youth that would shock her daughters.

'I bet you've got a whole lot of secrets none of us know about, Mum,' Laura said guardedly, throwing a nervous look at Frank as if afraid he was going to reveal them.

Frank's eyes were warm, like a shaft of sun on Alice's face. 'No, nothing really, just endearing. You were so young, much younger than Julian, and indeed me, but you had such a zest for life, a capacity for enjoyment, it's that I remember most about you.' His gaze rested on her and she remembered the good times they'd had, the sort of carefreeness when nothing went wrong and life held such promise.

All the time she'd known Frank she'd been in love with Julian and it had splashed her life with glorious colour, which had never really faded until Julian had died. How sad, she thought watching Laura, that her marriage to Douglas did not seem to hold the same magic.

But good though her marriage was, she wondered now why Frank, Julian's great friend and Laura's godfather, hadn't come to the house to see them on his visits to London, to see the children or the three of them go out to dinner together? Why Julian had said so little about him. She hadn't even known that Frank had a flat here. She was about to ask him when Laura said, 'I don't see why we have to have wedding speeches at all. They're always cringingly embarrassing.'

'I know what you mean,' Frank laughed. 'I'll keep it short. I better show you the draft first for your approval.'

'Just don't go on and on about me, will you?'

'Unfortunately I haven't been able to see you for much of your life, though your father always gave me news about you… about you both, he was very proud of you.' Frank smiled at Evie, who blushed and squirmed in her chair. Alice felt a pang of sympathy for her, guessing that she knew her father would not be proud of the predicament she'd got herself into now.

A little while later, Evie got up, saying she must finish some work before they went out to dinner, and she went inside. No one had mentioned her pregnancy, but when she had gone, Frank said, 'So this baby, when's it due?'

'Before the wedding, sort of end of October, I think,' Laura said, her mouth tight. 'Mum says to give her another month to get over it, so that's why we're having it in early December. Douglas has just to confirm the date though I think it's the 4th. We couldn't get a date we wanted in late November. You will be free to come, won't you?'

Frank nodded, 'Of course, I'll keep the whole week free for you.' He smiled, turned to Alice. 'These things happen, but at least she's keeping the baby. I suppose the boyfriend is too young and too broke to support her.'

Before Alice could answer, Laura chipped in again, 'Not at all, he's much older, and married with lots of children, legitimate and illegitimate. She was a fool to get caught.' She finished and Alice saw that even now, with her wedding day looming, Laura still harboured a kind of envy for Evie's involvement with Nick. If only this wedding was not taking place at all, Alice thought, wondering which was worse, to marry a man Laura didn't love enough, or yearning after such a roué as Nick. She wished she'd postpone her wedding for a while until she was sure she really loved Douglas, or found someone else unencumbered by an ex-wife and children.

The doorbell rang long and shrill through the house and into the garden. Laura jumped up. 'It's probably Douglas, he said he might come round after he'd finished at his mother's… if he could escape.'

When she was out of earshot, Alice said quietly to Frank, 'Nick, the father of Evie's baby, lives in Suffolk, he's married to a saintly wife whom he professes to love in his own selfish way, but he's like a magnet to some women, can't keep his trousers on, and as you see, Evie was seduced by him, willingly I'm afraid, she's thinks she's in love with him.'

'We can't always help who we fall in love with,' Frank said quietly, 'but now it's happened, even if you wish it hadn't she'll need your support for a while.'

'I know and I'll give it, she might stay here until the baby's born, she's still got quite a lot of her illustrations to finish. It might be easier to do them here,' Alice said, wishing she felt more positive about the situation.

'Support her through the birth and just after the baby is born but you mustn't give up your life for this, Alice. Evie is old enough to cope with this herself, I'm sure you'll help, love the child, but not, I hope, give up everything for her.'

'That's what Cecily said,' Alice told him.

He smiled, 'Ah, Cecily, I was so pleased to hear from her,

is she well? I must go and visit her, I haven't seen her for ages.'

'Yes, she's fine, but before Laura comes back,' she dropped her voice still further so that Frank had to lean close to hear her. 'I'm worried that Laura is... or thinks she is, in love with Nick too. He came round to the cottage quite a lot when we were there after Julian died. She's like Julian, takes things more seriously and I think she misread Nick's flirting as something more. We left to come back to London and he moved on to Evie.'

Frank looked grave, 'This Nick sounds a menace.'

'He is, but while I'm sure Evie, who's always had lots of men buzzing round her, will soon find someone else, if anyone is interested in taking on another man's child, I'm afraid that Laura is only marrying Douglas for the wrong reasons; a sort of one up on her sister or even hoping to make Nick jealous, which he won't be. I don't know, but I'm worried about it.'

Frank frowned, 'What's he like, this Douglas, do you like him?'

'He's nice and dependable but not very exciting... though that might be a mercy as we have enough excitement with Nick.' She smiled ruefully. 'I hope he has the best intentions towards her, though he needs someone to look after his children. He's divorced and their mother's a high-flyer and works in Hong Kong. I'm so afraid that taking all that on will be too much for her.'

Frank studied his glass, which still held a sliver of champagne. He said quietly, 'If she cares for Douglas, puts her mind to it and accepts she can never have Nick, who sounds a dreadful heart-breaker that no sensible woman would want anyway, and if Douglas is good to her, she has a chance. I expect she wants her own children and they will help her heart to heal.'

There was something about the way he said this that made Alice wonder if he had had his heart broken. He'd said he'd been through tough times, but she'd let it go. She was just about to gently probe him about it when Petra burst into the garden closely followed by Laura.

'Frank!' She approached him, her arms outstretched, her face wreathed in smiles. 'I just popped round on the off chance that you were here and here you are. I can't tell you how wonderful it is to see you again.'

Frank got up and Alice saw the question in his eyes as though trying to place her.

'Petra,' Alice said to help him, 'how did you know he was here already? He's only just arrived in the country.' She hoped she sounded calm but inside she was fuming. Trust Petra to barge in and, of course, be beautifully yet casually dressed with her hair and nails just done, before they had time to get to know Frank again.

'You haven't changed at all, still as glamorous as ever,' Frank smiled at her, allowing himself to be grabbed and kissed.

'I won't stay long, I'm sure you've got so much to talk about,' Petra said, settling herself down on the chair Evie had left and accepting a glass of champagne.

'But Alice,' she turned to her, 'whatever's happened to you? You look as if you've been pulled through a hedge backwards.' She regarded her with horror.

'She has, I found her up a tree,' Frank said smoothly, 'and I'm so relieved to find that she has not changed at all.'

Chapter 18

Frank took them to Mosimann's for dinner and it was obvious from the moment they entered that Frank was well known here. The staff greeted him with a pleasure that Alice thought was more heartfelt than normal courtesy. She wondered why they seemed to know him so well when he'd said he was hardly ever in London. This was a sort of exclusive dining club, so why would someone join it if they weren't going to use it fairly often? Surely this confirmed that Frank must come to London frequently, and if so, why had he never got in touch with her?

Laura and Evie gazed round the elegant restaurant with unconcealed delight and a little awe.

'This is very special,' Laura turned to Frank.

'A special place for special people,' Frank smiled, sitting down next to Alice, with Laura on his other side. 'Have you been here before?' he asked her.

'No,' Alice said, 'though Julian did talk of joining it once, before his illness took over.' In fact, she remembered now, Julian had wondered whether Mosimann's might be somewhere he could take clients to.

Had he dined here, with Frank? She wondered as the waiter fussed around them, whipping open their napkins for them and lighting the candles on the table. But if he had, surely he'd have told her? He often teased her by describing the mouth-watering meals he ate while on business, and he had eaten here, she knew that, but had Frank been there too?

Since Frank's arrival this afternoon she'd felt unsettled, not unsettled in a sexual way, like Petra obviously did, flirting away ten to the dozen, but as if this man from the past was carrying secrets, a part of Julian's life she didn't know about, and now he was gone she'd never know.

As she'd left him in the garden and gone upstairs to shower and change into something more suitable for a night out than grubby jeans and a faded shirt, she found herself thinking back to the conversation she'd had with Cecily about Henry, Frank's older brother and Julian's best friend, who'd died in an accident. A person she had never heard about until that recent conversation with Cecily. He was a close friend of her husband's whom he'd never mentioned, at least not by name. Obviously tonight was not the time to question Frank about it, but as he'd said he'd probably stay in London until after the wedding she hoped she'd get enough time with him – in between all the parties Petra and her girl friends were planning – to discover more about it.

The dinner was beautiful, each plate a work of art and delicious to eat. Alice felt herself relaxing, pushing away her fears, many probably imagined, as she was stressed with everything that was going on at the moment. Frank was in good form, telling them about his life living in France and travelling the world with his job.

'So your wife and children, they must come to the wedding,' Laura said eagerly. 'Perhaps they could be pages and bridesmaids?'

'They're far too big for that,' he smiled.

Alice, fortified with good food and wine turned to him.

'So how long have you been married? I seem to know so little about your life, Julian never told me much, just that you met up from time to time, and of course your wife and children must come to the wedding, I'd love to meet them.'

'Thank you but...' he glanced at Evie and Laura who were now whispering together about some of the other diners and their surroundings. He lowered his voice, leant closer to her, 'We're not together, we haven't divorced, but she has someone else and my children are at university, my son, Benedict, in America and Aline, my daughter, is studying fine arts in Italy.'

'I'm sorry, so your wife is French... I mean, your children have French names.' She felt out of her depth but shamefully a little relieved he was not committed to a wife, but then she reminded herself, the French were said to have different ideas about love, and perhaps he had a mistress or two as well.

'Yes she is. Simone is a lovely woman but it wasn't really right from the start, but as neither of us want to marry again we didn't get divorced. She comes from a very rich family, which certainly doesn't want to start carving up bits of the family wealth to hand out to failed marriage partners. We could have come to some agreement, I'm sure, I'm not a gold digger and would rather earn my own money than live off someone else's, but we get on well enough if we have to meet up for family things. We love our children and both of us are always there for them, so I don't think they have suffered too much.'

'But, when asked, you still say you're married.' He'd said it earlier this afternoon.

He smiled, 'Because it's true and...' he laughed, 'it's good cover if I get swamped by overexcited women.'

He surely meant Petra and she laughed too, feeling close

to him for a moment. 'All my girl friends who used to know you when we first married are after you,' she joked. 'You'll be entertained for ages while you're here. I just hope you'll keep the wedding date free.'

'Oh no, I don't want lots of parties,' he said in mock horror, 'but thanks for warning me. I'll make sure I've plenty of other commitments, but certainly...' his hand dropped on hers, a fleeting touch that sent a frisson of desire through her, catching her by surprise. She was just as bad as Petra and Margot and the rest of them. 'You and the girls will come first, if you need anything, you must tell me, and while we're about it,' he paused as if to collect his thoughts, 'I'd like to pay for the wedding.'

'But I... I can't possibly let you,' she stuttered. His offer was quite unexpected. 'They haven't decided on how it's to be yet, and anyway, Julian has left some money and...'

'Of course he has, but as he's not here and I'm Laura's godfather, it's my present to her. I'm sure Douglas has his own home already and doesn't need any more toasters or saucepans.'

'But this would be far more than saucepans,' she said weakly. She supposed he could afford it or he wouldn't have said it, and this wedding was not going to be one of those over-choreographed affairs that took a lifetime to pay off, though he didn't know that unless Laura had already told him.

'Julian was my dearest friend,' he said gently, 'and I owe him more that I can ever repay and it would make me so happy to give Laura the wedding of her dreams.'

'You're so kind,' Alice was near tears. The girls, sensing something was up, stopped their gossiping and turned to their mother, and she told them about Frank's generous offer and, while Laura was thanking him profusely, she wondered what Frank meant about owing Julian so much. Was it just the pleasure of his friendship, the pain of his early death, or was there something more?

Chapter 19

Seeing Alice again was more difficult than he'd imagined it would be. He'd assumed time and age would have diminished the strong feelings that he'd once carried for her, especially when he heard she was going to be a grandmother, which he wrongly thought would have toned down her adventurous spirit. But the moment he'd seen her, stuck in that tree, the full force of his love and desire for her swirled through him as though it had been waiting like the dormant seeds in the desert that suddenly spring into flower when the rains come.

He hoped he'd been successful in hiding his feelings. She hadn't expected him so soon in the day so she'd made no effort to smother herself in make-up as Petra had done, pushing in like that, inviting him to parties, determined to take over, flirting with him outrageously. Her behaviour amused him, but it didn't tempt him. Why did some women think all that war paint, and suggestive remarks and glances and fluttering hands that alighted on parts of him like tiresome butterflies, attracted him? Fine for a one-night stand, or perhaps a weekend of sexual desire, but for deep, long-lasting feeling there had to be something more, something you couldn't define, and Alice, after all these years of marriage, raising children and now bereavement, still possessed it.

There was a fragility about her that he hadn't remembered,

perhaps caused by Julian's death, and yet there was a strength to her that he admired as she struggled to cope with the new events that had struck her family. These feelings pulled him in, made him long to hold her, be close to her, but he must take care, keep his true feelings to himself, she was still in mourning for Julian and it would be crass of him to tell her that he'd always loved her and seeing her again confirmed it.

But there was more to it than curbing his desire, he wondered how much Julian had told her, if he'd told her anything. There was no doubt that Julian had loved her, and once Frank had been sure of that, he stayed away from her... it was as easy for him to live in France where he'd spent some of his childhood with his beloved grandmother as to be in London. It was up to Julian to tell her as much about the events in his life before he'd met her, as he wanted her to know.

It was hardly surprising that Alice and her daughters kept asking him – Julian's great friend – so many questions concerning Julian. They needed to talk about him, bring him back among them through their shared memories.

Then they were naturally curious about him too. They wanted to know whether he had a wife or girlfriend and children to bring to the wedding. Obviously Julian had not told them much about him, he felt miffed at that, he'd asked Frank to be godfather to his oldest daughter, and yet it seemed he had not spoken much about him. But perhaps they – by that he meant Alice – had not asked Julian about him.

But now they wanted to know about his life and so he told them about Simone, whom he was still fond of but their marriage had not turned out for either of them to be the great love they'd hoped for. They'd split up but still lived close enough to each other for the children to come and go to either house whenever they wanted. He told Alice that his wife had fallen in love with someone else but not that her lover – a politician – was also married and Frank couldn't stand her excuses and lies when her lover had suddenly called and wanted her to meet him somewhere, and so they'd parted. They'd both done their best with the children, but it was a relief they were now old enough to make their own lives, though he still saw them as often as he could.

He'd had his knocks, who hadn't, but it hadn't stopped him loving life, getting as much out of it as he could.

He enjoyed talking about his children, he adored them, they were both doing well, and he found himself boasting a little about his son's life at Harvard and his daughter's in Florence. But there was so much he had to keep hidden, guard his tongue and not let it run away with him.

Alice was obviously worried about Laura's marriage, though perhaps Alice was finding it hard to lose her so soon after Julian.

Evie reminded him of Alice when he'd first known her, the same fine features and a sense of adventure, though now she'd taken adventure too far with a child on the way and no man to support her. Laura took more after Julian and she was what would be described as a 'handsome' woman, an attractive woman, but not a great beauty as Alice and Evie were.

He understood Alice's anxieties for her daughters, but they were in their twenties, not teenagers, able, he thought, to make their own decisions, even though they – well especially Evie's – seemed to be the wrong ones.

Perhaps Alice was right, thinking that the girls' behaviour was a reaction to Julian's death. There was still time for Laura to call off the wedding, though she seemed happy enough about it when he'd questioned her. Perhaps she craved the security of a good man, and Alice described Douglas as a good and kind man, just dull, but he might not be dull to Laura, though she could confuse dullness with stability and a calm life. Taking on another person's children was a challenge however, but it was hardly unusual today, and Laura seemed capable enough and, as she'd said to him, she felt every child deserved a secure upbringing and she'd do her best to provide it to her stepchildren.

Not everyone was fortunate enough to spend their life happy and fulfilled with the person they loved. Perhaps the majority of people just took the best that was offered them, Mr or Miss 'almost right' and, caught up in the excitement of planning a wedding, imagined there was more to their romantic feelings than there really were, until the gloss came off with everyday living.

Evie's predicament was more of a concern than Laura's. She was different to her sister, bright and lively as Alice had been, still was, by the sound of her antics. Evie must have been lonely too without her father, easy meat for the sexy old roué who'd come to call.

He was so glad he was here. He felt Alice was in need of some support coping with her daughters' new lifestyles. He admired her courage faced with such problems, but she shouldn't have to shoulder them alone. He'd hang around in case she needed support, he told himself. There was no need to tell her he was still in love with her.

Chapter 20

A few days after the dinner with Frank, Evie insisted on returning to the cottage in Suffolk.

'I can't concentrate in London and with everyone about,' she said, her face moulded with defiance, her mouth tight with determination.

'But, darling, we're not about that often and the house is empty most of the day,' Alice's heart sank, wondering if Evie was feeling jealous with the commotion of Laura's plans for the wedding, the decision of whether to buy a dress or have Edith and Amy make it, the talk of shoes, flowers and all the trimmings. Alice didn't want Evie to go back to Nick, fearing he no longer wanted her, possibly because Freya had reined him in or, more likely, because Evie had lost her allure being so pregnant, or perhaps he'd already moved on to the next woman, but whatever it was, she wanted to shield her from the worst of the fallout of her unwise affair.

'I know, but I keep thinking of Dad and sort of waiting for him to come in here and ask me what I'm doing in his holy of holies,' she said sadly. Alice hugged her, saying that she understood, felt the same sometimes remembering how he hated his papers to be disturbed, even if they were sitting in a fluff of dust and once even a spider's web, beautifully woven between the lamp and a pile of folders when they'd been away.

'But don't you think it best to stay here for the moment?' Alice hoped she sounded calm. 'You could work in the spare room if you'd rather. We could fix up a table there and the light's good.'

'No, Mum, thanks all the same. I want to go back. I love it there, especially as autumn's coming and the colours are so stunning. I'm not going to let Nick spoil it for me.'

Alice wrestled to find the right words to say what needed to be said, afraid to provoke one of Evie's fortunately rare but spectacular rages, which, apart from winding her up, might upset the baby. She said firmly, 'But you, my darling, are in a way spoiling it for Freya and her children. No, wait,' she held up her hand as Evie began to protest. 'Like it or not, Nick is married to Freya and, unless she kicks him out, will stay that way. He also has his children to consider, the children he has with his wife,' she pushed on over Evie bleating, 'But I'm having his child.'

'I think you should stay away until things die down a little, and the baby's born, then see how things are and possibly go back then.'

Perhaps she should sell the cottage as Cecily suggested and put down something on a place for Evie, but she wouldn't get much in London and Evie would probably insist on somewhere in Suffolk, so the whole nightmare of moving would be pointless.

'But I'm all booked in for the birth there, I've got lovely midwives, people I know who'll support me. I don't know anyone in London and what if there's no room in the hospital here when I turn up, or I'm left alone in labour for hours as there aren't enough midwives to go round?' Her voice rose and Alice understood her fear, it was important to feel calm and confident while giving birth, especially the first time.

The telephone rang and she went over to the corner in the kitchen where it stood among her cookbooks to answer it. It was Laura, her voice hesitant, plunging Alice into yet more anxiety.

'I need to ask you a favour, Mum,' she started and then before Alice could speak burst out, 'I might have told you that Douglas and I are going to a wedding in Scotland this weekend of a great friend of his. The children were going to their mother's parents, but her father's collapsed, had a heart attack, or stroke or something, so they can't have them and Elspeth is tied up with some outing away with the National Trust.'

'So you want me to have them?' Laura's request filled Alice with anxiety; she hardly knew the children, whatever could she do with them, that poor little boy and his cocky sister?

'We've arranged for Zara to stay with a friend but it's Johnny, he needs to be with an adult we know, who'll take care of him, he's quite needy. If you can't, Mum, then I'll stay behind and Douglas can go without me,' she finished, her voice flat with disappointment, making Alice feel mean as she trawled her mind for an excuse to refuse. Like it or not she was going to be their step-grandmother and would surely have to take her turn in doing 'grandparenty' things.

'I'm sure I can, but let me just check my diary, darling,' she said, her mind blank now, not knowing if she had anything planned, and even if she did she'd probably have to cancel it. It would not be fair of her to make Laura miss the wedding with Douglas. They were a couple now and should be doing things together whenever they could.

She leafed through her diary, there was a lecture at the Tate she said she'd go to with a couple of friends of Julian's, but she didn't have to go, they had grandchildren themselves, so they'd understand. But Alice felt nervous of having Johnny, he was such an insecure little boy, but there was no reason why she couldn't have him.

'Yes, he can come here, but will he be all right?' she said anxiously. 'I mean, he's only met me once and that was with you and Douglas and his sister.'

'Oh, thanks so much, Mum.' Laura sounded relieved. 'He'll be fine, he likes drawing and Lego, he spends hours doing that, and we'll bring some with him.' She went on to tell her what to feed him as if he were some strange, mystical creature instead of a small boy who would probably be happy with hamburgers, pizza and chips, like the other children she knew. She half wondered if Elspeth would insist on doing a health and safety check on the house before he arrived.

It was arranged that Johnny would be dropped round at dawn on the Saturday on their way to the airport and they would pick him up on their way back the following evening.

Evie, who'd gone upstairs during the call, appeared and said, 'So how's the bride, is the wedding off?'

Alice recognised her resentment, her older, less glamorous sister had got herself a husband, a man who would stick by her and give her a home, while she'd been virtually dumped and left pregnant. No doubt in the beginning of this great love affair she'd felt exhilarated and secure, perhaps Nick had even briefly loved her in his way, made her feel he'd love her forever. Then she'd fallen pregnant, and perhaps she'd imagined that having his child would cement their relationship, but, sadly, true to form, it had not worked out like that.

'No, they're off to Scotland for a wedding but there's been a crisis over minding the children so I said I'd have...'

'Oh Mum,' Evie frowned, 'why should you have them? They have other grandparents.'

'They can't do that weekend, one's ill and... anyway they will be my step-grandchildren in a few months and you'll be their step-aunt. We're a family now. I'm only having Johnny and it's only for one night,' she said, annoyed with Evie's crabbiness, even though moments ago, Alice had felt the same way about the situation herself.

'Well I can't possibly do any work with a child rushing around, and I've got to get all this done before the baby's born and I'm behind already,' Evie said firmly. 'I'll take the train tomorrow, go back home. I'll stay out of Nick's way, I've heaps of other friends there.'

But now everyone knew about her and Nick would the friends still be there? Alice felt as if a great load had been dumped upon her, worried about the welfare of these inno- cent children in the line of fire of their parents' actions. She was about to remonstrate again with Evie when she thought of Cecily, who, never having had children and having been through a war when she was younger than Evie was, would no doubt expect her to let Evie get on with the mess she'd got herself into.

'If that's what you want,' she said wearily. 'But if things get difficult I think you should come back here.'

She dropped Evie at Liverpool Street station the following morning, giving her money for a taxi at the other end, not asking if she'd told Nick she was returning and expecting him to meet her.

She got up very early on Saturday to be ready for Johnny.

She'd just made her coffee when the doorbell rang and she opened the door to see Douglas and Laura standing there, their faces strained and Johnny clinging like a limpet to his father's leg.

'Morning Alice. Thank you so much for looking after Johnny at such short notice. Douglas tried to sound cheerful as if his leg was Johnny's usual form of transport, but it was obvious that the boy was terrified and didn't want to stay at all.

Laura threw her a despairing look. 'He'll be all right in a minute.'

It didn't look likely, but what could she do, his parents had a plane to catch and if they didn't leave now they'd miss the wedding. Johnny hid his face from her as she squatted down beside him.

'It's so nice to see you again, Johnny, we'll have such fun together and Daddy and...' she didn't know what he called Laura... 'will be back before you know it.' Whatever was she going to do with such a distressed child for two whole days?

Douglas eased him off his leg, saying sternly, 'Come on Johnno, we'll miss the plane. I'll ring you when we arrive and we're back tomorrow.' He yanked him off his leg and thrust him at Alice. Laura pushed his overnight bag, a box of Lego and a booster seat for the car after him. Johnny screamed louder but Douglas held him off. 'See you tomorrow, old chap, I'm sure you'll have a lovely time.' He put his hand on the door to pull it shut but Johnny stuck his leg out and Douglas had to bend down and shove it out of the way, a look of annoyed despair on his face. Alice took the child in her arms and pulled him inside and Douglas slammed the door and they were gone.

Johnny curled up on the doormat and wept, his skinny

little body shaking in misery. Alice was almost in tears herself; he was distraught. He should never have been left with her.

She sat beside him on the floor, wondering if holding him would cause him more grief. Then an idea came to her, she said, 'Remember we were going to check out paragliding, why don't we do that this weekend?'

Chapter 21

It was a thoughtless thing for her to say, unkind too, for she had no idea where on earth to go to paraglide, or how to set about finding a reputable place, but now she'd said it – in panic over his despair at being left here without his father – Johnny would surely expect her to take him, now, this instant.

He sat up, gulping back his tears, a shudder shaking his body, his mouth quivering. His misery tore at her heart. How could his mother dash off to Hong Kong leaving such a vulnerable child behind?

And what about Laura? What a start to her marriage. Would she be able to cope with such a child, fill up the void in him caused by his parents' bust-up and his mother – in his eyes anyway – all but abandoning him? What damage would that do to a child knowing that their mother had chosen to live without them? But then, a voice reasoned within her, his mother was obviously a successful businesswoman and been offered a prestigious job. If it had been Douglas going for it he wouldn't be criticised, accused of abandoning his children, though perhaps, if their marriage had been strong, she would have stayed or they could have all decamped abroad together.

It was wrong to make assumptions about people she didn't know – one of whom was going to marry her daughter. She'd been so fortunate with Julian. They both believed if children were born in a relationship they were equally responsible in raising them with love and security, but then they were happy together and the possibility of breaking up the home was never on the cards.

'When will we go?' Johnny asked, wiping his eyes with the back of his hand, gulping back tears.

She smiled to hide her anxiety. *Where* would they go more like? 'Let's look it up on the Internet,' she said, putting out her hand for him to take it so they could both get up from the floor. 'Are you hungry, did you have time for breakfast?'

Still holding his hand, she led him into the kitchen, offering him a paper handkerchief.

'We had breakfast,' Johnny said, his voice wobbling as he regarded her with agonised eyes. 'W... when will they be back?'

It struck her then that as he'd lost his mother to Hong Kong he might imagine that if his father went away he too might not return, and he'd be left here like an unclaimed parcel vainly waiting for collection. She put her arm round his shoulders; he was as delicate as a bird. 'Tomorrow, Johnny. They go to the wedding today and fly back tomorrow and will come straight here and pick you up.' She hoped she sounded positive but he smiled sadly.

'I s'pose they will.'

'Of course they will, they just couldn't take you to the wedding and you'd be bored anyway as there won't be other children. They'll tell you all about it tomorrow.'

She put her laptop on the kitchen table, clearing away the debris of her own breakfast and a pile of half-read newspapers, to make space for him to see, and turned it on. The telephone rang and, expecting it to be Douglas or Laura checking on Johnny, she moved slightly away from him, not thinking it a good idea for him to know it was them just as he seemed to be settling down.

'Alice, it's Frank, hope it's not too early.' There was an energy in his voice that lifted her spirits.

'Oh... Frank, how are you?'

'Fine, I know it's short notice but I wondered if we could meet up today. I have to go away tomorrow on business, something's come up, and I'll be away a week, a nuisance, but there it is. Would you like lunch?'

'I'd love to but I'm looking after Johnny, Douglas's son,' she smiled at Johnny, who was watching her with trepidation, 'my new step-grandson-to-be. Laura and Douglas have gone to Scotland for a wedding.' The thought suddenly hit her: Frank might know about paragliding. She went on, 'We have a problem you might be able to solve for us actually. Johnny wants to go paragliding, well, just watch for the moment, we might have a go when his parents get back, and I wondered if you knew of a place, a reputable place, near London.'

Johnny was holding his breath, his eyes huge on her face. She felt trapped by his anticipation.

'I do know a place, not too far away. I'll come round and take you both, I might even have a go myself if the conditions are right. What about you, Alice? I thought you said you wanted to do it, Laura said you did anyway.' He laughed, 'She's so like Julian and she's quite worried that you seem to be breaking out, test-driving sports cars, talking of doing extreme sports... good on you if you are.'

'I can't today because of Johnny, we must ask his parents' or, rather, his father's permission before he does it. Anyway, there's probably an age thing.'

'I don't know, but I've seen quite young children do it, after all they go up with an instructor, they're not let loose on their own. Give me an hour and I'll be with you.'

He rang off and she stood there for a moment feeling a mixture of relief and puzzlement. Why did Frank know all these things when he'd said he rarely came to London and then only for some quick business commitment. He lived in France and travelled all over the world wherever his journalistic work took him. She remembered Julian saying, not long before he became ill, that he wished Frank would come and live in London where there were surely more than enough legal articles to write and financial experts to interview. She hadn't questioned Julian on it then, she wished she had now, for she wondered why Frank didn't stay longer in London when he came over for work, and more importantly, when he was here why Julian never asked him home for supper or they all met up for dinner or something.

'Are we going?' Johnny broke into her thoughts, looking hopefully at her.

'Yes, I have a great friend, Frank. He's Laura's godfather. He's going to come here and take us to a club he knows. We won't be able to do it ourselves, you knew that didn't you?' Seeing his disappointment, she put her arm round him. 'I must ask your father's permission and he'd surely want to see you do it for the first time,' she finished lamely, suspecting that Douglas would never agree to having his insecure, little son skimming about like a kite high up in the sky, and after this, he, perhaps spurred on by Elspeth, might think Alice a bad influence and never let her look after Johnny on her own again.

Alice settled Johnny with his Lego and ran upstairs to make sure she looked her best, though Frank had seen her at her worst halfway up a tree and hadn't minded, so why was she making such an effort now? She was not Petra or Margot who never went out, or probably even opened their front doors, without glamming up, but she brushed her hair until it shone and checked her make-up before going downstairs again to wait for him.

He was not long and she opened the door to him with Johnny creeping behind her.

He kissed her on both cheeks, smiling. He'd recently shaved and his skin felt taut and smooth and the scent of his aftershave made her long to hold on to him. She sprang away from him, afraid of sending out the wrong signals.

'You look good,' he said, before turning to Johnny who watched him warily. 'So Johnny, you want to watch paragliding?'

Johnny nodded, his body twitching with shyness and excitement.

'Do you know somewhere we can go?' Alice said, really for something to say, for she was feeling slightly dizzy with all of them cramped together in the narrow hall.

'I do,' he followed her into the living room. 'It's in Sussex. I've been there but not for some time, so I checked if it was still open, and it is. So when you're ready we'll set off, my car's outside.'

He stood in the middle of the room, surveying it. He wore a pale pink shirt and a grey wool jacket and dark grey, wonderfully cut jeans and black loafers. The slightly continental combination could have looked effeminate on some men, but on Frank it seemed to define his masculinity.

She'd forgotten how attractive he was, or she hadn't noticed, being so in love with Julian. She must stop being foolish; she was behaving like Petra, always falling for any passable man. Her body sparked with half-forgotten desire, then sorrow grabbed her, she was missing Julian. She liked men, liked being around them, and now he'd gone there was a huge male void in her life.

'Would you like something to eat?' she asked him, 'eggs and bacon, toast, coffee?'

'No thanks, just had breakfast; I'm ready to leave when you are. We can have lunch down there too, would you like that, Johnny?' Frank smiled at him and Johnny smiled shyly back. He has a way with children, Alice thought, before remembering that he had his own.

'How old are your children?' she asked.

'Oh, much older than Johnny, seventeen and nineteen.'

'Do they come to London?' She wondered why Julian had never told her Frank had children, perhaps he was godfather to one of them, but if he were surely she'd have known that?

'Yes, sometimes,' he said, as if it was not important. He turned to Jonny and asked him if he was ready to leave and had his coat and everything.

Johnny nodded and ran to pick up his overnight bag that was still in the hall.

'We're coming back here tonight, you needn't bring that,' Alice said, but Johnny insisted and Alice, thinking he might feel insecure without it, said no more.

'We must put in his car seat,' she said to Frank, seeing it sitting in the hall; she'd forgotten about it. 'Will it go in your car?'

'I expect so,' Frank said, 'it's a long time since I've had one of those.' He smiled at Johnny. 'I expect you can show me how to fix it.'

'Daddy knows how to do it,' Johnny said, his lower lip quivering when he realised that Daddy was not here to do it.

'I'm sure I'll manage it,' Frank said to him. 'Come and show me which side you'd like me to fix it.' They left the house together, Frank adapting his pace to Johnny's, while Alice locked up the house.

The seat went in easily and they set off. When they reached the A3 and were settled on their way, Alice said, 'did you often come to London? It's just that everyone seemed to know you at Mosimann's, but I was under the impression you hardly ever came here, you never came to see us anyway.' She hoped her remark sounded casual, as if it were of no consequence, though she was determined to find out more about his life.

'I did come to London quite a bit, but it was always for work so I didn't have time to see you.' He glanced at her with a half smile,

'But you saw Julian?'

'Sometimes, but usually because we went to the same business meetings, but then I didn't come here for a while, I was dealing with some large companies in Asia, so I missed his illness and saying goodbye.' He turned back to the road, his face set hard as if he was controlling his emotions and she said no more for a while, then she remembered his nephew.

'You have a nephew who lives here, don't you?' she said.

He glanced at her warily and she felt he was startled by her question. She went on quickly, 'I think it was Laura who said you had a nephew staying in your flat and I was just surprised we'd never met him. We could have entertained him. Is he the same age as my girls?'

'No, he's older, almost thirty, and you know how the age difference matters when they are teenagers.'

'But all the same, we could have had him to a meal or something,' she said, waiting for Frank to say more about him but he didn't.

He seemed uncomfortable now. He stared ahead at the

road, deep in thought. Perhaps his nephew had some problem? He could be autistic, there seemed to be a lot of that about, or maybe he'd been in trouble with drugs or something, or... she'd better not pursue the subject. If Frank had wanted to tell her about his nephew surely he would have done. She mustn't pry into his life; it was none of her business.

She glanced at Frank surreptitiously, his profile serious now, wary – no she was imagining things, there was a lot of big, thundering lorries on the road, he was just concentrating on his driving. Having lived in France for so long perhaps he wasn't used to driving on the left any more.

He seemed to have changed from the charming, devil-may-care man he'd been when he'd first arrived back here and the time he'd taken them out to dinner, and even since this morning. He was obviously upset about Julian's death and was determined to do all he could for her and for Laura and he was so kind to give up his day for Johnny, but she felt now that he was a stranger and was keeping something to himself. She was pricked by anxiety, something about him was not quite right and she had no idea what it was.

Chapter 22

Fluffy white clouds drifted across the sky like islands in a sea of blue. Surely it was a perfect day to fly? Alice had watched people paragliding from the mountains in Switzerland, taking off on skis with an instructor, jumping over the edge of the mountain and then the sudden jerk as the airstream or thermals, whatever the technical terms were, caught the kite and it drifted like a strange bird of bright plumage over the snowy scene.

She'd wanted to have a go then, but Julian said, 'It looks wonderful, but there've been quite a few accidents, and what if you don't like it, you'll be stuck up in the sky waiting for the right current of air to bring you down?'

'But I'd be with an instructor,' she'd said, thinking how amazing it would be floating in that silent sky surrounded by the savage beauty of the mountains. She'd seen the anxiety in his eyes. To fly was expensive and she wouldn't be able to afford it herself, and she couldn't expect Julian to pay if he didn't want her to do it. The skiing holiday had cost enough as it was, and so she'd laughed, teased him about being afraid she'd fly away with one of the sexy instructors, and said no more about it.

Remembering that time now, she turned to Frank, who'd broken his brooding silence with an animated description of the times he had flown, in answer to Johnny's tentative question about how many times he had done it.

'Was there a reason, that you know of, why Julian was almost scared of such sports? I mean, we skied most winters and that can be quite dangerous, especially now with all those clowns on snowboards who don't know how to manage them.'

He shrugged, 'I don't think so, he just liked to live safe, he had a family after all.'

They had reached the club, Frank seemed relieved, he turned in, saying, 'Here we are Johnny, are you excited?'

'Yes,' Johnny answered, craning to look about.

They got out of the car; Johnny hovered close to her as they walked to the clubhouse, his eyes scouring the sky.

Frank said, 'It may not be time to go up yet, you have to wait until the conditions are right, Johnny, but there are quite a few people here, so I expect they'll go soon.'

'Will you do it?' Johnny was flushed with excitement; his face turned up to look at Frank.

'I'll see, I haven't booked and as it is the weekend there will probably be lots of people wanting to have a go, but this time we're here for you to watch.' He smiled down at him.

'But I'd like to watch you, *know* someone who's done it,' Johnny said eagerly.

It was the first time Alice had seen him so engaged, emerged from the shell he'd built around himself, and it was Frank who had achieved it. He'd listened to him, taken his views seriously when Johnny felt adrift with all the enormous changes in his young life. Frank caught her eye and she, full of warmth for his kindness, smiled back, unaware of how radiant she'd become. Their eyes caught and held and she had a sudden urge to be closer to him. It was like a scene in a film, she thought, the shot frozen as two people standing there among a crowd coming out of the clubhouse, suddenly becoming aware of each other, feeling a flare of attraction that surprised them. The spell was broken by Johnny pointing to the kites being loaded into a van, and Frank, with one last look at her making her heart race and wonder what on earth had got into her, followed behind them to inspect the kites more closely.

He soon got into a conversation with one of the instructors. Alice stood beside him with Johnny, listening to the jargon and then the instructor, a sandy-haired man with a rash of freckles over his face grinned, saying, 'I'm sure we could fit you in,' and looking at her, 'and your... wife and even,' he looked down at Johnny, 'your son, if he's over seven.'

'He's not my...' Alice began, 'and... I'm his grandmother, step... grandmother.' She stopped, seeing the confusion on the instructor's face. He'd thought her and Frank were married, or together anyway.

'Jeez,' the instructor swept his hand over his face as if to eradicate his mistake, 'sorry,' he grinned. 'You don't look old enough to be a grandmother.'

'It's OK,' she said. 'We've just come to look today.'

'But the man said seven, and I am seven, well nearly, in four months,' Johnny said, his eyes alight with excitement.

'We'll come back then, with your parents, I think we need their permission first,' Frank said. 'Now let's go and watch them fly, then you'll know if you really want to do it another time.'

'You could write permission,' Johnny regarded Frank with hope in his eyes.

'Not without asking your father first, and anyway, I'm sure he'd love to see you taking your first flight,' Frank said without much conviction.

They followed the van with all the gear to the place where the participants took off. They watched as the flyers launched themselves into the air, running while connected to a collection of straps and strings, a little ungraceful perhaps; large lumbering people until they were airborne and the brightly coloured kites dipped and soared like strange birds.

Alice watched, her feelings in turmoil; she was wary of Frank, feeling that he held a bundle of secrets that concerned Julian, their life together, the brother she'd only found out existed a few weeks ago, and, to her consternation, she realised she was strongly attracted to him. That moment when their eyes sent out signals to each other, she'd felt as if there were strong feelings between them and yet, apart from them both caring for Julian, they did not belong together.

Chapter 23

It was a relief that the day seemed to be progressing happily, well for Johnny anyway, Alice thought. Still a little shaken by his utter despair when he'd first arrived in her house, now he was eager and excited, showering Frank with questions, that, bless him, he answered as fully as he could.

Douglas telephoned when they'd arrived in Scotland, his voice tense as if he'd been tortured all the way up by leaving his distraught son curled up on her doormat, and after a quick query as to how things were, asked to speak to him. He was surprised and not a little anxious at Johnny's bubbling excitement of where he was.

'I'm here with Granny Alice and Frank and we're paragliding,' Johnny announced breathlessly and Alice, squatting down beside Johnny, heard the fear in Douglas's voice as he insisted on talking to her.

She glanced guiltily at Frank and took the mobile. Hoping she sounded cheerful, she said, 'So you've arrived safely, all's well here.'

'It doesn't sound it,' Douglas said sharply. 'I must say I'm disappointed in you... Mrs... Alice.' She heard Laura in the background, say frantically, 'What's happened, is he all right?'

She was aware of Johnny watching her anxiously, the joy draining from his face as if he'd done something wrong, and Frank mouthing, 'Shall I speak to him?' When Douglas began listing Johnny's insecurities and how doing something so dangerous with him would surely put him back months if not years, she pushed in: 'Douglas, we are at a paragliding club *watching* not *doing* it,' she said, emphasising the words, irritated by his attitude.

'But Johnny said...'

'He meant we are watching it; he can't do it until he is seven. We are just here having lunch, watching other people, it's a lovely day and Frank has kindly brought us here.' She knew she sounded impatient and hoped he wouldn't take it out on Laura and ruin their time together at the wedding. She was about to ask to speak to her when he spoke.

'I'm sorry, I jumped to the wrong conclusions, I'm just worried about him, he's been more affected by... by things, his mother leaving and all. He's quite a different character to Zara.'

His words mollified her and she accepted his apology, saying how much Johnny was enjoying the day and then passed the mobile back to Johnny. His spirits, having fallen at his father's anxiety, perked up again while he described the scene.

Frank asked her what Douglas had said and when she told him he said, 'Oh... perhaps we shouldn't have come. I hope I haven't made things difficult for you.' He threw her a wicked smile, 'Still not used to you being a mother-in-law, let alone a granny, but seriously,' his voice became more sombre, 'parents often cause more problems than they know, by showing fear of something themselves, making the child fearful, draining their confidence.'

'I know... I wish she wasn't marrying him.' She turned her back on Johnny and lowered her voice so he wouldn't hear.

'I can understand his worry about how his divorce and the children's mother leaving the country has affected them, but I don't want Laura to be involved in it. She's too young, I want her to marry a man with no complications, no previous children, so they can have fun together, just the two of them until they have their own family. That's what Julian and I had and it was a precious time.'

Frank took a couple of steps nearer to her so he could hear her lowered voice. He leant close and she could feel his breath soft on her face, but when she said that she and Julian had had a precious time together before the children came, he moved back a fraction, his face took on that closed look again before he said, 'Marriage is different today, it's easy to divorce, there's no shame in it as there used to be and some people leave for the most mundane of reasons. Laura's situation is very common, but she'll cope. I know she will.' He smiled, put his hand on her arm, kind and comforting, and she wondered if she'd imagined his closed expression a moment before. Her feelings were in tumult, her daughters' life-changing behaviour, her still learning to live without Julian and the ridiculous way her body was reacting whenever Frank stood close to her. She must stop imagining things, why shouldn't he disappear into his own thoughts without her thinking he was guarding all sorts of secrets, things that he and Julian got up to when they were together? No one owned anyone else, she reminded herself firmly, not even two people who loved each other and shared so much as she and Julian had done.

Johnny finished talking to Douglas on the mobile and handed it back to her, his little body seeming more crushed as he was cut off again from his father.

Frank noticed and said, 'I think it's lunchtime, let's go and get a table before everyone one else comes in. We might get one by the window then you can watch the people who are still flying.'

'OK,' Johnny said. He slipped his hand into Alice's as they went into the clubhouse and her heart went out to him, if only she could take his insecurity from him. Would Evie's baby be riddled with confusion too, saddled with its complicated family? She felt weak just thinking of it.

Frank took Johnny into the Gents with him to wash before lunch and Alice had a few moments alone in the Ladies. She inspected herself in the mirror. Her hair was blown all over the place and her face flushed by the wind. She tided her hair as best she could but left her face as it was, feeling her present 'sporty, open air' look was better suited to this place than carefully applied make-up. She didn't look too bad, she thought, not exactly soignée like Petra, but then she never had looked like that. She admired Petra for working so hard on her looks and spending so much time – and no doubt money – on exercise classes, diets and treatments, but apart from trying to eat sensibly, Alice couldn't be bothered to spend whole days on preserving herself. Petra attracted a lot of men, but what did she do when they spent nights together? Did she sleep in make-up and get up before they did to do her hair and everything? She sighed, why think of this now, was it because she was with such an attractive man as Frank? She must stop thinking about it and go and join them in case Johnny needed her.

Johnny looked happy enough when she found them already seated at their table. He'd ordered chips.

'But would you not like...' she studied the menu, 'fish fingers, chicken or spaghetti Bolognese?' She felt Elspeth's shadow looming, brandishing her list of 'dangerous' foods.

'No, just chips,' he said, looking as if he might cry, so she hastily agreed.

The food was not good and Frank apologised. Most of it was brought in ready-made and just heated up in a microwave and the one salad on the menu consisted of a lot of lettuce with a few slivers of chopped vegetables lurking in the leaves. There was 'gateau' for pudding, a large cardboard-looking cake inlaid with icing and tinned cherries on top; they settled for coffee and mints.

'Sorry,' Frank said, handing her the plate of mints, 'when I said I'd take you out to lunch I meant something better than this.'

She smiled, 'It's fine, we can't always go to Mosimann's.'

'No, but even a pub lunch is better than this.'

'You've done it for Johnny,' she said. He'd eaten his chips and drunk his water – she hadn't dared suggest he have anything fizzy and additive full – and had now turned his chair round towards the window and was engrossed in watching what was going on outside. 'Thank you for that.'

Frank smiled, his eyes soft as he regarded her. 'It must be quite a shock taking on someone else's children and suddenly becoming a grandmother.'

'I wish I wasn't, well at least not in the way it's happened. And what on earth will Evie do with a baby and no husband? She's just landed herself a wonderful job illustrating children's books – there's a whole series they want her to do, but I don't know if she'll be able to keep it up once the baby's born.'

He put his hand over hers, 'Of course you want what's best for her,' he smiled, 'but she's made the choice and even though it's a foolish one, there's a child's welfare at stake and she and the father, dysfunctional though he sounds, it's up to them to sort it out.' He took his hand away and she felt bereft.

'Life's so different from when we were young, isn't it?' She watched him grimace at the bitter taste as he finished his espresso. 'I mean, so many people having such complicated relationships, and all these poor children having to get used to new people in their parents' lives. I know I was lucky with Julian, lucky no one else had snapped him up before I found him.' She smiled.

'Yes,' Frank said. His expression a moment ago almost tender now became serious again, sending a chill into her. He'd told her his marriage was over, so did he think her sanctimonious for judging people who had not lived the same way as she and Julian had lived? When she'd known him all those years ago, she'd thought Frank more of a free spirit than Julian and perhaps he thought her too judgemental? Like she thought Elspeth was.

'I don't think, in fact I know Julian would have disapproved of Evie getting involved with Nick,' she said firmly, wanting to justify her remarks, insist that Julian shared them with her, wanting, she realised, for Frank not to think her mean-spirited.

Frank studied his wine glass as his fingers played with the stem. 'These things happen. Decent people make mistakes.'

'Of course, but Nick is old enough to know better; Evie's baby is not his first with another woman.' Her voice was edged with panic, in just a few weeks this baby would be born and change all of their lives. Evie needed to work and was so fortunate to have been chosen to do all those illustrations. There were surely many more, just as talented artists ready to snatch her place if she should fail. Alice did not want to be forced back into the nursery but nor did she want Evie to lose her job, her place in such a demanding environment. It was so easy for people like Frank and Cecily to say Evie had made her choice and must get on with it, but she knew, much though she didn't want to pander to it, she would not be able to stand aside if Evie and the baby – who, unlike Douglas's children, was part of their family, a part of Julian – needed her care.

Frank was silent and still. She guessed he was bored of the subject. He'd brought them out for a nice day, a day that revolved round Johnny, a child that had no link to him at all except he was to be the stepchild of his goddaughter. He, so used to delicious food, had had to eat this instant stuff that was already giving her indigestion and leaving a nasty taste in her mouth, there hadn't even been a decent wine to wash it down.

'I'm sorry,' she said. 'I won't go on about it; tell me about your children, do you see them often?'

He seemed relieved that she'd changed the subject, his expression lightened, he obviously loved his children and was proud of them and pleased to tell her about them. When he'd finished telling her his son was keen on sailing and his daughter good at riding and how she longed to ride in events, his face became less animated and she tried to encourage him by saying, 'It's an expensive sport, does she have a horse of her own?'

'Yes, but it's not good enough if she wants to try for the big time, and you need more than one.'

'Has she a chance? I understand it's very difficult sport to succeed in.'

'She's very good,' he said quietly.

He was worried about the expense, she thought, perhaps it was difficult to get sponsorship in France, or he had too much money to apply for it but not enough to fund her. He was quiet and, really to fill in the silence, she said, 'Does she get her talent from you or her mother?'

There was a long pause, he did not look at her but she could see the pain in his eyes. What had she said wrong? It was such a minefield if you didn't know someone well. She racked her brains for some light remark to ease the tension that had crept between them, but then he said quietly, 'She gets her talent from my father and my elder brother.'

'Henry?' His name shot out of her mouth.

'Yes,' his face was anguished, his eyes on her. 'Henry. No doubt Julian told you about him?'

'No,' she said, 'it was Cecily who told me about him, and only a few weeks ago. I never knew he existed, which was odd, don't you think, as he was Julian's best friend?'

Chapter 24

Why had his name slipped out like that? She was mortified; if she had always known it, his name might not be so readily on her lips. It had shocked Frank, who was struggling to compose himself, his eyes eloquent with grief.

'I'm so sorry.' She grasped his hand, 'I didn't mean to upset you, I just... well when Cecily told me about it I was surprised – upset that Julian hadn't told me something so obviously important to him. Forgive me, I won't mention it again.' She was near tears herself. Since Julian's death she became more affected by other people's grief than she had before.

The mood changed between them as if there was an unexploded grenade squatting on the table. Talking of the dead was painful, as she knew only too well. Sometimes it was easy, comforting to bring them back with some amusing story or a warm memory, but other times the grief gripped you by its teeth, refusing to let go.

'It's all right,' he attempted a smile, squeezing her hand. 'I... I just assumed he'd have told you about it, but maybe he thought...' His voice tailed off and he bent his head so she could not see his eyes.

'I expect it was too painful for him,' she said quickly, not wanting Frank to elaborate. Was it because she couldn't bear his pain, or talk of Julian, or... something else? Something that bothered her, made her feel she was faced with a Pandora's box and it would be a mistake to open it?

'Perhaps.' He took a deep breath, and confronted her with determination as if he had to tell her. 'Henry had this terrible riding accident, broke his back and all he could move was his head.' He stated it calmly now, although his face was tortured as he remembered it. 'He couldn't bear to be left like that. I miss him dreadfully, but when he died, it was a relief to know that he was free of it all.'

'I understand,' she said to comfort him. But it only threw up more questions she was afraid to ask. Such a tragedy would surely deeply affect Henry's family and friends. So why hadn't Julian told her about it? He'd told her so many other intimate things, things about his family, how he'd found it difficult to love his father who'd returned home a bully after the war, he'd even told her about a broken love affair, a woman he'd loved who'd hadn't loved him, or not enough to marry him. She'd felt quite jealous about it but understood that he was telling her everything important about himself before she committed to marrying him. But he hadn't told her about Henry, his death, or even the existence of his apparent best friend.

'Henry would be the last person to stop Aline, my daughter, following in his sport. Everyone knows riding can be dangerous, as can skiing, sailing, even driving a car, and I don't mind about those,' he smiled, 'enjoy doing them myself, but I find it difficult to let her ride, take it as seriously as Henry did, though I know I'm being unfair,' Frank said, his face calmer now.

'It must be hard,' she said, 'the fear of losing people we love is overwhelming, but just because it happened to him, it doesn't mean it will happen to Aline, and maybe her love of riding is just a phase and she'll pass through it.' There was a note of desperation in her voice; she wanted to wipe away Frank's pain, to return to their easy friendship of a few moments ago. She sensed they were in dangerous waters and she wanted to steer clear.

He seemed to guess her thoughts. 'Let's hope so,' he smiled, released her hand and turned back to Johnny. 'Shall we go outside and watch some more people taking off?'

'Yes... yes please.' Johnny's eyes shone with excitement, so different to the little boy of this morning. Frank had saved them from a difficult weekend; he'd given him confidence and something exciting to dwell on instead of the painful upheavals in his life.

Laura was part of that upheaval, though as far as Alice knew she had nothing to do with his parents' break-up. It was surely too much for her to deal with. After the wedding, Frank would return to his life in France and would not be here to take Johnny out on trips such as this, and she didn't see Douglas doing it. How difficult for Laura to start a marriage encumbered with his children. She remembered the early days of her marriage, just her and Julian drunk with love and passion, and apart from the disruptions of work, they could do what they liked – just please each other. The birth of the children had cemented their love, but that first year, before Laura, was one of the most precious times of her life. Laura would not have that, nor indeed would Evie.

Frank paid the bill, refusing to let Alice contribute, and they left the clubhouse and went to watch more people flying, Johnny running ahead but stopping and turning round every so often to make sure they were following behind.

'What are you thinking of?' Frank said, having seen how

quiet she had become. He linked his arm into hers.

'Just my girls and what strange starts they will have to their marriages. It was just Julian and I for the first year or so and I feel that was so important, like laying down firm foundations to build the family on. Laura and Douglas won't have the privacy, the space, to do that, and if Evie marries sometime, she'll bring Nick's baby into the relationship.'

'That's life today, and they must make the best of it. But you and Julian were lucky, Simone and I had time together before the children and our marriage did not last, perhaps there was not enough love to sustain it.' He smiled at her, squeezed her arm to him a second before letting go and calling to Johnny that he'd race him to the take-off site, leaving her feeling as if he'd taken something with him and she didn't know what.

Chapter 25

How strange that Julian had not told Alice about Henry. It hurt... shocked Frank deeply; he hoped he'd hidden his reaction from her. It had been a terrible time, the worst in his life; he'd idolised his elder brother. Henry was so good-looking, athletic, and so talented in almost everything he did. He was a brilliant horseman, shared such an affinity with the horses which brought out the best in them.

Henry rode for a couple of seasons as a jump jockey, done more for fun than to make a career of it, being too tall and therefore too heavy to be a jockey. He remembered his brother before that fateful race, laughing with the stable girl – the last time he had laughed with that sheer joy of being young and alive and about to ride – as he had countless times before.

He'd fallen at the third last jump, he was not ahead but in a group and it was no one's fault. Trojan, his horse jumped badly and both had fallen. Frank remembered the icy chill of shock as he saw it and the long stretched-out moments as he waited for Henry to get up as he had when he'd had other falls. Trojan struggled up at once but Henry did not. Then their lives took on a terrible momentum of hospitals and diagnoses and prognoses and, however it was put, the news was stark and unforgiving. Henry, that gilded youth with so much talent and charm, was imprisoned in a body that was useless. He would never again gallop over the turf, make love, even walk unaided across a room. It was a tragedy that affected all those who loved him, so how could Julian have kept such a monumental event from his wife, the woman he loved above all others?

But as Frank thought this over he realised that it was not as simple as that. Had it just been Henry's accident and death it would have been different, less complicated, and Alice had been very young and innocent then and might not have understood the whole story and, having been told it, might not have wanted to marry Julian. Then as time went on and they made their lives together and the girls were born, he imagined it became increasingly difficult to broach the subject, so it was pushed away, hidden under other things, perhaps even forgotten. Though when Julian became ill, faced his own death, had he not thought he should tell her then? Perhaps he had decided to do it, was waiting for the right moment, and though his death was not a surprise it was not expected to happen so soon, or he could have thought it too late to tell her Henry's story? After all *he* hadn't seen much of Alice over the years so perhaps Julian saw little point in telling her about something that had happened to his brother, a brother she had never known about.

Johnny kept them going most of the journey back by asking endless questions about paragliding and they got back to London at about seven. He'd have liked to have taken Alice out to dinner – to eat proper food after that lunch, but he obviously couldn't as she had Johnny to look after and he was now half asleep and couldn't come with them, so he'd said goodbye, kissed her chastely on the cheek and said he'd be back in London soon and he'd contact her as soon as he was.

He was going back to Paris on the Eurostar the next day

so he could finish that article on the way and be ready for his early appointment on Monday morning. Henry seemed very close to him tonight, a bittersweet memory. He could see his once strong athletic body prone in bed attached to various drips and devices and his eyes, those eloquent eyes, begging him.

He could talk, and talk he did, he didn't want to live like this, a vegetable unable to move. He'd understood, would feel that way himself if it had happened to him. Henry had been so full of life, a natural sportsman, riding, skiing for the army during his time there, climbing mountains. Their father understood, but their mother wanted to keep whatever was left of him. She would sit for hours holding his hand and talking to him, bringing him music, reading books, hassling the doctors for operations, treatments that would make his life better, but he didn't want it 'better', he wanted all or nothing, that was how Henry was and Julian understood it and so did Frank, but he did not have the courage to do what Henry begged.

He didn't want to be alone this evening with his thoughts of his brother. He had other friends, but they were probably away for the weekend or had plans already. If only Alice were free. But perhaps it was as well she wasn't, he must not get too close to her. There was Petra and Margot who'd begged him to come to supper, lunch, a drink, just drop in whenever he could. He was tempted, but he sensed they, Petra anyway, expected more than dinner and that would be a mistake and upset his relationship with Alice, though what was his relationship with Alice? Just being kind to her and the girls because Julian was no longer here? There could be nothing else because of the obstacles between them.

Surely Julian could have told her everything before he

died? If he hadn't told her about Henry, he obviously hadn't told her anything else about his earlier life. Alice was more mature now, knew that love was not all silver stars and sugary music. It would have shocked and saddened her, but she would have understood and accepted his revelations as things that had happened before she'd even known him. Julian was much older than she was after all, had almost twenty years of living before he met her.

He thought of Cecily, he'd always been fond of her, but perhaps it was too late to visit her. Although it was only eight o'clock, he'd ring her; Kalinda would answer if she were in bed.

But it was Cecily who answered. 'Frank, it's so long since I've seen you, of course come round. I hardly sleep, night is the same as day, and I'd love to see you. I have some good wine and some excellent cheese if that suits you.'

'Sounds perfect, though I'd like to take you out to dinner,' he said.

'And I'd love to go,' she laughed, 'but not tonight, dear Frank, but do come here. It will be wonderful to see you.'

He'd put a bottle of Moet et Chandon Grand Vintage champagne in the fridge hoping to share with Alice if they spent the day together – before he knew about Johnny – and this he took to Cecily.

'Champagne and one of the best.' Cecily's face lit up, and for an instant he saw the young and beautiful woman she'd once been. She was wearing a luscious dark red silk dressing gown, her face subtly made up and her thick white hair swept back with tortoiseshell combs. She looked wonderful.

'Kalinda, please fetch the glasses and one for yourself, it will be a rare treat to drink such a vintage,' she said. 'I'm so pleased to see you, Frank.' She gestured for him to sit down beside her on the sofa. 'I'm so glad we found you. I don't know if you ever got my letter but at least the telephone call got you in the end.'

'I'll get the letter eventually, Simone, my wife, or ex-wife really though we're not divorced, still lives there but she's away in the mountains for a few weeks, but I'm here anyway.' He went on to tell her about his day with Alice and Johnny then Kalinda came with the glasses and he opened the champagne and they all toasted each other.

Cecily said with a smile, 'And to Julian too, who brought you, Alice and the girls into my life and enriched it so.' Her words almost made him cry and he was grateful for the dim lighting that softened their features and hid his pain.

'Alice is worried about the wedding, or rather Laura rushing into it so soon and with a man she somewhat sprang on her. She'd never heard even a whisper of him before she announced they were getting married. Have you met him, Frank?' Cecily asked him.

'No, not yet, but I spent the day with his son, an insecure little boy.' And he told Cecily about their day watching the paragliding.

'Oh, did Alice have a go, she says she wants to.' Cecily laughed.

'No, we had Johnny and it was booked up being the weekend, but I'll take her another time, without Johnny. Just us two would be best. Laura probably wouldn't approve. I think she's quite cautious like her father.'

'You're right, she's not like Evie, who jumps before she thinks.' Cecily sighed, 'But Alice has the idea that Julian's death has pushed Laura, and indeed Evie, to make these drastic decisions. Evie's is worse of course, landing herself with a baby with a man who, by the sound of him, will not stay around.'

'We couldn't talk much today with Johnny there, but that could have something to do with it. Julian was obviously a good father and they must miss him dreadfully, he died far too young, but perhaps their decisions will make life more difficult for them, especially for Evie.' Privately he thought that both girls should have had more sense than to jump into such relationships, Evie anyway, he hadn't met Douglas so he couldn't judge that, but it was best not to say it and it was too late now for incriminations.

'It was foolish of her,' Cecily said as if she'd read his mind. 'Birth Control is readily available today. It was so difficult for us to get hold of it when I was young, especially if we weren't married, but now it seems it's almost handed out like sweets, which,' she smiled, 'possibly makes it compulsory to sleep with someone even if you don't want to, but one of them should have taken precautions.'

'Unless she thought if she had his child he'd leave his wife and stay with her,' Frank said. 'She wouldn't be the first woman to think that. She's old enough to know what's what, but missing her father makes her vulnerable to these so-called charming lovers.'

'I haven't met Nick,' Cecily said. 'I don't suppose he'll be asked to the wedding, so I never will.'

'Nor will I, unless I go to Suffolk, and there's no reason for me to go there.'

They discussed it more and time slipped by. They shared cheese and biscuits with a delicious red wine and fruit. Cecily did not seem tired; in fact, as the hours went on, she seemed more and more alert. It was comforting to be with her, she had been so much a part of Julian's life. 'She's so much more fun and easier to be with than my mother,' Julian used to say.

When Frank had first met Cecily she'd been working, travelling the world as a photographer, sending back pictures, usually of children – perhaps having none of her own, it was the closest she got to parenthood – children working on the rubbish heaps in India; little girls with their heads covered, posing in exotic marketplaces; boys flying kites in Afghanistan, their faces bright and eager or sometimes crushed by sorrows they were too young to understand.

Some of her photographs of the scenery of the countries she visited hung on the walls showing however cruel people were to each other nature still blessed them with wonderful sunrises and sunsets. The room with its warmth and soft lights threw up a feeling of intimacy and he said, his heart heavy now with guilt, 'I should have been here for Julian, were his last weeks very bad?'

She regarded him gravely, reading the guilt in his expression. 'We are born alone and we die alone, I learnt that in the war when so many people died such horrible deaths,' she said gently. 'His heart got very weak, there were various discussions as to whether to have certain treatments, even an operation, but before anything was decided he suddenly deteriorated and slipped away. I think that is what he wanted, not to go through painful procedures, sick-inducing drugs, just to struggle through a few more months of life.' Her eyes flickered towards the two photographs of the young men she'd loved on the table beside her.

'Without war we live longer, but it is the quality of life that counts, and I think he was ready to go, he hated putting Alice and the girls through it, though I've never said that to her. If he could have been made well again, it would have been different, but the medical world can only do so much, as you know with Henry,' she said quietly. 'Life means different things to different people and there are times when they should be able to choose their own exit.'

'So Julian...'

'No, it just happened with him, even the doctors were surprised he went so soon, though he could have lost the will to live, who knows? But he's left such an empty void behind him. He was like the son I never had, the one I would have wanted.' Her voice was soft; her faded eyes gleaming with unshed tears. He put his hand on hers and she smiled, 'But Alice will be all right, I know she will, she's been through hell, but she's getting stronger, it's just a pity the girls have landed themselves in such situations, but somehow it will work out, though perhaps not as happily as we might wish.'

Chapter 26

It didn't surprise Alice that there were repercussions after taking Johnny to the paragliding club. It wasn't as if he'd even done it, but having been almost mute when he arrived he now wouldn't stop talking about it.

She didn't care what the 'grisly grannies,' as she nicknamed them, thought of her, but it worried her that it seemed to have upset the balance between Douglas and Laura.

'Couldn't you have taken him to the Natural History museum like other grandparents do, Mum?' Laura wailed, having taken the day off work and coming round the morning after they'd collected him – which was very late so there was no time or energy for a post-mortem of the weekend then. 'You know what they're like, especially Elspeth, as Miriam, the other grandmother, is too tied up with her husband's health at the moment. Elspeth thinks it's bad to overexcite him. He's been let down, she said, because now you've taken him there, he wants to do something he won't be able to do, so it's bad for his self-esteem.'

'What nonsense, darling.' Alice was exhausted; she'd slept badly the last two nights, first listening for Johnny, and both nights disturbed by thinking about Frank.

'Poor child he seems so lost, so insecure, which is hardly surprising with his mother going off like that, but this outing made him happy, gave him an interest and Frank was wonderful with him.'

'It's not my fault he's so shy.' Laura slumped on the sofa in despair.

'Of course it's not,' Alice said hurriedly, hoping Laura wasn't going to start blaming herself for Johnny's insecurity. She should not be marrying Douglas, at least not yet. She was twenty-four and had no experience with children, especially not damaged ones.

The wedding plans were well on their way, but should she not find a way to ask Laura if she was really sure she wanted to take on this battered family? It was a rather sudden decision and might it not be better to postpone the wedding anyway until the following summer to give everyone time to get used to the idea? But Laura in the mood she was in would take it as a criticism of her choice of man, and she'd set her heart on this wedding. Who knew what the reason was, she certainly didn't.

'It might be love, good old common and garden love,' Cecily had said when Alice discussed it with her. 'Just because they are not all over each other all the time doesn't mean they don't feel it deeply; they could just be slow burners.'

Slow burners or not, Alice wished she was more convinced of their future happiness.

'Let's have some coffee, it's ages since breakfast,' Alice said, hoping to change the atmosphere.

'Johnny is dreadfully unhappy; sometimes he wakes in the night with nightmares. Douglas has to sit with him. I don't know what to do about it, perhaps he does need professional help, but no one will do anything. His grandparents think it's just a phase he's going through.'

'Did he have nightmares last night?' Alice asked.

'No, he slept right through. He was excited about the

paragliding,' she added grudgingly. 'It's just that Elspeth…
who rang us first thing, told Douglas it was wrong of you to
have taken him there. She thinks…' Laura looked guilty, as
if she were responsible for Elspeth's opinion, 'that being so
much younger than them – her and his other grandparents –
you… you don't have the right ideas.'

'I have *my* ideas,' Alice retorted. 'I think I brought you
both up successfully, didn't I? No, don't answer that,' she
said, expecting Laura to make some remark about Evie's
behaviour with another woman's husband. 'I shall do my
best, but I don't see why I should conform to the out-dated
ideas of the grisly grannies.'

Laura giggled. 'Oh Mum, what a name, but it's true, they
are a bit grisly, especially Elspeth. You'll meet her very soon,
Douglas wants to have a dinner with her and he wants to
invite Frank as he sees him as Dad's stand-in.' She looked at
Alice anxiously.

'I suppose he is,' Alice said. 'So when is this dinner?' Her
stomach cramped with dread.

'Sometime next week. Douglas also thinks Miriam and
David should come, if David is well enough, being the other
grandparents. He said the most important people are the
children, and it would be good if all the major people in their
lives could get to know each other.'

'Next week?' She knew she had to meet Douglas's mother
but had vainly hoped it wouldn't be before the wedding.
With luck the two of them not having much – if anything –
in common, need hardly ever have to see each other. It was a
bit daunting to have to meet the other grandparents as well
though she did see his point, but couldn't they meet up some
other time in the future?

'Yes, are you busy?' Laura eyed her accusingly.

'No, but let me know the date, Frank's away on business, but hopefully he'll be back in time.' She didn't think she could bear to go if he wasn't there. 'But David, is he very ill?' She changed the subject.

'No, it was what the doctor called a warning, but he's meant to rest. So we'll arrange it for the end of next week. What nights are you free and I'll text Frank to see if he'll be back, and what about Evie?' Laura looked uncomfortable. 'It will a bore for her won't it, to come up just for dinner?'

Alice understood Laura's reluctance to invite her now obviously pregnant sister to meet the family she was about to join. Elspeth would not approve, and if Evie were there, it might provoke a row, an atmosphere anyway. Evie would not take well to what she saw as sanctimonious remarks about the modern way of life as she practised it.

'She'll meet everyone at the wedding. You have the date the 4th of December, that's confirmed isn't it? The house you want in Putney is free and what about a church? Are you getting married in a church?' she asked tentatively, wondering if they'd have a religious service or just a blessing, or neither.

'Douglas knows a priest who'll give us a blessing in a little Victorian church on Putney Common, the reception's just down the road.' Laura took a brochure out of her bag and thrust it at her. 'A cousin of Douglas's had his reception there some years ago, but I'm sure it's all right, we'll go and look at it anyway.'

At least it wasn't the same venue as his first wedding. Alice leafed through the brochure. It had a picture of a wrought iron gate with the words 'Think and Thank' intertwined in it. This led through a small garden to a pretty house. The words made her feel that it depended on the thoughts, which for her were now like a swarm of stinging bees coming in her direction and she wouldn't thank anyone for them.

She accepted that Douglas was a good man, but she still felt that Laura, sad and lost without her father, had grabbed him as one might grab a passing branch if drowning in a fast river, regardless of what kind of tree it came from, whether it was a strong, supporting one or one that would splinter into pieces if tested. Even a strong marriage based on passionate love went through choppy waters, but if it was weak from the start, perhaps embarked upon with honourable but the wrong emotions, what hope was there then? But the thing that worried her most was that there were children involved, children who were already traumatised by the break-up of their parents' marriage, and that she felt put more than the usual pressures on to Laura.

Now was the time to speak her mind, perhaps she should talk about the children, and their reactions to it, suggest they wait until the summer when the weather would be better and by then Laura would have had more time to think it through and decide if it really was what she wanted. Or should she speak to Douglas about her concerns about Laura taking on his children, especially while Johnny seemed so vulnerable? But before she could muster the words together, the telephone rang and Laura jumped up to answer it.

'Oh, Frank, good it's you. Douglas wants to arrange a dinner to meet his mother next week and hopes you can come, what nights are you free?'

Perhaps he was not free at all, Alice thought, but that would not stop the dinner with Elspeth taking place and it would be far worse if he couldn't make it and be there to support her. Like it or not, it was going to happen and she must get on with it.

The dreaded dinner was fixed for Thursday. They all met at a French restaurant off Sloane Square, Frank picked Alice up in his car and he laughed when she told him how much she was dreading it.

'It's not obligatory to get on with the in-laws,' he teased her, 'but I understand, it makes the marriage more real for you, doesn't it? But it's Laura's choice and I think Douglas is a decent man. I liked him when I met him and I think he'll suit Laura very well.'

'Do you really?' she asked, and before he could answer she went on, 'But the children, I worry about her having to cope with them. I mean she's not just taking on a man, having time to get used to living with him before they add any more people to the household. Perhaps she ought to have lived with him and them for more than the occasional night or weekend, before deciding to marry him.'

'She'll manage, she'll bring them some security,' he smiled. 'Stop worrying, Alice, throwing up obstacles.'

The dinner brought out the worst in her. As she guessed, Elspeth disapproved of her on sight. She was a tall woman, slightly hunched, her hair styled neatly like an iron-grey cap on her head; she was dressed in a plain fawn dress and jacket, with a high neck and a calf-length skirt. She shook Alice's hand quickly as if she might catch something nasty from her and it was obvious as she looked her up and down that she thought her short, black lace dress was unsuitable. In her eyes, grandmothers did not do 'sexy'.

The other grandparents, Miriam and David, 'call me Dave', were easier to get on with. Douglas's ex-father-in-law had obviously recovered from whatever had prevented him babysitting that weekend Douglas and Laura were away. He eyed up Alice, leering slightly in her direction but in no more than an overgrown schoolboy sort of way, showing off to hide his nervousness when faced with an attractive woman. Frank came and stood protectively beside her, so he grinned good-naturedly and moved away. Miriam was very quiet, fragile-looking, as if her husband's boisterousness and perhaps her daughter's behaviour in running away from her husband and children had exhausted her, but she obviously adored her grandchildren and was pleasant enough to Alice, and even Laura, the two new women who were to share her grandchildren's lives.

They all sat down, Alice next to Douglas and Dave, and it was Elspeth who held court.

'We have a very delicate situation with Douglas's children,' she started before anyone had even looked at the menu or ordered any wine.

Alice said nothing, though she caught Frank's eye, glittering with mischief, giving her strength.

'We,' Elspeth started grandly, 'have written up some guidelines as to how best to bring them up. If we all set the same standards, then we can't go wrong, can we?'

'I'm sure Alice...' Douglas began as a waiter hovered for orders and Dave immediately asked for wine, 'Your house wine... a bottle of each,' which sent the waiter scurrying away to obey him.

'It's not your fault that you have had so little time with the children, and Laura, nice though she is...' Alice felt Elspeth's statement was pushed through gritted teeth, and glancing at Laura saw she felt the same, 'has very little experience with children and you know what they say about stepmothers, it is a very difficult relationship.'

'Only very misguided people say spiteful things,' Alice broke in, wanting to stand up for her daughter.

The wine waiter returned and went through the motions of opening the bottle and pouring the wine into Dave's glass to taste.

'It's a very difficult time for them,' Elspeth went on and Alice saw the guilt on Miriam's face, it was, after all, *her* daughter who, for whatever reason, had upped and left her young children.

Frank saved the day. 'I think the children are very fortunate to have so many decent, loving people to care for them,' he said. 'I very much enjoyed meeting Johnny the other day, he's a delightful child and we had a very good time together.'

'He's been overexcited after that outing for days,' Elspeth said acidly, eyeing Frank as if he were a danger too. 'He never stops going on about this *paragliding*,' she said the word as if it described something contaminating, like porn or lessons in knife crime.

Thankfully Dave muscled in, 'We all have the children's best interests at heart, Elspeth, now let's order, I'm starving, wasn't allowed to eat in the hospital, nearly died of starvation.' He laughed.

The dinner limped on and at last it was over. Douglas drove his mother home, no doubt to nag him all the way, and Frank drove Laura and Alice.

'Isn't she a witch,' Laura said as they drove down the King's Road.

Frank said, 'She is rather, but I expect it's because she's really worried about the children coping with yet another change in their lives. Once she gets to know you and sees how good you are with them, she'll be easier to get on with.'

Don't bank on it, Alice thought, but she said nothing, wishing with all her strength that the wedding would not take place.

Chapter 27

'I hear Frank's gone off again, he can't seem to stay in one place for a moment,' Margot grumbled, pushing a bowl of salad in Alice's direction, her eyes like searchlights on Alice's face as if to winkle out the slightest hint of her keeping his whereabouts a secret.

'He's only gone for a couple of days, he leads a very busy life.' Alice hoped she sounded disinterested, curbing her irritation of the fuss generated by her women friends by Frank's arrival. 'Mmm, lovely spinach and pomegranate,' she said, helping herself to the pretty pink and green salad, hoping to change the subject. 'I feel I need lots of iron after all our hard work.'

They'd spent the morning going through the accounts of their decorating business, having had a small resurrection with Cecily's curtains and a few other orders. They kept their accounts at Margot's house as Glen, Margot's husband, had a sort of office here and let them use his accountant from time to time.

Margot ignored the virtues of spinach and pressed on. 'I thought he was staying in London until after the wedding.'

'He's got a case, or an article or something, he's got to do, he'll be back.' Alice did not say that she missed him, that he probably wanted to spend time with whatever woman he was seeing, for surely there was one, if not more than one. She didn't want to talk about Frank and yet she did, talking of him kept him close, but that was foolish of her when he had another life in France without her. Margot knew her too well and the last thing she wanted was for her to imagine that she was attracted to him.

Margot could be secretive herself, namely about Glen's job in a prestigious financial company, which seemed to pay him staggering amounts. She often had a new piece of jewellery or a handbag, which she brushed off with some vague remark about Glen getting some bonus or tax rebate. '*Some tax rebate*,' people muttered darkly when they heard about it. She'd perfected ways to steer questions away from these extravagances, but she was like a terrier if she wanted to dig out gossip about other people.

'Do you know when Frank will be back? Petra and I wanted to give parties for him; he's so difficult to pin down. There's lots of people who remember him from when we were all young and he lived here and would love to see more of him,' Margot went on.

'I don't think he likes parties much,' Alice said warily before going on. 'I know this sounds odd, but seeing Frank somehow makes Julian's loss more final as I've only ever seen them together and so now he's here without him...'

'I didn't think of that, sorry, love.' Margot patted her hand. 'Of course it must be tough for you having him taking Julian's place at Laura's wedding.

Why had she said that about Frank and Julian? She hadn't meant to, even though it was true. Margot was smiling at her kindly and before Alice could stop herself she went on talking, as if by speaking the words she could make sense of them. 'I don't remember... well apart from a memorable ride

182

in his sports car – that I was ever really alone with Frank, he was always there in those days, just one of the crowd.' She attempted a laugh, dreading that Margot might realise that she had this odd yearning to be close to him, but that, she hastily told herself, was only because she missed Julian.

'Frank always cared for you, surely you knew that?' Margot said bossily.

'Oh, Margot, whatever do you mean?' She laughed.

'I just remember how he used to look at you, Petra noticed it too, but you were crazy about Julian so you probably didn't see it and maybe it was nothing, just a crush he had on you when we were all young. But I just wonder… now he's back and Julian is gone.' Margot scrutinised her carefully as if she was a casting director searching for a leading lady.

Margot's words unsettled Alice. She'd sensed Frank found her attractive, but he hadn't made any kind of pass, not even a jokey one, in fact there were times when she felt he was distancing himself from her. He was a kind man, an honourable man, Julian's great friend and Laura's godfather, determined to do his bit for her wedding, and he'd stuck up for her in front of Elspeth, but that was all. When the wedding was over he would be gone.

When they'd finished lunch and returned to their work, Alice said, 'Did you know Frank had a nephew living in London, or rather staying in his flat while he studied here?' She wanted to know if Margot – often the queen of gossip – knew anything about him.

Margot frowned, 'I didn't, how old is he?'

'Thirtyish. It's just odd Frank never mentioned it, or asked us to invite him to a meal or something. If Julian knew I'm sure he'd have asked him round, see he was all right. I don't think the boy's parents were around, not in London anyway.

He's a bit older than the girls, but all the same I'd have told Frank if one of them had gone to study in Paris.'

Margot laughed. 'You sure it was his nephew? Perhaps that's just a euphemism for Frank's love child. You know what the French are like, or supposed to be anyway. Cherchez la femme, I'd say.'

'Nonsense, Margot,' Alice laughed, 'anyway Frank is not French.'

'His grandmother was,' Margot said smugly, 'and blood will out.' She opened one of their work folders and examined it.

'Do you think we ought to cut these into tiny pieces to make sure no one finds credit card or bank details?' Margot pulled out a stack of old invoices, 'Our shredder is broken or we could have used that.'

'Who's going to look? Some of these are over ten years old. Have you seen odd people creeping round your dustbins?' Alice joked, 'Or do you fear the tax man?'

Her remark, not to be taken seriously, made Margot laugh rather frantically, 'Oh… no, no… well, I hope not.' She looked rather shifty and then, taking herself in hand, said more firmly, 'No, I just thought someone might see a credit card number or something and hack someone's account. You hear such a lot about hacking and things these days.' She picked up some scissors and began to cut the addresses and bank details into tiny slivers before pushing them into a plastic bag. 'Better safe than sorry,' she said with an awkward smile.

Margot's expression made Alice feel uncomfortable. It was none of her business what people did about paying tax and such and she knew they'd always given the correct information from their decorating business to an accountant and paid their dues, but that was just their own business, she didn't know what Glen did… or Margot with her own money for that matter, it wasn't anything to do with her.

'How well we did in those early days, we made quite a bit of money, didn't we?' She flicked through some of the invoices, 'Wish we could now.'

'Emma Bede made such a pretty Moses basket for her granddaughter, and I wonder if there could be a market in that,' Margot said. 'I'm sure our ladies in Suffolk could make some, they might be glad to do something different, glad of the work anyway.'

'That sounds a great idea, and we could line some baskets with little pockets to put the power, creams and such in; they'd make really special presents.' Alice was enthused by the idea. Would Evie be pleased with such a gift or would she dump all her baby stuff in with her painting things, possibly smearing the poor baby with paint instead of cream?

For the rest of the afternoon they looked up prices for plain baskets to cover with pretty material on the Internet and Alice drew some designs, including some for bags for all of a baby's kit and changing mats for travelling and cot buffers. They decided to ask Edith and Amy to make up a few samples and see how they went.

'I wish I had a daughter to make them for,' Margot, who had two strapping sons, said. 'Let's hope I have daughters-in-law I like.'

Alice, who had rather hoped one or both of her daughters might marry Margot's sons – boys she'd known since birth – said nothing. Apart from becoming a granny she was also about to become a mother-in-law to a 'nice but dull' man, unless Laura changed her mind, but she feared that now she was on the roller coaster of wedding plans she wouldn't be able to jump off in time.

It was early evening when Alice left Margot. She reluctantly agreed to go the long way home and drop an invitation through Frank's letter box to a party she and Glen were giving in a fortnight's time.

'I don't know exactly where he lives,' Alice said. 'I only have his telephone number.'

'Queen's Gate, you can take the 14 bus from South Ken home, it's just on the corner of Harrington Road, white door, his name's on the letter box.'

'You seem to know an awful lot about it, what's the flat like?' Alice teased her.

Margot blushed, 'I've no idea. I just know his address.'

Alice laughed, 'OK, I'll drop it off.' At least he was away and wouldn't see her hanging about as if she were a groupie.

Alice left Margot, both of them now fired up by their new nursery designs, and having ordered baskets and material online, Margot volunteered to drive them to Suffolk for Amy and Edith to make up.

It had stopped raining but it was almost as dark as a winter's evening. Alice turned out of Margot's street and into Queen's Gate and walked down towards Frank's flat. She crossed one half of the road, stopped in the middle waiting for a couple of taxis to pass before she crossed over the other half. A man came out of the door of Frank's block of flats, hovered on the pavement in front of her and then crossed the road towards her. Her heart stopped; it was Julian. She saw his profile as he turned to check for traffic and the way he stood and his long, purposeful stride as he crossed the road.

'Julian,' she called, her arm reaching as if to catch him, but he didn't hear and crossed the road behind her, walking quickly away.

She was mad, of course it wasn't Julian. This man was far

younger, and Julian was dead. It was a trick of the light or rather the shadows, that was all.

She pushed Frank's invitation through his mailbox beside the front door and turned away towards South Kensington and the bus. She was tired, she had too much to think and worry about with her daughters' new life choices, and yet for a moment she'd been so certain it was Julian, if only it had been and she could see him one more time.

Chapter 28

The telephone rang, waking Alice abruptly, drilling through her subconscious. She'd barely slept, tormented by her anxieties, and had surely just dropped off when she was so violently woken. Mechanically, she stretched for the phone on her bedside table. 'Hello.'

'Alice, or should I say Granny, glammy granny as Evie calls you,' a teasing male voice addressed her. 'The baby's come, born early.'

'What?' She sat up as if electrified. 'Nick, is that you, what's happened, is Evie all right?' Fear clutched at her, she struggled to be calm.

'Everything is fine. It's a boy. It happened quite fast for a first child. She went into labour about midnight and he was born about half an hour ago.'

'Is he premature?' Fearfully, she envisaged a tiny scrap of humanity attached to wires and monitors, fighting for life.

'Not really, she probably got her dates wrong. He's fine.' His voice was defensive as if *his* babies were of a superior kind, who never got born too early or were any less than perfect. 'Evie so hopes you'll come.' He sounded as if *he* wanted her to come to take charge, let him off the hook. Though what was his role going to be in all this anyway? Had he been there at the birth? Taken Evie to hospital?

'So were you there?' she asked.

'No, that's women's work. She got a friend to take her in, you know Suzie who lives in the thatched cottage at the start of the lane, and it was very quick and then she texted me, told me to ring you.'

'So you haven't seen him, gone to see how they both are?' She was shocked, yet what did she expect from such a selfish man?

'No... I will later.' His voice was impatient now, almost dismissive, and her heart went out to Evie and this poor little boy.

'So you'll come... today, dear grandmamma? You must surely be the most beautiful granny there is.' His voice became syrupy sweet with flattery and she despised herself for the surge of warmth it provoked in her. Poor, sweet Evie, no wonder, sad and lost without her beloved father, she'd been easy meat to this devilishly attractive man.

She said briskly, 'I'll come today. Has Evie got her mobile, can I ring her, do they allow mobiles on the ward?' She longed to hear her daughter's voice, find out how she was after the ordeal of childbirth, which was bad enough to go through with a loving husband by one's side, a doting father keen to welcome his child into his life. Now he was here she would love him, she couldn't bear not to love him even though she wasn't ready for him, wasn't ready to be a grandmother.

'Her mobile's run out, but she said she'd call you on Suzie's mobile when she's back in the ward. So she'll ring soon, I expect. Goodbye then, Alice.' And he rang off, his voice subdued now as if he had suddenly realised the magnitude of what he had done and was... hopefully, ashamed of himself.

She collapsed back in bed, the silent receiver still in her hand. 'Julian, you should be here, we're grandparents.' Her face was wet with sudden tears. Here was one of the most sacred, precious moments of her life and she was facing it on her own.

She got up, and not bearing to be alone with her news, she rang Laura from her mobile.

'It's just past six, Mum, are you all right?' Laura sounded scared.

'Yes, Nick rang, Evie's baby is born, just now, it's a boy,' she blurted out, still not quite believing it.

'Is it... he... all right, isn't he too early?' Laura said irritably as if he were a guest who'd arrived before the party was ready.

'He's fine; she may have got her dates wrong. I'm waiting for her to ring me; I'll go there today. People don't seem to stay in hospital long these days after childbirth if all is well.'

'So Nick was with her?'

'No, but he rang me.'

'Do you want me to come with you?' Laura said, surprising her.

'But you have your work,' she said, wishing Laura could come, not wanting to do this alone.

'It's Friday and I'm sure they'll understand. I'll tell Douglas and I'll come back on Sunday. You're a granny,' she said suddenly, 'and I'm an aunt, scary.'

'It takes some getting used to,' Alice said, 'but if you could come, darling – but don't get sacked or anything – it would be lovely.'

'I'll call Douglas, then I'll come round and we can leave.' Laura rang off.

The phone rang again and it was Evie. 'Oh Mum... it was agony and there wasn't time for the epidural and I'd been promised it. I'll never go through that again, it was terrible.' Evie sounded near tears.

'But the baby is safely here, I'm longing to see him... you too, of course, darling,' Alice said, the pain of childbirth now the least of her worries. 'And... how is he, what does he weigh?' She worried he might be too small if he was early.

'Just under seven pounds, He's fine, but it was a shock him coming like that. I'm not ready for him, I thought I had another month, everyone says first babies are late... and I won't meet my deadline for my illustrations now,' she wailed, perhaps realising for the first time how much her life would change.

'Well he's here now and Laura and I will come down today and get things ready for you. You have got most things, haven't you, darling?' She wondered if she should rush out and buy stuff, but what?

'Some things: a Moses basket, nappies, I don't know. Suzie says she'll lend me things. Nick might come.' Her voice was flat and Alice suffered for her. Perhaps she and the baby should leave Suffolk so she wouldn't have to bump into Nick all the time, expect things – love, care, interest – from him that she wouldn't get, but now was not the time to discuss it and, after assuring her that she and Laura would be there early afternoon, she rang off, dressed and packed a bag.

Laura turned up soon after she was ready and they had breakfast together.

'Douglas says he'll cover for me, we had a few things we should be doing this weekend but he understands,' she said, buttering her toast.

'But if he needs you...' Alice felt torn, both her girls now had their own commitments and she couldn't expect

Laura to drop everything and come with her.

'No, it will be all right,' Laura said firmly. 'I'll come back on Sunday. Will Evie and the baby come here, do you think?'

'I've no idea, we'll see when we get there,' Alice said, impatient now to be off.

The baby was naturally their main source of conversation but Laura soon began to talk about Nick, wondering how much input he'd have as a father.

'Not much I shouldn't think.' Alice was annoyed with him for causing so much distress to her family, and to his own, and afraid that Laura, who also seemed to love him, or thought that she did, would get hurt. Was her eagerness to come with her more in the hope of seeing *him* than her sister or the baby? Did she imagine that he'd spend the weekend at the cottage seeing his son and she, while her sister rested, would have access to him? Perhaps she needed to see him before she married Douglas, who was, Alice imagined, only second best.

'We mustn't forget that he is married to poor, long-suffering Freya and has children with her. He has behaved very badly,' Alice said sternly, a feeling of helpless apathy creeping over her at the troubles ahead.

'She might chuck him out, I know I would if Douglas behaved like that,' Laura said firmly.

Alice refrained from saying that Douglas was not the type of man to set female pulses racing. 'But who would take him in?' she said instead. 'Does any self-respecting woman really want to be lumbered with a man like that?' She meant her remark to be a warning to Laura, not a criticism of Freya.

'If they love him enough he might change,' Laura said determinedly and Alice warned herself not to say that if

Laura was thinking she could save him with her love she would be severely disappointed, after all no one could love him – or understand him – as well as Freya did. To change the subject and perhaps remind her that she'd already made her commitment to Douglas, Alice questioned her on her wedding, asking how their plans were going and had they had any answers yet to the invitations Laura had sent and their discussion lasted all the way to the hospital.

They went inside and after asking the way were shown to the ward, having to pass a security check in case they were baby-snatchers, Alice assumed, remembering how friendly and free it all used to be when her girls were born. Evie was dressed, looking pale and fragile, sitting on her bed, waiting impatiently for them to arrive. The baby was in a plastic cot, asleep beside her.

'I can hardly walk, I'm so sore,' she greeted them. 'It's agony having a baby,' she said to Laura. 'If I ever have another I'll insist on being knocked out.'

'Let me look at him.' Alice bent over the cot. The baby was sleeping on his back, his arms thrown out behind him. He was the image of Nick and she remembered how Freya said you never needed a paternity test where Nick's babies were concerned. 'He's perfect' she said, hugging Evie, who clung to her for a moment as if afraid of what she'd done. But it was too late now, the situation had to be faced and a baby cared for. Alice regarded him again; he was so small with pale fluffy hair, two tiny fists escaping from the blanket. She felt a rush of love, a yearning to hold him close to her.

'Are you allowed home, darling?' she asked Evie.

'Yes, I've got all these papers, and they said I could go when you came.' Evie said. 'And Suzie lent me those,' she gestured to her case and a car seat both under the bed. 'You have to have them as soon as the baby's born. I don't know how you fit them in the car.'

Laura was staring down at the baby, her face impassive. Was it making her feel broody or jealous, seeing he looked the image of his father and she was wishing Nick loved her or even that the baby was hers?

'Right, if you're ready let's go,' Alice said, handing Laura the car seat and picking up Evie's bags. 'Can you manage the baby, darling?' She wondered if she felt safe carrying him along the corridor and down in the lift to the car park.

'Fine, I've practised already,' Evie said, picking him up and they followed her out of the ward.

With difficulty, they got the car seat in the back of the car and the baby strapped in. Evie sat in the back with him. Alice wondered if there was any food in the house and was tempted to stop at the supermarket, but perhaps it was best to get Evie back home, she'd go out later if necessary.

No one really talked on the way back to the cottage. Evie was obviously tired and sore and not a little shocked at suddenly becoming a mother, Alice too was exhausted and emotional, wishing Julian were here to see their beautiful grandchild. Laura was strangely quiet and Alice forbade herself to imagine what, or whom, she was thinking of.

There was a lot to do when they reached the cottage. Evie had a shower and went to bed, complaining that she hadn't slept at all since the night before. Alice held the baby, feeling him snuffling into her neck. How she'd dreaded his birth, but now he was here she loved him unconditionally.

When Evie was in bed, Alice handed the baby to her, hoping she'd get over the shock at having him so soon. Laura wandered in and the two of them made up the Moses basket

– lent by Suzie who'd also left a pile of stuff for Evie in the hall, including a well-used pram. While she sorted things out, Alice told them both about Margot and their new ideas for Amy and Edith to make nursery things, and said she'd get them to make a basket for the baby's creams, wipes and such, for her.

'What are you going to call him?' Laura asked, sitting on the bed watching everything going on with a slight air of amazement. 'Are you going to choose his name yourself or ask Nick?'

Evie said, 'It's my baby, so I'll choose his name. I thought I'd call him after Dad.'

'Oh, 'Alice was surprised by a sudden rush of tears.

'I thought you'd like it,' Evie said, frowning.

'What does Nick think?' Laura asked.

'I don't know, we never talked of names.'

'Has he seen him yet?' Laura asked.

Evie shook her head, 'He'll come by soon. But I can't think of another name I like. I thought he'd be a girl, I've lots of names for girls.'

She shouldn't be surprised at Evie's choice of name for her son but it had come as a shock. She didn't want it, not as a first name to hear it all the time, but she wouldn't say anything now knowing how fragile a new mother's emotions were after birth, especially a first baby and it perhaps it would be worse in Evie's circumstances.

'It's early days, darling and you're tired. Try and sleep a little, you'll feel better in a day or so.'

There was a sound of a car pulling up outside in the lane and Laura made for the door. 'I wonder who that is, I'll go and see for you.' She ran out of Evie's bedroom and down the stairs.

Alice braced herself for seeing Nick. Naturally he would come and see his child, but she didn't feel like seeing him so soon and before Evie and the baby were settled. She heard a woman's voice on the stairs and, going on to the landing, she saw a rosy-faced woman in a dark coat, with Laura following disconsolately behind.

'Hello there, I'm Ruby Spence, come to see how mother and baby are settling in. I pass the cottage on my way home so I thought I'd pop in; see if everything is all right. I'll be back in the morning as well.'

'How kind, thank you.' Alice was grateful to see this cheerful, confident woman. 'I'll leave you to it and be downstairs should you need me.' She smiled and made her way downstairs. She was obviously one of the midwives looking after Evie and it was probably best to leave them alone.

Laura stood listlessly by the door, staring out at the garden, obviously disappointed that the visitor was not Nick. He did not come, or even telephone for the rest of the day, leaving all three of them anxious. His mobile was on call back and Evie left a message saying they'd been discharged and she was home, in case he'd gone to the hospital to see them. Her voice was sad and waif-like, breaking Alice's heart.

When they were together in the living room, out of Evie's hearing, Laura wondered anxiously if he had had an accident 'as surely he'd want to see his son?'

'Nick is the accident,' Alice retorted, her emotions muddled, relief that Evie and the baby were safe and love for the tiny boy, but anger too that both her daughters seemed to be so strongly under Nick's spell.

Chapter 29

The weekend was spent settling in the baby, who was still un-named and so referred to as 'the baby'. Laura protested that she didn't want him called after their father as he'd remind her of him in a sad way and Evie got upset and said it was none of her business. Alice had to step in and take Laura aside and explain that having just given birth, and especially in such circumstances, Evie's hormones were all over the place and it would be best not to say anything that might upset her for the moment.

'Well, Dad wouldn't like this mess she's in,' Laura said petulantly, 'and giving the baby his name won't make it right.'

'She's not doing it for that reason.' Alice was exhausted trying to keep both her daughters calm. Perhaps Laura should not have come, seeing Nick's baby so soon.

The baby, though, stole their hearts, but he too was unsettled and they all had a troubled night, disturbed by his cries. The feeding was not going well and he cried fretfully, obviously hungry, adding to the tension, and Alice was relieved when Ruby the cheerful midwife turned up again. It was so different from Alice's own happy experience of having the girls, a loving home and, most important, a loving and supportive husband and father for the children.

Ruby wasn't at all fazed by the baby's parentage. 'That's

nothing compared to some we have,' she said when Alice went with her to her car, hoping for a few words of advice about how to cope with the situation. 'Evie will be fine in a week or so. Becoming a mother for the first time, especially when the father is absent, is always a bit of a shock, but she has you and her sister to support her, and those lovely drawings,' she smiled. 'At least she can make a living at home.'

'But his father, I don't know...' Alice tailed off.

Ruby sighed, 'He's a bad boy; this baby is not the first of his I've delivered. If I was his wife I'd cut off his balls, but at least he does pay maintenance, although that's about all he does. I hope Evie doesn't expect more.' She regarded Alice seriously as if to make sure she understood what she was saying.

'I know Freya well and like her and I know she'll never leave him. My husband died two years ago and Evie was here alone and missing him and Nick... well he can be so persuasive.'

Ruby put her hand on her arm, her eyes soft with concern. 'I know and I'm sorry. It will be difficult, but I'm sure she'll be fine and you'll all love him... I see you do already,' she smiled. 'He's a beautiful baby. Well, I must go on to the next one, not such a happy story, I'm afraid, the baby was born with a serious stomach disorder and needed immediate surgery and many more operations to come. I or Stella, who Evie knows too, will come by tomorrow.'

'I'm so sorry,' Alice said, thinking of the family of that baby. What agony to go through all that with any child but especially a new born baby. Despite their circumstances her family *was* lucky, luckier than most, Alice told herself firmly – Evie's baby was healthy and he was loved, it was impossible not to love him, and Evie would keep on working, somehow, around him, after all the publisher had known she was pregnant soon after giving her the contract. The only problem was Nick.

Everyone in the district knew what Nick was like and why would he change for Evie? Though sadly, like so many girls before her, Evie had convinced herself that he loved her that their child was living proof of that and Nick would stay with her. But he was Freya's husband and father of *her* children, and even if Freya did chuck him out, she doubted he'd stick by Evie. Nick liked a varied love life without commitment, and it appeared that there was no shortage of women ready to jump into his bed, and Evie, having had his baby, was probably now banished from his playground.

'Mum, phone, its Frank.' Laura came out of the cottage holding out her mobile. 'He wants to speak... to congratulate you, I think.'

'Frank?' He'd become a hazy memory in this new world of babies and keeping her daughters from going for each other. Laura did care for the baby, often held him and rocked him, though Alice felt she was sort of hoping Nick would suddenly appear and see her with him and... well she didn't know what, it was all so confusing.

She took Laura's mobile and stood on the doorstep where the signal was strongest.

'Hello Frank, it's lovely to hear you. How are you? Are you back in London?'

'Yes, I was hoping to see you all, but Laura's told me you're with Evie. Congratulations on being a granny, you're far too young and glamorous for it, but lucky boy, you'll be so good with him.'

'I don't know about that, it's frightening how much I've forgotten about tiny babies and how exhausting it is to lose so much sleep.' His praise warmed her and this time she was not annoyed by it. Frank meant it; he was not trying to seduce her or to curry favour with her.

'How long will you be there? Laura says she's coming back tomorrow.'

'I'm not sure, just until Evie's settled, which shouldn't be long. I might even bring them back to London for a while. I'll see how it goes.' She had a sudden yearning for Frank to arrive in one of his fast cars and whizz her away, to feel the wind in her hair and that wonderful exhilaration of being alive and free.

'I was hoping to take you paragliding.' She could hear the energy in his voice. 'You said you wanted to try it and so, if you want to do it, I thought I would book a place, then later, if his parents agree, we could take Johnny.'

'It sounds wonderful, Frank. I would love to do it when I get back.' She looked up at the sky, there seemed to be so much more of it in Suffolk, wide and open, clear blue scattered with froths of cloud, what would it be like floating across it with Frank?

They talked a little more about how the wedding preparations were going and she promised she'd contact him when she returned to London.

She took Laura to the station on Sunday. 'I think it so odd that Nick didn't come to see his own child, don't you, Mum? Has he finished with Evie? She hasn't said they've split up. Surely he'll still see her if only to see his child, Freya would have to allow that.' Laura turned towards her; Alice stared straight ahead at the road, not wanting to see Laura's expression in case she saw hope there, hope that would never be realised, of Nick coming to her. It worried Alice, not just because of Nick's despicable treatment of his wife and family, but because Laura was engaged to marry Douglas and it did not bode well for their marriage if she was lusting after someone else.

'I've no idea,' she said firmly, 'and anyway, no one must forget that he is married to Freya and she loves him and despite his appalling behaviour she is determined to stay with him for their children's sakes. He had dysfunctional parents apparently, and she thinks that's one of the reasons he behaves as he does, but she doesn't want their own children to go through a family break-up so, for the moment, she'll stay with him.'

'I can see Freya wants to keep their family together, but she'll have to let him visit his own son,' Laura said. 'He's a beautiful baby, do you think Evie is pleased she's got him, she didn't seem that interested to me,'

'This is not the first time poor Freya has been through this and we must allow her to cope with it in her own way,' Alice said firmly, relieved that Laura was returning to London and Douglas. 'Evie will be fine, it's all been a bit of a shock, giving birth earlier than she thought, but she'll soon get the hang of being a mother.'

The weekend had been a strange one, she was glad Laura had come with her and yet Alice sensed there were bad feelings simmering between the two sisters. Evie was too shell-shocked to do much about it and she had warned Laura not to pick any quarrels with her sister so soon after she'd been through childbirth, so both had kept their feelings in check, but she feared that when they met up again they would erupt. Did Evie know that Laura thought herself in love with Nick? She'd be surprised if she did as Laura usually kept her feelings close. She hoped Evie would never find out and tease her about it and what would Douglas think of such a thing?

They arrived at the station and Alice said, 'It's been a stressful yet exciting weekend, so thank you for coming, darling, it's much easier to cope with things as a family.'

'That's all right,' Laura said, lingering as if she had something to say. There were a few minutes before the train was due and Alice felt she must voice her concerns, she wanted no more emotional accidents.

'You are sure, darling, about the wedding? I mean, you could have it next year, next spring if it was easier, gives you more time to organise it?' She hoped her voice was light and Laura wouldn't imagine or, worse, hear the truth behind her question. Inferring that she didn't think the wedding should go ahead until Laura had sorted out her feelings towards the two men.

There was a long silence and Alice braced herself for Laura to say she wanted to get out of the wedding but with the children and everything she didn't know how, but she gave a little laugh, 'Of course, Mum, some of the invitations have gone out and we'll get the rest done this week. Douglas is very efficient, we've booked the place and they have their own caterers and Beth from school will do the flowers. There's just my dress, if I'd known the baby was coming now I'd have brought down my designs for Edith and Amy to see.'

'Of course, sorry darling, this baby's arrival has addled my mind. I didn't know you'd made up your mind to use them and not buy one in London, though we hardly had time to go over and see them this weekend. You did say you didn't want the hassle of making trips up here if you found one in London.' Alice thought to remind her of that, afraid of Laura making trips to see Edith and Amy here in case she ran into Nick and he was on the prowl again and found her a willing conquest.

'I sort of know what I want, I'll work on it this week and come down for them to fit me,' Laura's face was hopeful again. 'Must go or I'll miss the train.' She kissed her and jumped out of the car, her step lighter as she disappeared into the station, no doubt thrilled to have another excuse to return to Suffolk and hopefully see Nick.

A few days later, Alice went over to Amy and Edith to see how the nursery stuff was going. Margot had dropped the baskets and material with them and had called in at the cottage on the way back.

'Sweet baby,' she had said, vaguely peering into the basket. 'Where's Evie?'

'Working, she's got a deadline,' Alice said. 'She hoped she'd finish before the baby came, but he caught us all out. But it's strange, since his birth, her work seems to have taken on a new energy, glowing with life and colour.'

'Well, don't get sucked in,' Margot had warned, mistaking her feeling of wonder for Evie's talent for being swept back into the nursery again. 'I saw Frank yesterday, he asked after you.'

Alice had ignored a surge of warmth, 'Oh, how is he?'

Margot had spent the next twenty minutes telling her, saying what fun he was and so interesting compared to everyone else, which was probably due to him living abroad, and Alice was relieved when at last Margot had said she must hit the road as she and Glen were going out that evening.

When Alice told Amy and Edith that Laura wanted them to make her wedding dress, they were thrilled. Alice knew that whatever fears she had about Laura hoping to see Nick, these women were the best bet for a beautiful dress as they had been properly trained in making couture clothes.

They had made a couple of nursery baskets, which were

beautifully lined with pretty material and pockets to hold all the baby things. Margot was going to arrange to have them photographed and hopefully get them into a few magazines.

Alice ordered one of the baskets for Evie, wondering what the two spinster sisters thought of married men fathering children around the place as blatantly as Nick did.

On the way back to the cottage, Alice stopped at the supermarket to buy some food, she had a long list with her as she thought she had better stay with Evie until the midwives stopped calling. As she walked towards the supermarket, she saw Freya and Nick coming towards her. Nick saw her at once and pretended he hadn't but then Freya saw her and came towards her, pushing the overloaded trolley in front of her like a battering ram.

Nick for once looked sheepish and began to walk faster as if he were in a hurry and would pass her, no doubt with some quick excuse, but Freya stopped the trolley and said, 'Alice, nice to see you, though the circumstances are hardly good. But is Evie all right and the baby?' She ignored Nick, who had taken out his mobile and was studying it intently as if he had nothing whatever to do with the baby's existence and had far more important things to do than stand here chatting.

'Yes, she's fine they both are thank you. I'm sorry...' If only Nick were not here and she could say how upset she was for the pain Freya must be feeling, but it was difficult with him standing there with little sign of contrition on his face, so she asked Freya about her coup with the V and A instead. 'Have you sent any of your work there yet? I must go and see it, I'm sure it will be wonderful.'

'First lot go next week,' Freya said. 'I'll be coming up to arrange it in the shop. If you're back in London, we could perhaps meet up.'

'I'm not sure if I'll be back by then, I don't know what's happening just yet.' Alice felt so awkward standing here talking to the wife of her daughter's lover and mother of his children – both were mothers of his children – it was like some awful farce, only neither of them were laughing, though Freya became quite animated as she talked about her order from the V and A and Alice was pleased for her. Perhaps she'd put more of her energies into her pottery if it took off, but perhaps that would make Nick behave even worse if he felt eclipsed by her talent.

'No, it's early days. Well, we better get on,' Freya moved to leave. Nick threw Alice a regretful smile as though he were a small boy caught stealing sweets.

This infuriated her, fathering a child with her unmarried daughter was not as trivial as taking sweets and it goaded Alice into saying, 'So Nick, I hope you'll take your responsibility seriously for this child, give Evie maintenance for him and all.'

Freya looked away, her face set hard, Alice was upset for her but she might not see Nick for ages. Julian would have said the same if he'd been here.

'Of course,' he looked affronted as if she'd accused him of dishonesty. 'I haven't been to see him as new mothers need time to bond, but I'll set up something with my bank, you know I will.'

But I don't, Alice said to herself. 'Thank you, Nick, please do it soon,' she gave him a stern look.

'So bang goes our skiing holiday,' she heard Freya say to him as they reached their car close by. 'If you do this again, Nick, I really will chuck you out, in fact I think I'll book you in for a vasectomy.'

Nick's hand shot down to the front of his trousers.

'Don't say such a thing,' he said. 'It's barbaric.'

'Perhaps castration would be better,' Freya said darkly, wrenching open the boot of the car, making him winch even more.

Pity she hadn't done it before, Alice thought, geld him like the tomcat he was.

Chapter 30

The days blurred into feeding, changing and snatching sleep when they could. The baby, who was still without a name, summoned them at all hours of the day and night with his petulant cry. Alice struggled out of bed to go to him hoping to give Evie some rest, but he woke her too, his cries drilling through the walls demanding attention. He was Nick's child all right, Alice grumbled to herself as she stubbed her toe in the dark as she crossed the landing to go to him. She kept the lights out, hoping he would slip back to sleep, and crept, feeling her way like a blind person, to his door.

'He can't want more to eat,' Evie called from her bedroom. 'My milk's obviously not nutritious enough, he'll have bottles tomorrow.' Despite the encouragement from her friendly midwives, Evie hadn't taken to breastfeeding and after a week of 'persevering' had decided to give up, her breasts were sore and so it hurt to feed him and she needed to get on with her illustrations, keep as near as she could to the deadline. If Alice could take over the feeding with bottled formula, she could get down to it and not keep having to interrupt her work to feed him, especially as it took so long and didn't seem to satisfy him.

Alice picked him up and tried to soothe him. He wept pitifully, snuggling his downy head into her neck, snuffling against her skin, his warm mouth searching, and she was overcome with a great wave of love for him. Poor little boy, did he feel the rejection of his father already? Nick had still not come to see him, though he had put a sum of money into Evie's account, not much but enough now for his small needs, and Evie's mind, she had to admit, seemed more focused on her illustrations than her child, but it was her work and she had a deadline, and each picture took so much time, being so intricate, the colours shimmering like jewels.

'I was expecting to have another month free before he arrived then I'd have finished this lot and could have a break until the next book,' Evie said. 'I didn't know a baby could take up so much time, but thanks for being here, Mum, to love him and, after all, you know what to do having had us.' She gave her a quick hug.

Alice hugged her back. 'But I can't stay for long, darling, just until you're on your feet again.' She thought of Cecily's advice. She'd been right, Evie would expect her to take charge and she mustn't fall into that trap, she was happy to be here, settling them both in, but she had to get back to her own world and the longer she stayed here, the more Evie would come to rely on her instead of picking up the reins of motherhood herself. There was also the wedding to think about so Laura needed her time too, she reminded herself, feeling slightly overwhelmed with it all. Laura was coming down for the weekend with her dress designs to show to Edith and Amy.

Despite her moans, Evie had had an easy birth, and coping with a baby, especially for the first time, even for happy and secure couples was a shock, but she'd been here nearly two weeks now and it was time Evie got on with motherhood by herself. Her drawings were almost finished, and Alice had agreed to take them back to London and drop them safely with her publisher. Then Evie could concentrate fully on being a mother.

Various women friends had called round and offered to help, and there were the kind midwives for any dramas so Alice knew Evie was not going to be deserted… except it seemed, by Nick.

Alice picked Laura up from the station on Friday night. Almost the first thing she said after greeting her and getting in the car was, 'Has Nick seen him yet? Does he love him?' Her last remark tinged with longing.

'No, Nick hasn't visited yet.' Alice was rather dreading the weekend – or rather just tomorrow, as Laura was going back on Sunday for Elspeth's birthday lunch. It was disastrous *both* her daughters loving the same disreputable man. 'Nick's very busy apparently, lots of gardens to see to, but he's not forgotten her, and is paying maintenance.'

'Doesn't he want to see his own child?'

He has too many to see, Alice thought, but didn't say it, instead she said, 'You know many men, even the most loving ones, often don't show much interest in tiny babies. It's when they start to do things, relate to them, that they become good fathers.'

'Was Dad like that?' Laura looked hurt.

'No, he wasn't, he loved you both from the start. But then he hadn't had any children before, and perhaps Nick, having had so many, is not so excited. After all it's not as if they are married and raising him together,' she paused, not wanting to seem to put any blame on Freya. 'He has to think of how this affects his wife and their children and it's hurtful enough without him spending lots of time with Evie.'

'But not to come to see him even once,' Laura said in disbelief, 'or Evie. Have they broken up?'

'I'm sure he'll see him soon.' Alice didn't want to talk about Nick, or see the hope in Laura's eyes, though, as she was rarely here, how could anything develop between them? Not that she wanted anything to develop. Nick's affairs all went the same way and after a few sexual encounters that would be the end of it, leaving Laura – if she ever succumbed to him - distraught.

It was quite late by the time they got to the cottage. Laura was tired too after a hectic week at work. She admired her sister's magical illustrations, and Evie, in her turn, praised Laura's design for her wedding dress, which was simple, high-necked with a low-cut back well fitted to the body and a fullish skirt that swirled softly from the hips.

'I showed it to Frank and he said it must be made of the best wild silk for extra wow factor and he'll pay for it.' Laura glanced at Alice to see her reaction.

'I won't let him pay for it, it's for me to take care of and he's been generous enough already,' Alice said firmly. 'Did you see him, how is he?'

'He took us both out to dinner the night before last. He sent his love and hopes you'll be back soon.'

'Mum's waiting until I finish my work so she can take it back to London for me,' Evie said.

'So how long will that take?' Laura demanded. 'I've lots to do for the wedding and I need Mum to help me with that, flowers and things.'

If only she could fold up into a tiny shape and slip away, her girls were too demanding and yet she wanted to help them, it was just unfortunate that both such important events had occurred at the same time. 'Let's discuss it in the morning,' she said quickly, hoping to soothe the turbulence that threatened the atmosphere. 'We're all tired now and we'll feel better in the morning.'

A beautiful basket of flowers arrived for Evie that evening. Alice answered the door and took them into the living room where both girls were sitting.

'Wow, they are awesome,' Evie said, taking them on her lap and opening the card tucked in beside them.

They must be from Nick, Alice thought and guessed the girls did too by their faces: Laura's slightly jealous, Evie ecstatic. She opened the tiny envelope and her face fell. 'Oh, they're from Cecily, lovely of her,' she said, touched but obviously disappointed that they were not from Nick.

'How sweet of her,' Alice said, longing suddenly to talk to her, feeling the need for her advice.

Evie rang Cecily and thanked her and then passed the telephone to Alice.

'Well, my dear, I'm glad he's arrived safe and sound and I'm sure you're besotted with him.' Her voice was warm.

'I am, but I'm coming back to London in a couple of days when Evie has finished her work.'

'Good, I'll be glad to see you. Frank is back and he said he wants to take you paragliding,' she laughed. 'I'm looking forward to hearing about that.'

'Me too,' Alice said, feeling suddenly alive.

After breakfast the next morning, Alice and Laura set out for Edith and Amy. It was a fine morning, the sun a deeper gold now the year was nearing its end, gilding the fields and hedgerows with its touch.

'I sometimes wish I could live here, stay for weeks like we did as children,' Laura said, gazing out at the flat countryside dotted with old oak trees.

'It is lovely in the summer, nowhere better,' Alice said, wondering if this was the prelude to something else, like Laura saying she didn't want to marry Douglas after all but leave London and start a new life here. Or did she want to be in Suffolk to be closer to Nick? If she was going to call off the wedding, she hoped she'd do it before Edith and Amy started on the dress.

'Though remember how cold and gloomy it could be in the winter? We spent most of the winter in London, didn't we? It didn't seem so cold and damp there.' Alice turned to her, wondering if now was the time for confidences but not wanting to push her, knowing she'd retreat like a snail going back to the safety of its shell.

'Yes, I remember but... Mum... is, well, has Evie taken the cottage, is it hers now?'

'No, of course not, it belongs to all of us. She is just using it for peace and quiet while she does her illustrations. You... and Douglas and the children can come here for a holiday or weekend whenever you'd like to. Arrange it with Evie and she can come to London or be here too, there's enough room, the baby can go in with her.'

'We might. Obviously I'm giving up the flat and moving in with Douglas when we're married and I just wondered...' She tailed off, staring out of the window.

'You're sure you want to do this?' Alice said, before she could stop herself.

'What, have the dress made by Edith and Amy? Of course, it may be a bit of a hassle coming up here for fittings, but the dress will be just how I want it and I hate going round and round shops with pushy sales people gushing over me, saying hideous dresses look wonderful on me when they don't.'

'Of course it will be beautiful, far more beautiful than anything you could buy in a shop,' Alice scolded herself for being too much of a coward to bluntly question her daughter about her feelings. Laura would take it the wrong way, imagining that her mother thought she was not capable enough to be marrying Douglas and taking on his children.

Edith and Amy, bright-eyed and eager, glowed with excitement when Laura showed them her design. They measured her with great precision, congratulating her on her figure; draping some purple silk round her to see the effect of the skirt. 'It will be cut on the bias, so it will hang without bulking out the hips,' Amy said, writing down the measurements in a finicky hand, so small Alice could barely read them.

It was a restful morning sitting in their workroom, French windows looking out at a small, well-kept garden. There was a comfortable intimacy about discussing materials and styles, calming Alice's fears. She could almost hear Cecily warning her: *You did your best to bring up your children and now they must fly free to make mistakes, like everyone else.*

Because they were still connected to the couture world, Edith could order the right silk for the dress at wholesale prices and Amy produced a book of swatches of gleaming silks. Laura chose a cream silk with a slight sheen to it that made it seem as if it were alive, which, indeed, Amy explained, in a way it was and must be carefully treated, kept in a linen cover not a plastic one so it could breathe.

Their mood carried on for the rest of the day. The baby now slept longer. He was nicknamed 'Bunny' by Laura who said he looked like a rabbit when he wrinkled his nose and Evie still could not decide on another name, though she insisted his second name would be after her father. Laura took him for a walk while Alice curled up with the newspaper and Evie drew. Later that evening Alice dropped Laura at the station to go back to Douglas, leaving her feeling bereft, thinking of her daughter going back into her new life. You can't have it both ways; she scolded herself, when only last night she yearned to be free of her girls and their dramas.

'Julian, if only you could send me some sort of sign that you are somewhere close,' she said out loud. There was no answer, just emptiness stretching on ahead of her forever, but just as she reached the turn to the cottage Frank came into her mind, bringing a surge of pleasure. He wanted to take her paragliding; she could almost feel the rush of air as they took off, the gentle drift through the sky. How long would it be before she would see him again?

Evie finished her illustrations. She felt better in herself, the wounds of childbirth had eased and her deadline had been met, so she finally had time to enjoy her baby, scooping him up, wrapping him in a sling against her chest and taking up the reins of her new life. But still Nick had not come to visit. Perhaps he was waiting for her to leave, Alice wondered, she'd be gone in a couple of days, as Evie had now taken over.

The day before she left Evie, Alice went into Bury St Edmunds to do one last shop for her, planning to cook a few dishes for the freezer so Evie would be able to give more time to her baby. She took him with her to allow Evie to pack up her illustrations for her to take to London. She parked near the square, unloaded Bunny into his pram and set off to the shops.

She'd forgotten how useful a pram was to carry things, though there wasn't much room with all the paraphernalia Evie had insisted she take.

'We're only going to Bury, darling, not on a polar expedition,' Alice had joked, 'and we won't be long.'

'Take it in case,' Evie had said, as if afraid something vital would be left behind and Bunny would become distraught.

To humour her, Alice obeyed, but now she was here she left most of it in the car, after all she could come back if something was desperately needed.

She rather enjoyed the sensation of pushing a pram again and after doing her shopping she decided, as the sun was out, to wander round the Abbey gardens and leave Evie in peace a little longer to finish any last touches to her work, wash her hair and search out some clothes that fitted her.

She had just reached the ancient arch leading into the garden when she heard someone call her name and she saw Freya crossing the road behind her. She was dressed in a dark red coat with a multi-coloured silk scarf swirling round her shoulders.

'Thought it was you, Alice.' She kept her eyes firmly off the pram, 'You're still here? I thought you might have gone home... though of course,' her laugh was shrill, 'here is your home too.'

'I'm going tomorrow, I've just been waiting for Evie to finish her work so I can take it with me to hand over to her editor. Safer than posting it, I hope so anyway.'

There was an awkward silence, the pram and its occupant like a huge embarrassment between them. Alice held firmly to the handle, wondering whether to make a remark about wanting to see the gardens and saying goodbye, or waiting for Freya to make her excuses to leave herself. Before she could make up her mind which was the best option Freya said, 'Well, as he's here I suppose I'd better look at him, it's not his fault, poor little mite.' She leant over and peered into the pram. He was sleeping, looking pink and perfect and the image of her wayward husband.

'I can see a little of Evie about him. How is she, is she happy?' Freya's face was hard now as though she'd clamped a mask over it to control her real feelings of pain and fury. Whatever must it be like to not be able to trust one's husband, wonder how many more of his offspring would appear in the neighbourhood? How fortunate she'd been with Julian.

'I'm so sorry, this must be so awful for you,' Alice said, ashamed it was *her* child who had caused such mayhem.

'It will be his last, any more and he is out, I've told him that. But Alice,' Freya took her arm as if she was about to break some bad news, 'I hope Evie is not waiting for him to turn up and love her. He won't you know. His affairs, and often there are more than one going on at the same time, run their course and then it is over. He might break her heart if she still loves him.'

Alice thought of Laura, her heart was more fragile than Evie's. Evie might be furious to have been taken in, annoyed with herself for being such a fool, but she'd get over it, she had Bunny, and perhaps more importantly for her pride, her exquisite drawing and the chance of a brilliant career before her, whereas Laura only had Douglas, kind and dull and probably safe but without the excitement of Nick.

After a few more moments of discussion they – or rather Freya – decided to have tea in the hotel on the square. There was room for a pram there and it was quieter than some of the smaller places in the town.

They had just ordered, and Freya, sitting back in her chair, confronted her as if she was about to interview her, asking what Evie was going to do and if she was returning to London. Alice had no idea; they hadn't discussed it, with Evie's mind having been more preoccupied with her deadline than the future of her and her child. She was about to explain this, thinking that as Freya was an artist too, she'd understand, when to her horror she saw Nick coming in, towing a skinny, red-headed girl behind him.

Freya was sitting in a hefty winged chair facing her and could not see her husband, and Nick had not seen either of them. Alice seethed with anger: how dare he be unfaithful to his wife and Evie too. Freya, catching her expression, frowned and turned round in her chair and at the same moment Nick saw them. Not to be outdone, the baby woke and began to cry. Alice desperately rocked the pram but his cries became louder, and then a waitress brought their order. Alice picked Bunny up and held him to her, throwing Nick a despising look.

He'd been intent on making for a quiet corner in the room and not seen them until he was almost upon them. He started, turned to leave, but Freya stopped him in his tracks, saying coldly,

'This is your last baby, Nick. Be thankful he is healthy, you're getting too old to have children now, old fathers can produce dud offspring, you know. Anyway, if you stray again you might lose us all. My patience with your tomcat behaviour is exhausted.'

As she spoke she did not even glance at the red-headed girl behind him who, faced with them, looked scared, creeping closer to Nick as if for protection, unsure what to do.

'My darling, what a funny remark, I don't understand.' Nick laughed awkwardly, glancing at his son. Alice turned him round so he could see his face. Nick made no attempt to touch him but studied him intently a moment as if, Alice thought, he wanted to reassure himself he had fathered him.

'I don't think it funny at all, nor, I'm sure, does Alice,' Freya said, picking up the espresso that sat before her and taking a large gulp. 'Now you're here, Nick, you can give me a lift home and come to the supermarket on the way. We need to stock up and I can do that now you're here to help.' She took another gulp from her coffee, reached towards him and put her hand into his pocket and took out his wallet and, extracting a £10 note, put it on the table to pay for their tea, waving away Alice's offer to pay.

She got up from the table, and blew Alice a kiss, and firmly taking Nick's arm led him out of the hotel, preventing him from any further contact with his son, though he showed no inclination to want any. She ignored the red-headed girl, who looked stunned, obviously not knowing that Nick was already married and throwing a horrified glace at Bunny, who now was red in the face and screaming for his bottle. The girl turned and scuttled away, no doubt relieved at her lucky escape.

Chapter 31

Alice missed the baby, her grandson.

To her relief she didn't feel any older, or for that matter any more staid and sensible now she had reached this milestone so much earlier than she had wanted. She kept reminding herself that she was now a granny, and after Laura and Douglas's wedding she would also be a mother-in-law *and* a step-grandmother to two other children. 'Glammy granny,' as Evie called her to flatter her, hoping to make the situation she disapproved of sound exciting. She didn't feel glamorous, she felt exhausted by the last few weeks and lack of sleep while Bunny had settled into life. So, apart from delivering Evie's illustrations to her publisher, she stayed quietly at home for a couple of days before ringing Laura.

'Oh, you're back, I thought I'd come down and see you all at the weekend... see how my dress is getting on,' she added as if to convince Alice, and perhaps herself, that the main reason she was going was to check on her dress, which was coming along wonderfully.

'Yes, I'm back. Evie's finished her work and has more time to devote to motherhood, while she waits to hear if she has to redo any of the drawings or produce more.'

'That's good.' There was a pause and Alice braced herself for Laura to ask about Nick but she did not, she rushed on,

'Oh, Frank said to ring him when you're back. He said he'd take you paragliding. Is that a good idea, Mum, I mean you're not old but… you know it's…'

'Not for grannies, you mean, darling. Grannies come in all shapes and sizes, these days and it won't stop what I want to do. I didn't expect to be a grandmother so soon, but now I am I'm still the same person I was before.'

'You're not really, Mum. You've changed since Dad went. I mean, doing all these mad things; you'd never have done them if he were still here. I don't know why Frank suggested it…'

'I suggested it, and I'd love to do it. You're too like your father, darling, not wanting to do anything risky.' She didn't add, although you are rushing into a marriage and taking on someone else's children when you're still quite young yourself, which is very risky indeed.

She telephoned Frank after she put the phone down to Laura, before she lost her nerve. She wanted to see him and yet she felt wary of him, though she didn't know why. Was she afraid she was becoming attracted to him, that her body would betray her by wanting to be in his arms, in his bed?

She'd no idea how today's 'dating' worked. Petra was the only person of her age she knew well who indulged in it and it seemed to be awfully hard work, keeping fit and keeping one's eyes open for any passing, attractive man, going on dating sites, trawling through photographs of men as you might trawl through a clothes catalogue, and perhaps not as tempting. She didn't think she could be bothered with it all.

'Alice, you're back.' Frank sounded pleased. 'How are you… and Evie and the baby?'

The sound of his voice made her heart leap in the most annoying way. She was about to say 'I'm exhausted' but she did not. 'Fine, thanks, but it's good to be back and important for Evie to learn to cope by herself.'

'It is. Now, do you feel like celebrating your return by going paragliding?'

She laughed, 'Yes... when can we go?'

To her surprise he said, 'Why not today? Being a weekday we'll probably get a slot. I'll make the arrangements and pick you up about ten thirty, that OK? Oh, and wear boots that support your ankles, we could land on rough ground, and warmish clothes as sometimes it's cold up there.'

'Lovely, yes, see you then.' She rang off and sat there a moment, his voice lingering in her ears. She must not be like Petra, ready to leap into bed with any half-decent man and some not decent at all, though why was she thinking of going to bed with Frank when he'd only offered to take her paragliding? No doubt he had a swarm of women buzzing round him and would not want to complicate his life by getting romantically involved with her. She'd never had a proper sexual relationship until she met Julian and she'd never wanted to stray, but now she was alone and still young there were times when her body felt cold and lost, but that didn't mean that sex with Frank was on the cards, she told herself firmly.

They arrived at the club late morning. 'I've booked a session almost immediately. I thought we'd fly in tandem if that's all right.'

'So we go up straight away then?' She tried to ignore a lurch of panic in her stomach.

'You're not turning chicken on me are you, Alice?' he laughed. 'I've been here a few times while you were with Evie and they are all well trained. Would you rather go up with one of the younger men, or a woman, they have some female instructors too?' He turned to her, his eyes sparkling with merriment.

'Are you able to take me up?' she asked. 'Do you need some sort of safety qualification... Health and safety and all that?'

'I've done it enough to be qualified to fly tandem, but it's up to you if you'd feel safer with one of the instructors. I won't mind. I'll fly up on my own at the same time and we can drift across the sky together.'

Alice thought a moment, wondering if he'd prefer to fly alone but she trusted him, would rather be with him than some young, perhaps over zealous person who might show off with some scary manoeuvres. 'I'd rather fly with you if that's all right,' she said, warmed by his sudden smile.

'Of course, it's all right,' he said. He turned into a parking space and turned off the engine. 'Trust me, you'll love it,' he said before getting out to open the door for her.

They were warmly welcomed, and as if the instructors guessed her fear they started at once to fix her and Frank up with the two-seater kite; Frank was to sit behind her and control the kite, all she had to do, she was assured, was sit back and enjoy it.

She, Frank and a couple of cheerful instructors, Ben and Cherry, went down to the take-off point. Today, the wind being where it was, they were going to jump off a hill. Better not to think too much about it, Alice thought, while she tried to concentrate on Cherry telling her how to stand, take off and land.

She felt afraid yet excited too; she'd wanted to do this for so long, ever since she'd seen it in Switzerland while staying at a skiing resort, the colourful kites drifting above the mountains in the clear, blue sky.

'Ready?' Frank said in her ear and she nodded, fear suddenly taking hold of her, but they were running, running over the drop. Panic clutched at her but then they were up floating in the sky and it was so vast, so beautiful and silent, that for a moment she could not speak, she was so intoxicated by the wonder of it all. Frank searched for thermals in the air and they were soaring up, floating above the landscape. He was close behind her, just the two of them alone in such beauty.

'OK?' Frank said behind her.

'Awesome, absolutely awesome.'

He pointed out a few landmarks and there was the sea, brilliant blue, eating away the land and then a forest, a mass of green heads clustered together, tiny houses tucked into the countryside, glistening ribbons of rivers chasing to the sea; she was spellbound.

She didn't know how long they were up there, time stopped, she'd never be able to explain this exhilaration, floating in the silence of the sky, but Frank understood and she would treasure sharing this intimate time with him.

Eventually, they landed in a field, surprising the sheep grazing there who regarded them balefully while munching the grass.

Alice took off her helmet, shaking her hair free. She was hit with a keen sense of loss: up there they were different people, fused together by the kite, now here on land, standing together, she felt shy of him, even though he'd been on the edge of her life for so long, she felt she knew so little about him. She'd just experienced the most wonderful sensation, an experience so difficult to describe, showing how insignificant they were against the mighty expanse of the universe. Now back on the ground again she felt insecure, adrift.

Frank rang the club on his mobile, stating where they were so they could be picked up.

'They'll be here in about twenty minutes,' he said to her. 'We might as well sit on that tree trunk and wait until they come.'

He seemed withdrawn into himself; perhaps he too was overcome by the majesty of the sky. When they were sitting rather awkwardly side by side on the tree trunk, felled by some storm and left to lie there, she had a sudden vision of the young man whom she'd mistaken for Julian coming out of his block of flats. To fill the silence she said, 'The oddest thing happened when you were away, I went past your flat to post Margot's invitation for her party and I saw a young man the image of Julian. Well an image of Julian when he was younger...' She stopped, Frank's face was ashen, he choked, tried to smile.

'It obviously wasn't Julian, but he did look so like him,' she went on with an attempt of a laugh, wishing she hadn't said it now, he'd think her mad, having delusions.

Frank stayed silent, his eyes fixed on the ground by his feet. Perhaps mentioning Julian suddenly like this had upset him. She struggled to think of something to say to make things easy between them, but before she could, he said quietly, still gazing at the ground.

'Did Julian ever talk to you about... things in his life before he met you? After all, he was many years older than you and it was not surprising that he knew other people... other women, had other relationships.'

'Of course I knew that, he told me, early on in our relationship that he'd had a serious love affair but it hadn't ended in marriage... He was so attractive it would have been odd if he hadn't had a few love affairs.' But even as she said it, there was a chill inside her, something was not right and it scared her. 'He didn't tell me every detail of his life before we met, after all he didn't tell me about Henry.'

Frank lifted his head, stared ahead into the distance. 'No, that did amaze me, I must say. They were such friends.'

'And yet he never spoke of him. I only heard of him by chance from Cecily not long ago. I find that very strange, don't you?' She faced him, determined now to find out more.

Frank sighed, said after a moment, choosing his words carefully, 'Perhaps he didn't think you'd understand and maybe you wouldn't, remember how young you were. My father, and indeed Cecily, understood, as they lived through the war, but no doubt Julian found it too hard, too painful to talk about when he first met you, and then as time went on, it became too late, and perhaps not necessary, it happened long before you came into his life.' He glanced up the lane as if he hoped to see the truck clattering up to fetch them so that he need not go on, but it was all quiet except for the wind rustling the leaves and the occasional baa from the sheep on the other side of the field, and the far-off sound of cars crawling along the motorway.

'But it's not difficult to understand, Frank. Your brother was very badly injured in a riding accident and he died. Why couldn't he tell me that?' she said firmly, determined to know.

'Because there were things... things that happened that Julian probably didn't want to burden you with, that you might not understand,' Frank said slowly.

She felt rather impatient with him now, she understood how difficult it must be for Frank to talk of his brother's death but all she was asking was *why*, during twenty-five years of marriage, Julian had never even mentioned his best friend's name, let alone his death. She started to say this when Frank stopped her.

'As you insist, I'll tell you,' he said, 'though you are not to be judgemental.'

'I won't be... but...'

He carried on as if he must get it over with. 'In the war, when soldiers were moving on, escaping from the oncoming enemy, they couldn't always take the seriously injured with them, they couldn't leave them to be humiliated, tortured by the enemy, so they made sure they were safe, made sure they were dead. It wasn't easy but it was what they had to do. Henry and my father understood, and Julian helped them; I hadn't the courage.' Tears glazed his eyes. 'We never told my mother, but it was the best way. If you had known Henry, you'd understand. He was a brilliant sportsman, an outdoor man, and to be chained to a bed or a chair by his injuries, to not even be able to feed himself or scratch his nose for the rest of his life...' Frank's face was haggard as he remembered it. 'It was what Henry wanted and we understood.'

'I see.' Alice felt drained by the enormity of what Frank had told her, crushed by his grief, still so potent after all these years. She felt sick with the horror of it. No wonder Julian hadn't told her. Had he... and Frank's father committed a crime? The word *murder* lurched into her mind.

'I shouldn't have told you,' Frank said. 'I can see you are shocked but if you'd been there...' He let the words hang in the air.

'I'm sorry I made you tell me,' she said at last, vowing to leave it now, not to dwell on this private act of love that she did not need to know. To change the subject she said, 'But still it gave me a turn, seeing that young man so like Julian. I must have been thinking of when I first met Julian and he was younger, and then I saw that man... and it was quite dark then as it had been raining...'

Frank said nothing and his silence spooked her.

'There's something else, isn't there, Frank?' she said quietly.

'You better know it all,' he turned to her, 'though this too happened long before he met you. I have a sister, Sarah, in between Henry and I. She spent a lot of time with Henry and Julian so it was not surprising that Julian fell in love with her. She's such a lovely person. Their affair came to a natural end as she was going to study in America. When she'd gone, she discovered she was pregnant.' He took Alice's hand, held it close in both of his. 'I thought he would have told you. Edward... Ned, he's Julian's son.'

'No.' His news was like an arrow to her heart. 'His *son*.' She could not grasp it, why had Julian not told her? Her mouth was dry, the news thudded round her brain, how could he have been so intimate with her... his wife, and not told her about such a monumental event? He, who was such a good father to his daughters, how could be have left his son? Though *had* he left him? Or had he lived his life between both families? Was that why Julian sometimes came back from business trips some days later than he planned? Or did he take trips to visit this son and tell her he was away on business? Her mind spun with questions. She wanted Julian here so she could interrogate him. So much he had kept from her. She'd thought she'd had the perfect marriage but she had not, it had been a marriage of secrets and he had deceived her.

Still keeping hold of her hand though she tried to withdraw it, Frank went on, 'Ned was born and lived in New Jersey. Soon after she arrived, Sarah met and fell in love with Greg.

They married and Greg brought him up as his son, though Ned always knew Julian was his biological father and saw him from time to time. Ned stayed in London in my flat in Queen's Gate for a few months here and there while he studied and did an internship, though that was mostly after Julian's death. Had he been alive when he was here I'm sure he'd have introduced you all.' He did not sound very convincing.

'I don't think he would after he'd kept him secret for so long,' Alice said sadly, struggling to understand. 'It was just a sheer fluke that I saw him in Queen's Gate that day and if I hadn't mentioned it to you I would have never known, would I? Or my girls that they have a half-brother?' It hit her hard as she realised that her daughters had a brother, what would they feel about that?

'You must not blame Julian, Alice, he loved you, more than he loved anyone. He met you after Ned's birth and for some reason he didn't tell you. When you asked me some time ago why I hadn't introduced my nephew to you, I waited to see if you mentioned Julian's son, but you did not. So I said nothing,' he said quietly.

'I wish you'd told me.' She turned to him her face anguished.

'It was not my story to tell. Perhaps Julian meant to tell you but time went by and he put it off and then it probably became too difficult, I don't know, but you mustn't hold it against him, he loved you and your girls and that is the most important thing.'

'But Ned, is related to my girls and...' She burst into tears. It was too much. All these years she'd been married to a man she didn't know, their marriage, the marriage she thought she'd had, was a sham and she felt that Frank too had conspired in the betrayal.

Chapter 32

To his relief, Frank saw the truck lurching over the rough ground to pick them up.

Alice saw it too and took a deep, shuddering breath, struggling to control her tears. He moved to hold her but she leant away from him, scrabbling in her pocket for a handkerchief to wipe her eyes. She turned her face away, watching the truck approach, adding to his pain and confused anger with himself for telling her so much, and with Julian for not telling her anything. And yet had not that been one of the reasons Frank had been reluctant to see her, afraid of the secrets he shared with Julian? He and Julian rarely spoke of them, though they both sometimes felt them hovering between them like ghosts.

He had fallen in love with Alice himself in those early days but he took himself out of the way by moving to France, not wanting to be hanging around their marriage. Coming back all these years later, he found to his surprise that he still loved her. Now he was here, and she was alone he wanted to stay close to her, though the bombshell that Julian had left behind had now destroyed anything that might have blossomed between them. Even if he'd kept Ned secret, as Julian had done, it loomed too large between them for a loving relationship to flourish.

Ben was steering the truck with one hand and leaning with his free arm on the open window. He stopped beside them, jumped out, his face split with a grin, looking from one to the other. 'So how was it? Did you enjoy it?'

'Very much,' Frank said. 'Alice has just got to get her breath back,' he added, hoping to save her having to explain her tears, but she had her back to them, bending down to sort out the tangle of seat, kite and ropes to hide her face.

She said, 'Lovely, really enjoyed it.'

'Good, you must do it again. No, leave that I'll do it.' Ben came over to her and yanked up the kite and its para-phernalia to bundle into the truck. 'Great conditions today, hope to go up myself, later.'

Frank helped him load up. He longed to comfort Alice, hold her in his arms, but she had closed in upon herself and wouldn't even look at him. He felt angry with Julian, why had he not told her about Ned before they married? He had not asked him about it himself, perhaps feeling that it was between Alice and Julian and now he thought about it, he'd just assumed that Alice knew about Ned and as he never saw her it was not discussed. He understood why Julian hadn't talked about Henry, helping someone to die – even though Henry had begged them to do it and had dictated a letter outlining his wishes – was a crime.

It was the fact that Julian had not told her about Ned that infuriated him. She might have been upset at first, but she was a sensible woman and would surely have seen that the relationship – which happened before they met – held no threat to her and their family. Hiding it like Julian had done made it seem like there was more to it than there was. It was not as bad as Evie's baby, openly fathered by a man cheating on his wife, who was too careless to bother with birth control. Ned had been conceived by mistake, Julian and Sarah had been in love but not enough to marry. Ned was well balanced and happy, knowing that he was loved and wanted, even if his conception had not been planned.

Sarah and Julian's relationship had started soon after Henry's death, both perhaps needing the other after the trauma of it all. They'd both known that Sarah was going to study in the US. She had no idea she was pregnant when she left Britain, indeed didn't find out until she was over three months gone. Julian offered to marry her but by then she'd met Greg, who'd stood by her and accepted Ned. Julian then met Alice and for some reason he could not fathom, he had not told her about his son. If only she hadn't – by some unlucky quirk of fate – seen him. Sod's law that Ned was only in London for a few days and he'd come out of the flat just as she passed it. He glanced at her; she was watching a couple of kites circling above them, her hands clenched in her lap, showing her pain. He shouldn't have told her. He should have brushed off her story of seeing Ned as a strange coincidence.

Ned had been in his life as his nephew so long Frank no longer gave his beginnings much thought. He wondered now if Ned knew about his half-sisters? He knew Julian was married but it was another life to him, he'd lived and was educated in New Jersey and had his doting family, friends and interests there. He had always seen Greg – who was there all the time – as his father, and although he was fond of Julian they never had enough time together to bond strongly as father and son. Now that his nephew was working in corporate law, the same field as he was, they had much in common and there were many interesting cases Ned wanted to discuss with him.

Ned had just started work in a prestigious firm in New

York so had not come over from the States to go to Julian's funeral, and he himself was too far away and tied up with a difficult case to go either. He still missed Julian, but now he was furious that he'd left behind these secrets for him to break to Alice and surely ruin any loving relationship they might have had together.

Alice got into the truck beside Ben, who was chattering on, and Frank squeezed in himself. There was not much room in the cabin and they sat close together, their bodies touching. She did not move but stared ahead as Ben turned the truck and started back along the track, their bodies swinging against each other as the truck rattled over the dry, ridged earth. Ben talked all the time, which both of them found a relief.

They reached the clubhouse and Alice disappeared into the Ladies. They were supposed to be going to a good pub he knew for a decent lunch, but he'd lost his appetite and he imagined she had too. He hung about waiting for her to emerge, intently studying the photographs on the wall, taken of the landscape from the air.

She came out at last, she'd done her best to hide the ravages of her distress by re-doing her make-up, but it was there in her eyes, in the way she moved, and it crushed his spirits.

'Do you feel like something to eat?' he asked quietly. 'I know it was a shock and I'm so upset that I was the one who had to tell you.'

'I'm sorry, Frank, but I just want to go home.' She moved towards the door and he followed her to the car. It seemed so long since their flight, the beauty and the calmness, the magic of floating together in the sky. He'd felt so close to her, as if they were the only two people in the world, their own worlds latched together as one.

232

He felt a surge of resentment against Julian. Had he imagined that, because Ned lived most of his life in the States with his family he need not tell her? Ned had been about four years old when Julian and Alice married and it was true Julian barely saw him at that time, but later when as a young adult he'd come to London to study, surely he could have told her then?

They reached the car and got in, he drove out of the club and up the road. 'Look,' he said to break the silence, 'I assumed that Julian must have told you about Ned when you married but if there is anything you want to know please ask me. It happened long before he knew you, so it wasn't as if it happened behind your back, not like... Nick and Evie. I know it's been a shock, but when you've had time to think, you'll come to terms with it, I know you will.'

'It's not that,' she turned to him in anguish. 'Of course if he had affairs and sex and... as Evie reminded me sex makes babies, I'd have understood, asked Ned round to meet the girls... his half-sisters.' She gulped on the words. 'What hurts me so much is that Julian didn't tell me, didn't include his son... introduce him to us. He lived – when he was in London – close by and yet we never had an inkling about his existence. Why was that? Was he ashamed of him, ashamed of us?'

'Of course not.' He clutched the steering wheel, his feelings in turmoil, not wanting such a conversation now when they were driving. 'Julian was hardly a saint, he made mistakes like the rest of us and, for what it's worth, I think he made a mistake not to tell you, but for whatever reason, he didn't. Look, Alice, can we stop somewhere, talk about this quietly?'

'No, I just want to get home, please Frank. I'm sorry...

the flight was wonderful, I'll never forget it and I'm sorry it ended this way.'

He was chilled by her words; did she mean she didn't want to see him again? Banish the 'messenger' of such news. But he'd promised to be at Laura's wedding to take Julian's place. He was doing too much for Julian, he thought, now sorting out the mayhem he'd left behind, which had ruined Alice's opinion of him.

'As you wish, Alice, but please don't blame me for it; you can blame me for telling you about it, but not for what happened.'

He'd been in love with her so long, though when she'd asked him to come and give Laura away, he'd convinced himself that time would have changed her and that his love for her would have died a natural death. Besides, hadn't he often thought that there were too many complications between him and Julian for them to have a life together? But when he'd seen her again, his feelings for her were as strong as ever and he kidded himself that the secrets that bound him to Julian were in the past and now she was alone they might have a chance to be happy together.

He struggled to bank down his fury; Julian knew that he loved Alice. He'd even asked him if that was why he'd upped sticks and gone to live in France to put some space between them. He'd been rather vague with his answer and to his relief they'd been interrupted before the conversation got too deep.

Had Julian set up these hurdles knowing that he would find them too much of a barrier to nurture a love between them when he'd gone? He'd known for years that his heart condition would kill him early and he was older than he was, had he, could he, knowing them both so well, stymied any hope of them coming together?

No, Frank scolded himself for thinking such a thing. He was overwrought with the ruination of the day and Alice's pain, Julian would never think like that, would he?

Chapter 33

Alice stared out of the window at the passing scenery as she and Frank drove back to London. She felt disorientated, as if she didn't know herself, the person she once was, the wife, now widow of such a man. She wondered if Cecily had known about Julian's past life too, kept them from her all these years? Alice had been young, barely twenty-one when she'd married Julian, but not so young as not to have understood about Ned, accepted that Julian had had a liaison that resulted in a child before he'd even known her.

Who was he really, this man she'd loved and married? He felt now like a stranger. Had she conjured up the kind and caring man who'd professed to love her? But he had loved her, she told herself, surely he had, for how could he have kept up the act for so long? And he loved his daughters, there was no doubt of that. But why had he not shared this part of his life with her, did he not trust her, respect her enough to do so? Surely he loved his son too, but if so, why hadn't he told them about him, included him in the family, especially as he'd been here in London from time to time, living so close to them?

They drove in silence most of the way back, both of them reluctant to speak in case more disclosures would reveal themselves. Frank dropped her off home and as he stopped the car she tried to apologise for her mood, conscious that he was unhappy, disappointed in how the day he'd taken so much trouble to plan had ended. She wished now she hadn't mentioned seeing Ned, had stayed in blissful ignorance about Julian's past. For whatever reason he hadn't wanted her to know or he would have told her.

'The paragliding was wonderful, Frank,' she said, 'I'll never forget the experience of floating together in the sky, it was every bit as wonderful, more so in fact, than I imagined. Thank you so much.'

'Shall I come in with you or is Laura there?' he asked, turning to her a moment, his face stern as he struggled with his emotions, dashing any hopes she had of feeling easy with him again.

'No... thank you.' She opened the car door, she wanted to be alone to try and make some sense of it.

'Please ring if you need me, Again, I'm sorry I had to be the one to tell you all these things, but it's better out in the open and I hope you come to terms with it.' He said, inwardly cursing Julian.

'I'll be fine, goodbye and thank you for the paragliding, I loved it, I really did.' She got out quickly and shut the door, almost slamming it in her anguish. She couldn't bear to hear another word, have Frank floundering on, making excuses for Julian, adding more insecurity to her muddled thoughts.

Frank was out of the car too and came and stood beside her and she had to almost touch him as she made for her front door. She struggled with a sudden wish for him to hold her, comfort her, and take away the chill of Julian's betrayal.

She had her door key in her hand and she passed him quickly and went and unlocked the door, the whine of the alarm picking up. 'Goodbye,' she said, scooting in and turning off the alarm before shutting the door. She leant against it, listening to Frank slamming his car door and the throb of the engine as he started up the car and roared away down the street, leaving an overwhelming sense of loss. Not only Frank's loss but Julian's too, the very memory that she still clung to was flawed.

She passed a miserable night and the next morning she took the bus to see Cecily. She'd telephoned first, knowing how she often played bridge with friends or could even be out on some expedition with Kalinda, but she was there and Alice craved her advice and comfort.

'My dear, whatever has happened, you look dreadful?' Cecily greeted her from her usual place on the sofa, the day's newspapers strewn over the cushions. She pushed them on the floor, patted the place bedside her, 'Sit down, nothing's happened to the girls or that baby has it?'

Alice shook her head, struggling with her tears.

'Here's Kalinda with some coffee for us,' Cecily said, smiling at Kalinda. 'Thank you, we might need a nip of brandy in it if we have to face bad news.' She touched Alice's arm in sympathy.

'No, not unless you want some,' Alice said, ashamed now of dashing round here as though the world had ended, though for her, in a way, it had.

'It depends what you're going to tell me,' Cecily said. 'We better have it in case, please Kalinda.'

Kalinda fetched the bottle from the drinks tray that stood by the window. 'There you are, call if you need anything.' She patted Alice on the shoulder as she left. She too understood suffering, and again Alice felt ashamed, she'd had a happy life compared to them.

'You're the only person I can talk to about it, Cecily,' she started. 'You might know all about it but it came as a terrible shock to me. I went paragliding with Frank yesterday, it was wonderful but then we landed and had a little time to wait for the truck to pick us up, I told him I'd seen a man that looked just like Julian, a young Julian, coming out of his block of flats and he told me...' she dashed the tears from her eyes, 'he was Julian's son.' She watched Cecily carefully but she looked as shocked as she'd been.

'His *son*? You don't mean godson?'

'No son. He had a son with Frank and Henry's sister, Sarah. After Henry died, she went to America to study and she didn't realise she was pregnant for some weeks, and by then she was in love with someone else whom she married.' She went on to tell Cecily about Julian's part in Henry's death.

'I guessed that,' Cecily said. 'He never said anything to me about it and I didn't ask, but I saw how much he suffered over it. I'd seen that situation in the war. So many beautiful, strong young men came back with appalling injuries and not a lot could be done for them. Julian told me Henry died, but that was all and all I expected to hear. Some things should remain private between those concerned, and it is not for us to judge.'

'I know and it's not that I judge him for but for having a son, a half-brother to the girls, that he kept secret from us. It happened before I knew him, but still, he had a son. Did you know anything about it, Cecily?'

'No, we were close but he didn't tell me everything. Anyway, at that time, I was travelling and working and we didn't see much of each other. When did he find out?'

'Soon enough, before Ned was born... he offered to marry Sarah, but she'd met someone else. Ned spent his childhood in America, Sarah had more children, but then Ned came here to London to study, work, I don't know. And then I saw him… and I thought he was Julian.'

Cecily sat quiet for a moment, digesting the news; her hands clasped loosely in her lap, her faded eyes faraway. She said at last, 'And Frank told you all this yesterday?'

'Yes, and I was furious, it spoilt our lovely day. I made him take me home, miss the lunch he'd planned. I just couldn't be with him, knowing he'd known all this about Julian, Ned is his nephew after all, and no one told me.' She swallowed her tears, the injustice of it digging into her.

'Did you feel, perhaps, as if you were not deemed important enough in their lives to be told?' Cecily watched her.

'Yes, I suppose I do, insignificant, compared to Julian's bond with *their* family, and yet we were married, had children together and all the time he had this secret family. He often saw Frank when he went to Europe on business or here in London, but he never suggested we meet up, have him over to the house as we did with our other friends.' She frowned, trying to think back to the times Frank might have been here.

'I think, am sure, you've got it wrong, my dear.' Cecily put her hands over hers as they twisted in her lap. 'Julian loved you, loved you and the girls more than anyone, you must not lose sight of that. But he was also close to Frank because of Henry and what happened to him and there was a bond there, a deep bond that has nothing to do with his love for you and it seems there's a bond through their sister too. We do not belong to each other, Alice, and we should be allowed some privacy, don't let this destroy you, destroy the love you and Julian shared, be thankful you had it for so many years.' Her eyes skimmed over the pictures of her dead fiancés, 'No one can take away that love you shared, whether it lasted a long time or hardly any time at all. It is there in your make-up and cannot be lost unless you choose to destroy it.'

She'd been lucky with her family and Julian, Alice knew that, and yet she still felt angry – torn to bits – that such a secret was kept from her and she was angry with herself for taking it out on Frank when it was Julian who was to blame. Cecily guessed her thoughts. 'It's very hard to accept some things in life, but you must accept this or you're in danger of ruining everything. The loving life you shared together, the good memories you stored up. Tell the girls about Ned, their half-brother, ask Frank to introduce you. Does Ned know about you all?'

'I don't know.'

'Well get Frank on to it, and, Alice, don't blame him, give him a chance.'

'A chance for what?'

Cecily smiled a rather annoying, secret smile. 'Just give him a chance, he's a good man, he deserves happiness.'

Alice was weary of secrets. She had felt close to Frank when she'd seen him again, but now she felt that she and Frank could never be comfortable together after this. He was an honourable man and he'd do his bit at Laura's wedding and then he'd leave and go home to France. Apart from wishes at Christmas and perhaps occasional visits if he came to London they would not see each other again.

Cecily obviously thought she'd said enough on the subject and asked how Evie was getting on juggling baby and work, and how the arrangements for Laura's wedding were going. 'Almost a Christmas wedding, candlelight, evergreens with bright berries, possibly even snow, it will be lovely,' Cecily said. 'Keep looking forward, my dear, the past is past and there's no going back.'

'It's just the consequences of it that mess up the future,' Alice said.

When Alice left Cecily she walked all the way down Park Lane to Hyde Park Corner to the bus that would take her home. She passed the showrooms of the gleaming cars and wished she could drive one on her own to a time before she known these secrets.

Chapter 34

'But we can't possibly have Nick at your wedding, Laura,' Alice protested, still poleaxed from Frank's revelations, feeling she'd lost him as her ally in this venture.

'Why ever not? He's part of our family now, like it or not, and Freya's coming, I've asked them both. I asked their little girl Lexie to be a bridesmaid, or rather she asked me and I couldn't refuse her,' Laura said. 'Apart from Zara, I don't know any other small children and I just want little bridesmaids and Lexie's so pretty,' Laura finished defiantly, her eyes hard on Alice; they were having tea together in the kitchen. She leant over to help herself to another biscuit and bit savagely into it.

Alice was furious. Nick had caused enough trouble in her family and was not welcome at the wedding. He'd even had the audacity to suggest he'd give Laura away before they found Frank. His arrogance was too much.

'But... what does Douglas think about it and... his mother?' Alice said, not wanting a row with her daughters and rather shamefully hoping that Elspeth's opinion would count against him. She certainly wouldn't put up with the married lover of her son's sister-in-law and father of her baby at the wedding.

'She's fine about it, well we didn't tell her too much, just that he and Freya are old friends of the family, which they are, Mum. We've known them for ever; Dad knew them and liked them.'

'We both like Freya, but your father would have thought differently about Nick if he'd been here now,' Alice retorted, though he might understand, having been in this predicament himself. Though, unlike Nick, he hadn't cheated on anyone. Perhaps they should ask Ned and Sarah to come too, for all to see the scandals of their family. She hadn't told her daughters about Ned; she hadn't told anyone except for Cecily. Besides, the girls should know the story before she told her friends. She must tell her daughters calmly, not let the anger she felt leach out, and she must tell them both together, but they weren't all going to be together until the wedding, unless she joined them in the cottage when Laura next went down for her last fitting.

She poured herself some more tea, wishing she had some brandy to slosh into it to give her strength. Cecily's idea was a good one. 'It takes the edge off shocks and other nasties. Far better than antidepressants and all those drugs they push at you these days at the slightest upset,' she'd said, before pouring them both a good slug.

The wedding plans were progressing. It was to be a small affair and there had been much heartache as to who would have to be left off the guest list. It hadn't occurred to her that Nick... and Freya would be asked, let alone their daughter be a bridesmaid.

'None of the London people know about him and Evie, and Lexie is Bunny's half-sister, we can't get away from that. Freya's all right about it, I did ask her. I saw her and Lexie in Bury when I went down for my dress fitting.' Laura took another biscuit. 'Freya and I chatted awhile and Lexie was dancing about and when she heard the word wedding she said, rather wistfully, that her friend was being a bridesmaid in a "fairy" dress and could she be mine, and somehow I couldn't say no.'

'But surely Freya doesn't want...'

'She told her to be quiet, saying she'd be a bridesmaid another time, but Lexie grabbed my hand and looked at me with such longing saying, "please, I'm little I won't take up much room," I couldn't find a way to refuse her. So I said yes, and then of course she jumped about so excited that Freya had to give in. But it will be fine, Mum, they won't be the only people there, after all.'

'Has Nick been in touch with Evie?' Alice asked. He'd seen his son only because he'd come across them in the town and she had pointedly held him up to show him.

'I don't know, Evie didn't say, but she doesn't mind him coming to the wedding,' Laura said. 'We found Zara's dress in Laura Ashley and Lexie will have the same.'

'So it seems as if it's all settled then, and I suppose it would be unkind not to let Lexie come if she's set her heart on it,' Alice said, going on to ask if Laura had seen Frank lately.

She was haunted by how badly she'd treated him, when it was Julian she wanted to blame, not Frank, the messenger.

She'd tried to telephone him the day after she'd seen Cecily but it went straight to voicemail and she couldn't think what to say so she'd rung off. That was almost two weeks ago and she hadn't heard a word from him since. Had he gone back to France? Would he come back for the wedding?

'Frank, yes, he's rung a couple of times, asked how everything is going.'

'Is he here or back in France?' Alice asked.

'Here, I think. Hasn't he been in touch with you recently, taken you paragliding again,' she teased.

'No… we must take Johnny again, we did promise,' she finished lamely.

'Let's wait until after the wedding, perhaps in the summer,' Laura said, clearly hoping Johnny would have forgotten about it by then. 'Was it scary?'

'No, well just for a moment before we took off, but it was wonderful, so peaceful floating in the sky.'

'Did you do it alone, two kites side by side?'

'I didn't fly on my own, we flew in tandem, Frank's done it before. He flew behind me and controlled everything, searching for thermals and all that. We were perfectly safe and I loved it, would like to do it again.'

Frank would not ask her again but the instructors were nice; she could go up with them, the ever-chatty Ben or the girl whose name she'd forgotten, though it wouldn't be the same, that special magic she'd shared with Frank.

There was a pain whenever she thought of him, and a desperate wish that she'd never mentioned seeing that young man.

'Well don't say too much about it to Johnny. He's stopped going on about it a bit. Anyway, they've been away with their mother, somewhere expensive, a sort of kids' club with endless games and sports to occupy them all the time, while their mother…' her mouth twisted at the word as if she had a bad taste on her tongue, 'lay about with her lover.'

'I expect she's exhausted with her high-powered job,' Alice said weakly. There were too many complications, too many people pushing into their lives, sending it askew. Were all families now so complicated, with their musical chairs of changing partners and children?

Laura's approaching wedding was like a train out of control, surging on to the end of the line. Perhaps it would all work out in the end but her main thought now was how her daughters would react to the news that they had a half-brother to add to this crazy mix of families.

Evie had her drawing to ground her and surely she now realised that Nick would not stand by her. But there was more fallout to come. Julian's illness and death had been difficult enough to come to terms with, and both of the girls had retaliated by making such life-changing mistakes. How would they cope with the fact that their beloved father was not the man they thought he was but had led a double life, a life he kept hidden from them all?

Chapter 35

The 'nursery' baskets took off – as much as they could with
only two people making them and just word of mouth and
one small advertisement in a free magazine. Margot and Alice
kept their sewing ladies stocked with pretty fabrics and baskets, which, to Alice's relief gave her mind a rest from her
family problems.

Frank had still not contacted her since the day he'd told
her about Julian's son, and she had not tried to contact him
again. Whenever she went to Margot's house, she kept an
eye out for him, and even Ned in case he'd returned. She
often took the bus to South Kensington, even walking up
Queen's Gate, scouring the faces of the people she passed.
Occasionally her heart lurched at the sight of a man of
Frank's build, the glimpse of a profile, the sharp cut of a suit,
but it was never him, perhaps he was no longer in London.

He kept in touch with Laura and it was through her that
she heard that he *was* still in London working on some article
about the affairs of a large financial company who'd employed
a firm which specialised in so-called 'legal' tax dodges.

'He can't be distracted, he's got a tight deadline but he'll
be at the wedding,' Laura told her when they met in a hurried
lunch hour to discuss the menu for the great day.

'So you're often in touch with him?' Alice asked, squashed

into a corner of the busy restaurant, hoping she sounded casual, though just the mention of Frank was like snagging a wound inside her.

She was ashamed now of blaming Frank for telling her these important things that her husband should have done. It wasn't as if Julian hadn't had plenty of time and opportunities – and what other secrets had he hidden?

In the lonely, dead hours of the night, her mind sometimes trawled through all those years she'd trusted Julian when he was away on business and the times he'd told her he couldn't make it home as there'd been a crisis at work.

'We speak or text most weeks.' Laura raised her voice over the chatter in the restaurant and she leant forward, her eyes on her. 'He says you do too much.'

'Too much of what?' Had they been talking about her behind her back?

'Oh, this and that.' She looked away, her face awkward. 'I think he means things with us, well really Evie's baby... I mean she's landed herself in it, hasn't she, Mum? Just when she got that great commission she got pregnant with a man who'll never stay with her. Do you think she did it to get out of doing that? She did feel it was quite a challenge and I know she's afraid her work won't be thought good enough and they'll dump her.'

'No, I don't. She was thrilled to get the job, naturally she worried she might not be good enough or get it done in time, but that was a positive feeling, it made her work extra hard. People who think they are wonderful at things often just drift on,' Alice said, impatient with the psycho rubbish spewed out today. 'Nick is very attractive and very good at seducing women. I think he chose Evie because she was vulnerable after Dad's death, and alone in the cottage.

249

Evie should have known better, or at the very least not got pregnant, but I blame him more than I blame her. There's something weak about a man who only seduces vulnerable women and I despise him for it,' Alice finished sternly.

'Oh, Mum, that's rubbish, it takes two, and it's not Victorian times when women knew nothing about sex,' Laura snapped. 'Evie didn't *have* to sleep with him or have his baby. She was on the pill, so I wonder why she stopped it.'

Alice hadn't known Evie was on the pill, though it seemed sensible if she was planning to sleep with someone, but Laura was right, why would she have stopped taking it? Had she not planned to sleep with anyone after Julian's death, so stopped taking it or had Nick's seduction of her been so over powering they hadn't time to take other precautions?

Since Frank's revelations Alice found that she admired Freya even more for putting her children's welfare before her heartache over Nick's behaviour, though they were young children still dependant on their home life.

Later, after lunch, Alice went on to meet Margot at her house. It was a relief to discuss colours and materials and choosing pretty ribbons and braid to trim the baskets. They added lined laundry baskets to their range and whole matching sets of baskets for the nursery.

'Sam says we should have a website, sell on the Internet,' Margot told her of her son's idea. 'We'd have to find more people to help Edith and Amy and we don't want them to feel we think it is too much for them.'

'Let's see how this lot go first,' Alice said. They'd had quite a few orders from their advertisement. 'How many have they done already, should one of us fetch them?' She didn't want to go to Suffolk, but she did want to see Bunny, he'd captured her heart, as she'd known he would. Whatever the circumstances of his birth, he was not to blame and he was part of the family now, a person to be treasured.

'I can't go just now.' Margot looked cagey. 'You should go, see your grandson, stay a night down there? We do need to have some finished baskets up here to be able to sell in London and see if some of the small children's shops would stock them.'

It was on the tip of her tongue to ask Margot why she couldn't go to Suffolk. She'd always managed before to take her turn on driving there and she liked to see Edith and Amy and keep an eye on their work, but she kept quiet. Alice had an uncomfortable feeling that something was not quite right. Margot had been withdrawn all afternoon, staring into space, and though Alice had asked if anything was wrong, Margot said hurriedly, 'No, why should there be?' in a tone that forbade further questions.

'OK, I'll go then. Laura wants another fitting. So I'll take her with me,' Alice said, remembering Laura saying at lunch that she wasn't sure she liked the sleeves of her dress. 'I'll text her and see when she can manage it.'

'Thanks, I'll go next time,' Margot said, starting to pack up the fabrics and the ribbons for her to take.

They left for Suffolk a couple of days later, Laura now stressing that she'd put on weight and wouldn't fit into the dress,

'You're never fat, darling,' Alice reassured her. Laura was a larger build than dainty little Evie but she wasn't fat.

The drive was slow with many lorries on the road, Laura fell asleep and Alice, left to herself, was hit with a sudden thought that buzzed into the back of her mind like an annoying wasp. The three of them would be together, alone in the cottage tonight. It could well be the last time before the wedding. She must tell them about Ned.

She'd asked Cecily's advice when she'd last seen her a few days ago. 'I'm dreading telling them, upsetting their image of their father. Do you think I really have to? Julian didn't think it worth telling me, so perhaps...' Her anger with him burned, how could he have died and left this bombshell behind?

'I don't know what he thought about it or why he didn't tell you, but I think you must tell them, they are adults after all and secrets can often cause more upset than the truth,' Cecily said firmly. 'Think how it distressed you, finding out, and how angry you are with Julian for not telling you, disturbing your good memories of him. You don't want them finding out some other way and thinking the same of you, far better to get it out in the open.'

'You're right, I'll have to tell them, but look how they reacted when Julian died.' Her stomach churned with the dread of telling them.

'I know. That was unfortunate, but surely they're over that. Evie won't have another baby now she's juggling one with her work, and from what you tell me, Nick has moved on. Laura's about to get married, and unless she calls it off nothing worse will happen.' Cecily smiled, took her hand, 'Alice, it's not you who did this but Julian and he shouldn't have left it for you to do. These things are never easy, perhaps Frank would help you tell them, after all he was there when it all happened, and knows Ned well.'

'Oh, no, that won't work,' she said hurriedly, she couldn't possibly involve Frank.

Cecily regarded her thoughtfully before saying, 'It was Julian's doing and Julian's responsibility. I'm very disappointed that he never told me that I had a great-nephew, especially since Ned lived in London for a while, but for whatever reason, he chose not to tell us and we can do nothing about it now.'

'He should have told you, Cecily, I wonder why he didn't.'

'That was his choice, it's not something you want to share with everyone,' Cecily said. 'But once you've done it you'll feel better about it, have them to share it with, but don't let it ruin your happy memories of Julian. Remember they are all you have left now so cherish them.'

Alice thought of Cecily's advice as they trailed along the busy road, held up again by roadworks. It was a great relief when they at last turned down the lane to the cottage and arrived.

Evie and Bunny came out to greet them, Evie asking why it had taken them so long, seeming pleased to see them.

Bunny had grown and become more alert and seemed a cheerful little boy, though he called out often for attention, which Alice was happy to give him, bouncing him on her knee or cuddling him while she fed him or he slept. She noticed that Evie appeared to be glowing with some inner joy. Motherhood obviously suited her. She'd finished her illustrations, they were much admired by the publishers and she had a few weeks respite before having to start on the next book.

'I've decided to call him Raphael, Raffi for short, and Julian after Dad, for his middle name, so he can choose which one he likes best when he's older,' she announced proudly when they were all sitting together with tea and a rather battered chocolate cake Evie had baked for them.

'A good choice. Unusual,' Alice said, wondering how she'd come to settle on the name.

'Raphael, who do we know called Raphael?' Laura

stared expectantly at her sister as if waiting for some fascinating revelation.

Evie blushed, a soft rosy glow covering her face. She turned away from them, fiddling with some late flowering roses she'd picked from the garden and put in a vase in the living room. Alice waited. 'Someone I know suggested it,' Evie said vaguely. 'Bunny's a bit... well we don't want it to stick, do we?'

'No, Raphael... Raffi is perfect,' Alice said hurriedly. 'Now we'd better get over to Edith and Amy and we'll all have supper together this evening. I'll get something nice on the way back.' She didn't feel like eating, perhaps none of them would when they'd heard what she had to say.

When they left the fitting, the car was full of pretty baskets, making Evie exclaim and beg to have a set for herself.

'I've already ordered one for you,' Alice said, 'but we need these to try and sell in London.

Later they ate supper together, though she could hardly swallow, and then, just as Evie said she was going to have a shower before settling down to a television programme she liked, she said, 'Just stay a second, darling, sit down – I've something to tell you, something difficult, but it has to be said.'

Both girls exchanged anxious looks with each other. Evie sunk down on the sofa close to Laura, who put down the magazine she was flicking through.

'You've got some terrible illness,' Evie blurted, her eyes round with fear.

Laura leant over and touched her, her voice raw, her eyes wild, 'You haven't, have you, Mum?'

'No... nothing like that. No. It's something to do with your father...'

'Don't say he's not really our father,' Evie said, the relief that her mother was not ill struggling with her new fear.

'No, he *is* your father, please listen, it is difficult for me to tell you but I must, you have a right to know. Frank told me. Your father never even hinted about it, so it came as a great shock to me.' The tears, tears of fury as well as betrayal, surged up in her. She thought of Cecily; she would be strong, face it squarely, and tell it as it was. 'You know Frank is one of your father's dearest friends, well Dad's real friend was his older brother, Henry, and Henry had a terrible riding accident and died.' She was never going to tell anyone about Julian's part in this, that would be kept private. 'Naturally they were all very upset and then Dad fell in love with their sister, Sarah and...' she paused and Laura said quietly, 'I suppose they had a baby, did they marry? Were you and Dad married, properly married I mean?'

'Not bigamy,' Evie burst out. 'Don't tell me Dad had two wives and two lots of children at the same time.'

'No.' This was turning into a farce. 'They never married. Sarah left Britain to study in America and found later that she was having Dad's baby. She fell in love with someone out there and married him.'

'So what you're saying is we have a half... what, brother or sister?' Laura demanded.

'A half-brother, Ned, only Dad never told us about him.'

'Perhaps he didn't know,' Evie said. 'You said the girl only found out she was pregnant when she'd left here.'

'He did know, he often saw him. Even though Ned lives in America, he studied and worked in London not far from us, in Queens Gate, and he never told us.'

Chapter 36

Alice couldn't sleep and tossed and turned in one of the single beds in the spare room. Evie had taken over the master bed since she'd been alone with Raffi, putting his cot into the en-suite bathroom so she could hear him easily in the night, and for that Alice was glad. She didn't want to feel Julian's presence in the dark beside her, remember how often they made love here, more often than they did in London, as being in the cottage always had a relaxed, holiday feel about it.

She had told them the truth, it was over and she should be relieved. They hadn't been as shocked as she had, they'd even found it exciting. 'A brother, great, I've always wanted a brother,' Evie exclaimed, and even Laura seemed pleased. 'Babies do get born to people who aren't married,' she said pointedly. 'Do you think she did it to trap him, wanted to marry him herself?'

'I've no idea.' Alice didn't want to think about it, let her imagination take wing and throw up all sorts of lurid scenarios.

She'd cried when she told them, saying how hurt she was that Julian hadn't told her about it. They'd been together all those years and he'd never even hinted at it, and though the girls hugged her, begged her not to cry, they saw it differently.

'He didn't want you to be upset and you would have been,

you'd have interrogated him, Mum, wouldn't you? Making it worse than it was,' Laura said kindly. 'It happened before he knew you, it would be much worse if he'd sloped off and had an affair behind your back.' She threw Evie a sharp look, though Evie didn't see.

'I think it makes Dad rather exciting,' Evie said. 'He made us think he was a very cautious, careful man and all the time he'd led this secret life.' Her eyes shone as if she'd suddenly found out that her father was really James Bond.

'It's not the sort of excitement I want, and at the very least he could have told us... me.' She'd dreaded the girls being upset by their father's betrayal but in fact they seemed to admire him more because of it.

The next morning after they'd all had time to absorb the news, Laura and Evie bombarded her with questions about Ned. Could he come to the wedding, if only she'd known about him, Laura said, *he* could have given her away.

'But you've asked Frank and he's accepted and is paying for most of the wedding, you can't put him off now. I don't know how much Ned knows about us, if anything. He's got to get to know us, and there's no time with the wedding only weeks away. I think it best to take it slowly. I can't get my head round it just now, there's been too many things to think about,' Alice said. She'd have to accept Ned in their lives if the girls wanted to get to know him; after all he was their half-brother. But would *she* want him in her life, a clone of his father, a reminder of a life she'd never known about? 'Also imagine the drama if people found out he was your father's son, it will spoil the day for you, Laura, it's *your* day after all.' Alice knew what it would be like if Ned came to the wedding, all the attention would be on him and she couldn't bear it: the gossip, the whispers, and the incredulity.

'I've told Douglas and he's amazed,' Laura said. 'He wonders why Dad didn't tell us ages ago.' She regarded Alice warily.

'It is odd he didn't tell, I mean I'd tell my husband or whatever about Raffi,' Evie said, lurching the baby over her shoulder to wind him.

'Perhaps men feel differently, and as you say, Mum, the girl didn't know she was pregnant for ages. There wasn't much sex education when Dad was young or reliable birth control, was there?' Laura said. 'But I do wish he'd told us. I'd have liked to get to know Ned.'

'You're sure he is Dad's?' Evie frowned. 'I mean, you all seemed so unclued up about sex and all then, what if Ned is the other man's, the one she married?'

'No, I'm sure Ned is his,' Alice said. 'I saw him.'

'What! Why didn't you tell us?' Both girls chorused together.

'We didn't speak, he didn't even see me, and if he had he wouldn't have known who I was. I saw him coming out of Frank's block of flats and crossing the road and I thought he was Dad.' She went on to explain the scene to them, the shock of seeing him, mistaking him for Julian and realising that it couldn't be him. She didn't tell them about the sorrow she'd felt and now the anger that he had died and left behind an image of himself to taunt her.

As the girls, especially Evie, discussed it, they made excuses for their father's behaviour. 'I think he feels more human knowing this about him,' Evie said.

'Being like you, you mean,' Laura retorted.

'No squabbling, girls,' Alice said weakly.

While Laura and Evie were finding excuses for their father's actions, Alice felt they skated round Nick, who was hardly a good example of a loving, caring father and she wondered if they would compare their own father to him. Had Julian just left Ned to be brought up by Sarah's family, opted out, as Nick seemed to be doing with Raffi?

Her daughters, or anyway Evie, might pretend they didn't know what was said about Nick's inability to keep his trousers done up and habit of fathering children with women other than his wife. Would some people – Elspeth, Laura's dire future mother-in-law, came to mind – say the same things about Julian when they heard the story, giving her something else to disapprove of?

She should be above caring what people like Elspeth thought, but it was Laura who'd bear the brunt of it. Julian had changed in Alice's mind; she could no longer feel the presence of the man she'd loved for so long. He'd gone, leaving behind a stranger, setting her adrift from the person she'd thought herself to be.

Chapter 37

Alice and Laura got back to London late on the Sunday night, and Laura stayed over, leaving early the next morning for work. Soon she'd move back home, having given up her flat, and in a few weeks she'd be married.

Laura had never lived with Douglas, perhaps because of his children being there. Alice knew there were times when the children stayed with their mother or grandparents and the two of them would spend some time together alone, but perhaps not enough time. Having to go to school and all, the children spent the majority of their time with their father, so there couldn't be much privacy and time for getting to know each other.

It was difficult to know what was right. Some of her friends' daughters had moved in with boyfriends and then the relationships had turned sour and they'd been cast out with nothing. On the other hand, if two adults had never lived together they might find it hard to settle into each other's rhythms. Alice had been so young, able to adapt easily to Julian, and he came alone, unencumbered with children – well, so she had thought at the time.

Now she'd become too set in her ways to dovetail into another man's life, especially as she was just beginning to enjoy her independence, and, though she'd welcome Julian back, the man he used to be, the man she'd believed he was, she didn't know that she wanted to live with someone else now.

She was contemplating this over her third cup of coffee when the doorbell went. It must be the postman or some delivery; things for the wedding were coming in most weeks now. She opened the door with a smile on her face: it was Frank.

The two of them stood there regarding each other a moment, then Frank said, 'May I come in? I know it's early but I want to see you and Laura told me you came back from Suffolk last night.' He didn't wait for her answer, walking in and standing in the narrow hall, watching her.

She couldn't think what to say, her heart was doing a sort of jig; perhaps she'd have a seizure and collapse on the floor, though there wouldn't be room for both of them in this narrow passage. She was relieved that she was dressed and made up. She always liked to start the day ready for it, lounging about her in nightclothes made her feel sloppy and lethargic.

'I suppose you want to talk about Julian and Ned and all of them.' She turned her back on him and walked through the house into the large kitchen. The sun shone through the window, touching the room with syrupy light. She faced him. 'I told the girls about Ned this weekend.'

'I know, and did it cause fainting fits, hysteria, outrage and hatred of their father?'

There was an edge of laughter in his voice and she hated him, hated him for keeping such news from her, for ruining the picture she had of Julian and now seemingly taking it so lightly.

'You don't understand,' she said, 'it might be old news to you, even a joke but it's not for me, finding out that my husband was leading a double life, a life that it seems you colluded in. Is there any more to it than you told me?' Her mouth set firm, her eyes glittered with angry tears.

He was standing close to her and for a second she felt he'd touch her, take her hand perhaps, or put his arm round her, but he stepped away, walked over to the glass door to the garden and stood there looking out at the last roses, their petals dropping onto the paving stones.

'Don't let this ruin your love for him, the happy marriage you shared,' he said, still staring out into the garden. 'You're making more of it than you should, Alice. I think he knew you would, that's why he never told you.'

'So put the blame on me,' she snapped, not wanting to admit there was some truth in what he said. 'What a typical male thing to do.'

'Don't blame anyone,' he turned round to her, his face grave. 'I thought better of you, Alice; it happened before you met him, years before, and was over quickly. Ned was not planned – it surprised them both. By the time Sarah found out it was too late for a termination and anyway she didn't want one, and Greg married her before Ned was born, and most people assumed Ned was his.'

Her legs felt like cotton wool. She sat down at the table in front of her cooling coffee, ashamed of her anger, and yet it was so hard to accept Julian was not the person she thought he was, the man she'd built him up to be. Today people felt differently about such things, and it was ironic when birth control was so easily available today that people were so lax about it and babies were born to the most unlikely couples, who didn't stay together, never would have done, like Evie and Nick.

'So how did your girls take it?' he asked more gently. 'Laura didn't sound shocked at all.'

She shrugged, 'When I said I had something important to tell them, Evie thought I had some frightful illness, or that Julian wasn't really their father.'

'Thank God it wasn't either of those things, Alice. They didn't mind so much, did they? In fact, they want to meet Ned, are excited about it.'

'You've obviously spoken to Laura about it,' she said.

'I rang her on Friday, to find out where you were so I could see you. She told me where you'd all be at the weekend, so I guessed you might tell them. She rang me herself later to tell me, said she wanted to meet Ned, asked if he could come to the wedding, but I said it was better to wait until it was over, He's working hard in New York and he can't leave just now anyway.'

'I feel as if my life is a tangled mess, so much has happened: Julian getting ill, then dying, Evie having Nick's baby and Laura taking on Douglas and two children, making me a grandmother, and now this.' She regarded him intently. 'I hope there's nothing else to find out.'

He took a step towards her, his eyes tender, a slight smile on his lips. 'Perhaps if Julian had told you, or the girls had not reacted the way they did to his death, you would have taken it better. He loved you, only you, and you must never forget that or let your misguided feelings sour it.'

His voice was soft; she felt the sincerity of it soothing her. She was battered by the recent events in her life. She wanted to be in Frank's arms, have him hold her close to him and she half rose from her chair to go to him, lay her head against his heart, but the telephone rang, loud and strident like a

263

warning bell across the room, cutting through her feelings.

As if he guessed her intention, his face fell, he shrugged, a little helpless movement. 'You better answer it.'

With regret, she crossed the room and picked it up, if it was someone trying to sell her something she'd swear at them. It wasn't: it was Margot in tears.

'Alice, thank God you're there, please help me, the police have come and arrested Glen and taken him away.'

Chapter 38

'Arrested, Glen?' All sort of lurid scenes swam through her mind. Margot was usually so cagey about her marriage, had he been involved in some sort of accident? She must stop her imagination whirling out of control. Perhaps she'd misheard, Margot sounded in a terrible way, her voice distorted with hysteria. 'Tell me slowly, Margot. I'll come round at once, but tell me what's happened.'

Frank, hearing the conversation and seeing Alice's distress, came over to her. She slightly released the receiver from her ear and he bent close so he could hear Margot's terror.

'The police came; some of them are searching the house. Glen said there was trouble at work but it was a misunderstanding, he couldn't say more, he looked terrible.' Margot broke into fresh sobs.

It was his work, she should have guessed, not a car crash.

'I've got Frank with me; we'll both come round now. Don't talk to anyone else. Frank is in Glen's world, finance, law and all that, so he may be able to help. Wait until we come, sit down, have some tea... or something stronger.' She thought of Cecily's bracing nip of brandy. 'Oh Margot, it might not be as bad as all that. We're coming now.'

With a few more words of encouragement, Alice put down the phone, her mind whirring in overdrive. 'Do you mind coming with me, Frank?' He was so close she could feel the warmth of him and for a moment she wished he would hold her close but he stepped away, his face stern as he digested the news.

'I'm... sorry, Frank, I sort of dumped you into it, but I don't know what else to do, she sounds distraught. Why would they arrest Glen, what could he have done?' She fired questions at him while she ran about the kitchen like a mad hen hunting for her bag, her keys and her Oyster card, she couldn't take her car, there was nowhere to park.

'I'll drive you,' Frank said calmly. 'I have resident parking for that area so we'll be fine. Remind me as we go whom Glen worked for and a bit about him. I know Margot, of course, but I hardly know her husband.'

She locked up the house and followed Frank to his car, all her thoughts for Margot.

'So,' he said as they started off, 'tell me about Glen, where he works, what he does.'

She told him Glen was in the financial world, watching his face as he concentrated on the road and then seeing his expression tighten, become grim when she mentioned the name of his firm.

'Do you know something bad about it?' she asked fearfully. 'I'm sure Glen's not dishonest, others might be, but not him.' She couldn't bear it for Margot, for their sons.

'I've been researching various firms and the tax schemes they use, and his firm is one of them,' Frank said. 'But don't let's jump to any conclusions. It could be nothing, but the police need to question everyone who has dealings with the company.'

Alice tried to make sense of his words. She and Petra sometimes wondered why Margot rarely discussed her husband's work, she'd skilfully change the subject if she was questioned, but that could be because she was slightly embarrassed by the amount of money he earned, their large house and expensive holidays things her old friends, Petra and Alice, couldn't match.

Frank went on,' I'm not making any judgements while I'm still working on it. I'm writing some articles for the *Financial Times*. Quite a few people sail a bit close to the wind over their taxable income and the government is rightly clamping down on it.' They stopped at the lights and he turned to face her, 'I don't suppose Margot knows anything about it, people who do these things don't usually tell their wives or husbands. Some people don't give fiddling the books much thought, they pay what they think is a large amount of tax and see nothing wrong in trying to keep back a bit more.'

Alice thought of the jewels, the beautiful presents Glen had bought Margot, and their expensive house filled with lovely antiques.

'Could he go to prison?' How on earth would Margot cope with that?

'These are complex cases and some people have rather savvy accountants, to say the least. But some of the laws, especially about tax, should be tightened. It would be best, Alice, if you didn't say anything to Margot about me working on this. It could have nothing whatever to do with Glen, but he's been swept up with the rest. Let's just find out what has happened first.'

'You're right, Frank. Oh, I'm so relieved you're here.' She turned to him and saw the warmth in his eyes.

'So am I,' he said softly, turning into a parking place in Margot's street.

He turned off the engine and got out and as Alice followed

him she thought of their nursery baskets and how well they were selling, and she wondered if they too were somehow caught up in this tax thing. She was about to ask Frank when they reached Margot's door. Frank rang the bell, his expression inscrutable as if his mind was taken up with his work, thinking up questions for his article.

Sam, one of Margot's sons, opened the door to them. He looked very young and frightened, his hair tousled, his clothes creased as if they'd spent the night on the floor and he'd pulled them on all anyhow. Alice hugged him. 'Things will work out,' she said feebly.

'Hope so.' Tears glazed his eyes, he swallowed, 'Mum's on the sofa, she's in a bad way.'

'Do you know what this is about?' Frank asked him, laying his hand on Sam's arm, offering support.

Sam shook his head and Alice went into the living room and saw Margot lying on the sofa as if she was in the last stages of a mortal illness. She knelt down on the floor beside her and took her in her arms. 'Margot, I'm so sorry, what happened, do you want to tell me?'

'I don't know. We were woken by a terrible banging or I was, Glen was already up. I heard the front door open, Glen call out he was coming while he unlocked it and the police rushed in. I thought we were being robbed, though they kept shouting police, but I got confused, I mean anyone can shout out police, can't they?'

'I suppose so, I...'

Frank came into the room and, seeing him, Margot sat up, pushing her hair, damp from her tears, away from her face. 'Glen had to go with the police and they've left these others here to go through his things. Oh Frank, don't write about this, will you? I know you write legal things, but you could find out about it, couldn't you?'

Frank sat down beside her and put his arm round her. 'Tell me what you know, Margot. It will be in complete confidence, I promise you. Has Glen said anything, behaved strangely... been worried about things at work?' He took out a clean, white handkerchief from his pocket and gently wiped her face. 'Take your time.'

Alice sat down close to her on her other side, concerned for her, for all the family. But Frank would help despite wanting copy for his article, she was certain he'd do what he could to support them.

Poor Margot. The sound of drawers being opened, people moving about in Glen's study, appalled her. Was nothing sacred in one's own home, family photographs, private letters and cards all scrutinised by strangers? And what about the papers concerning their interior decorating business, would they be snatched and pored over too? She was about to ask when a policewoman passed outside the room with a bulging black sack. Margot didn't seem to notice but Frank did and caught her eye, gave a tiny shake of his head as if guessing Alice was going to remark on it, so she stayed silent.

Margot said, 'Glen told me there'd been trouble at work; he wouldn't say what, in fact he was very bad-tempered, sort of edgy, difficult to live with.' She didn't look at them as if she found it hard to admit to. 'I... I said he was working too hard and why didn't we have a holiday, even just a weekend, to get away.'

'And what did he say?' Frank asked her.

'He was rather vague, said he'd see. I was worried he was ill, one of his colleagues had a heart attack the other day, I thought he was doing too much... but this... oh Frank, why would the police come in like that as if he were a murderer?' She clutched at him, her eyes wide with fear.

Frank hugged her closer. Sam had come into the room and sat down miserably, staring at Frank as if he were their lifeline. 'There are various stories buzzing about and the police sometimes go overboard in their zealousness. I know it's easy to say, but try not to worry unless you have to,' Frank said.

'It must be a mistake, but why couldn't they have telephoned, asked to see him instead of this... this barbaric behaviour. I mean we're not in somewhere like Russia,' Margot protested.

'There has to be an element of surprise in this sort of thing in case people have time to destroy any evidence of wrong doing. They are probably in the company now, doing the same thing,' Frank said. 'You need a lawyer, have you a good one?'

'There's Paul Cartwright,' Sam said, 'his family have been friends of ours forever. Shall I call him?' There was hope on his face as he thought of him.

'Aren't you a lawyer, Frank?' Margot's voice lifted, she clutched Frank's arm.

'Not practising, but I write legal articles, mostly to do with business.'

'So you must know a lot. Couldn't you go to the police station and get Glen home?' Margot begged him.

'No, Margot, I'm afraid I can't. Let's call this friend. Whatever the reason the police raided you this morning, Glen needs a lawyer.'

The doorbell rang and everyone froze. Margot brightened, half expecting it to be Glen, explaining that it had all been a dreadful mistake. Sam ran to open the door and they heard him exclaim, with relief, 'Oh, Uncle Richard, what can we do?'

Margot burst into tears as her brother came into the room. 'Richard, thank God you're here. I don't know what's going on.'

'I came as soon as I could.' He kissed Alice, 'Good to see you, Alice.' He was introduced to Frank before turning his attention to Margot. 'So tell me everything,' He pulled up a chair and sat close to her.

Frank caught Alice's eye and moved to leave now that Margot had her brother with her. 'I'll go and see what I can find out, Margot, I'll contact you later, let you know if I find anything,' he said, hugging her again before getting up.

Alice was unsure what to do, but now Richard was here, Margot had support. She turned to Sam, 'Try and keep strong, you can both come and stay with me if you want to, get your mother away from this.' The shock was beginning to wear off now, leaving her fearful but determined to be supportive.

'I don't know what Mum wants to do... or Dad.' His voice trailed off, he threw her an anguished look and she knew what he was thinking, what if his father was arrested?

'I'll stay if you want me to,' she said, wanting to leave with Frank and yet she could not abandon her friend if she needed her.

'I don't know, Uncle Richard's here and Lucas is on his way,' he mentioned his older brother.

Margot seemed to brace up with her brother there and she assured Alice she felt better now, it was bound to be a mistake and Glen would soon be back. 'Thanks for rushing round, Alice, but I'm sure you've lots to do with the wedding and all. I'll ring you later.' She seemed to slip back into her shell of silence that Alice knew so well when certain things, namely Glen and his work, were mentioned.

'If you're sure,' Alice hugged her, 'but ring me on my mobile if you need anything.'

A few minutes later Alice and Frank left the house, neither spoke until they were in his car.

'Is it very bad?' she asked, fearful of his answer.

'There are a lot of questions about the company, but we'll have to wait and see how deep Glen is in it. Poor Margot, it must be such a shock for her and her boys.'

Alice stayed silent, afraid for her friend. Much though she longed to confide in Frank, she decided she must not say anything, however innocent she thought it was, in case he used it in his articles. She would not tell him how reticent Margot was about gossiping about her husband, though maybe she didn't want to lay out their lives to be picked over, even by her dearest friends, but did she ever suspect things were not quite right and had chosen to ignore them, or was she afraid to upset the balance of their marriage and question him? Or had she questioned him and he'd reassured her that all was well and she accepted it?

She'd always liked Glen, he was charming and amusing and very good company, but was he hiding something under all his charm, just as Julian had hidden his son from her? She'd learnt a hard lesson that people were not always who they seemed or who you wanted them to be.

Chapter 39

Frank's mind was now on his work. He was relieved that Margot's brother had arrived and one of her sons was there. Alice, dear Alice, was being so strong, so kind, even though she was probably being over-optimistic about Glen's part in it all. He'd seen it before, perfectly decent people being a little lax with the truth, perhaps once making a mistake on their tax return form, getting away with it and thinking it didn't matter, then doing it again and somehow kidding themselves that it was all right, their hard work and long hours brought in so much revenue into the business and therefore to the country, so surely it did no harm to cream a little extra off for themselves? So often it became too easy and they got lazy or too cavalier and they were caught.

'I suspect there are some dodgy deals going on and no doubt they've arrested everyone high up in the company as a matter of course and will soon release him when they've got the ones they want,' Richard had said as they left. 'I'm sure Glen hasn't done anything wrong.'

Frank was aware then that Alice was watching him as if she was willing him to agree with Richard, explain the usual procedure of investigating suspected malpractice in these companies, but he wouldn't meet her gaze, he said goodbye again and left the house. He didn't want to say that

273

he needed to get round to the company Glen worked for as soon as possible. There had been rumours floating about for some time about it, and he must find out how today's activities would affect the article he was working on.

He'd left them with some trite remark, like, 'Don't worry, these things often seem worse than they are,' though inwardly he felt they were very serious indeed. Though Glen could have had nothing to do with it, might only get his knuckles rapped for not keeping a more thorough eye on things. He didn't want to think about the fraudulent people he'd written about, who'd managed to get away with their dishonesty so long just because they *were* so charming, seemed to be so honest and decent, that no one suspected them of foul play until it was too late.

Alice was silent now beside him in the car, her face turned away as she gazed out of the window. He wished he could get close to her, get back to the easy feeling they'd had between them before she'd asked him about Ned.

He'd slept badly ever since, worried about her, tortured if he were honest, by her blaming him for Julian's secrecy. It had to be sorted now, before things festered further, and he'd gone round this morning determined to have it out with her. He understood how upset she was, wondering why Julian hadn't told her about Ned and if there was more to it than the simple truth.

The first time he'd met Alice with Julian he'd been drawn to her but it was obvious that she was madly in love with Julian. Ned happily secure with his mother and stepfather in the US didn't feature. He couldn't remember now if he'd ever asked Julian if he'd told Alice about him, probably not as he assumed it was Julian's business to do so. Alice never mentioned him and in those early days there were so many other things they talked about. Then after their wedding he'd gone to live in France and he hadn't seen much of Alice and Julian together.

He'd heard of Julian's death through a friend, though he'd known he was ill and had seen him a few months before. Perhaps he meant to tell Alice about it when he became ill but died before he could, but now he would never know.

But his early morning mission to go round to her and make his peace, and hopefully spend the day with her, had been scuppered by Margot's problems, which had obviously taken over, and he must now go to the company and see what was happening, so he couldn't stay with Alice today anyway. To his relief she seemed to have forgotten her anger with him, or perhaps Margot's problems had overshadowed it.

She broke her silence. 'It's so scary. Do you think Glen was up to something he shouldn't be? I mean, that house cost so much more than the one they sold in Fulham and the presents he gives her, Julian often talked about it, wondered how much money he was earning and he thought the so-called shares were quite dubious.'

He hated to see how worried she was; there was nothing she, any of them, could do, except stand by Margot. She could count on Alice. She wasn't the sort of person to dump her friends if they were in trouble and he so hoped she wouldn't distance herself from him because he'd told her about Julian and Ned. He'd kept away from her all these years because he loved her and she was Julian's wife, but now he wanted to stay and hope that she might grow to love him...

Shaking himself from his thoughts, he said, 'I don't know, but I'll find out. I'm afraid I've seen quite a lot of this sort of thing; it's the bulk of my work after all, reporting on various frauds and mistakes. Perfectly decent people can get sucked into things and then keep quiet as they are afraid to lose their job, lose the money they are spending on their children's education, good holidays, a better house and all the rest of it.'

'So he could be guilty of something?' Alice asked, her face strained. 'And Margot, do you think she knew?'

'Let's wait and see what happens, not speculate until we know.' He smiled at her. He knew all about wives accepting expensive gifts and believing whatever story their husbands chose to tell them as to how they suddenly had money to burn. It worked both ways: he'd come across a few women who'd defrauded their company and convinced the men in their lives it was legal too.

Margot was an intelligent woman, and Alice had told him that she was apt to be cagey about discussing her husband, so did she suspect he was up to something? Or feel, as so many people did, that by pretending nothing was wrong it somehow wouldn't be? Or was she like most wives and mothers often juggling work and home and being too busy, or just too tired at the end of the day, to confront it and demand to know what was going on? Had Alice wondered about Julian, wondered why he, Frank, never came to their house? Or was she too occupied with their busy life to care?

He went on, 'There are troubles in that company, but I won't tell you about it, as they might not be true. I'm sorry but I must go there at once. I wanted to talk to you about Julian and Ned, but I'll have to leave that until this is over. I'm so sorry, Alice.' He turned to her, wishing he could hold her but he couldn't, not without causing a terrible crash on the Gloucester Road.

'It's all right,' she said. She turned to him, her face anxious. 'It's frightening that you can live so intimately with someone for many years and they can keep such things hidden – Julian with Ned and now Glen and Margot. I've known Margot since we were six and she's one of the most honest people I know. She never had much money until she got a job at Colefax and Fowler, and yet she never grumbled or tried to get hold of money she hadn't worked for. She married Glen and he had a good job and things got better for them as he climbed up the greasy pole of success in the City. Then she and I started our decorating business and made quite good money at the beginning, hardly enough to live on, but enough, and now it seems to be taking off again. But I'm worried now the tax wasn't paid on it, we left it to Glen's accountant.'

'You must have some correspondence to prove it was paid.' He was worried for her now. Who was this accountant, was he responsible for any tax dodges Glen was involved in?

'We do. We went through the papers the other day. It all looked all right, and we're hardly talking mammoth sums of money here.'

'Have you got them at home, I could check them for you?' He couldn't do it now but perhaps he could come back this evening, take her out to dinner.

'No, they are with Margot. Oh God, I suppose the police will have taken them won't they, in their black sacks?' Her voice was anguished. 'If they were wrong, we'll be in this too. Will we be arrested?'

He pulled over and turned to her, taking her hands in his. 'Alice, I don't know what, *if* anything, Glen was up to. But if you paid the tax on your business and had confirmation back, you'll be in the clear. All the papers will be scrutinised, and it will take ages.'

'But we've just started a new line which is going quite well, will we have to stop it?'

'I don't think so, but it may be better to keep all the papers to do with it at your house. When Margot's calmed down a little ask her if any of them are still around. Do you have all your contacts so you can keep trading?' It was so hard seeing her like this. She'd had so much to bear, Julian's illness and death, her daughters' drastic actions, then finding out about Ned and now this.

'By luck I took our contact book home and it has the dates of our recent orders so we can finish those.'

'Good, but fortunately your business is small fry compared to this huge financial firm. Does Glen finance your business at all?'

'No, we were determined to do this on our own and not ask either of our husbands for money.' She smiled, 'It is entirely ours, so neither husband could boss us about.'

He laughed, 'Good thinking. Was Julian very bossy then?'

'No, he wasn't, not often anyway, but we wanted to use our own ideas and not have too much input from outside. We did our tax returns but gave them to Glen's accountant to file, so...' she shrugged. 'I just hope he did them correctly.'

He wanted to kiss her, hold her; she was so brave fighting on without Julian beside her. He wished he could help her but she was too proud to let him, too annoyed with him for keeping such secrets and no doubt felt he was ganging up on her, him and Julian together.

He could not tell her that he'd always loved her and that he felt it prudent to move away from her. As time went on he buried his love for her deep in his memory and met and married Simone, and they'd been happy enough, though their marriage had failed, and they got on better now they lived apart. He'd made a good life for himself and had two wonderful children.

'Let me out here, please Frank, I want to go on to Peter Jones and get some ribbons for our baskets, if we still have a business,' Alice said, seeing the lights were about to change. 'I'll leave you to go on to work. Thank you for coming with me to Margot's. I'll ring her later, see if she wants to come and stay with me for a while.' She got out of the car before he could stop her, then leant back in. 'I know I mustn't ask you what's going on, but if you find anything out about Glen, please tell me.'

'I'll have to see about that, but if there's anything, it's bound to come out. Take care. Let's meet soon.' He blew her a kiss and she blew one back, quickly as if it were a reflex action.

'I know you'll be busy with this for some time, just turn up at the wedding, that's all you need to do.' With a smile she was gone and he watched her through the driving mirror, her slim hips swinging elegantly as she moved away from him and out of sight.

Chapter 40

Glen was released on bail, and Frank, when Alice, egged on by Margot, telephoned him that evening to ask what was going on, said vaguely that various complicated scams had been discovered in the bank and he couldn't say anything about them just now.

'They'll take ages to get to court and these things are often hard to prove so they'll probably get away with them,' Frank said, 'but don't say that to Margot. It could be all over the press tomorrow though, so warn her. I'm sorry, Alice, there's nothing I can do to stop things coming out, other journalists have got hold of the story now.'

'Thanks Frank, I'll tell her.' She was dying to hear more, though she guessed by his tone of voice things were more serious than he was letting on. She assumed he wasn't allowed to say or encourage any rumour before he wrote his article.

'I'm afraid I'll be working flat out for the next few weeks,' he said, 'and I so wanted to talk to you about Julian, I can't bear for you to think badly of him, he loved you more than anyone, please hold on to that.'

'I will,' she said, though she felt empty inside, as if some familiar part of her had been destroyed.

'I'll be in touch when I can and certainly be there for the

wedding and… do ring me if there is anything you need, Alice.' There was a slight edge to his voice now, which she interpreted as him having other more pressing things to do.

The case was not widely reported in the press and was only in the financial pages, which was a relief for those concerned. Margot chose to believe that Glen was innocent and most of their friends went along with that, though he and the other directors were suspended from work, and he and Margot escaped down to Cornwall to recover, or possibly hide, from the ordeal.

'I'll be back for the wedding,' she promised Alice. 'I just want to leave London, can't stand all the suspicious looks people we know give us, though they say to our face that they're sure Glen is innocent. Our best friends like you are fine but some of the others are envious about the money Glen earned and can't believe he didn't do something dishonest to get it.'

Alice understood that Margot wanted to escape, though she wished she were still here as their nursery basket business seemed to have suddenly taken off, so it was now left to her to choose the fabrics and take everything down to Suffolk, not that she really minded as she could see Raffi, and Laura needed one last fitting of her dress. But there was so much else to do with the wedding that needed her attention, find her own outfit for a start, and because she enjoyed baking, Laura asked if she'd mind making her wedding cake.

'They cost a fortune if you have one made and it won't taste nearly as good as yours anyway. You make one every Christmas and it's the same sort of cake, so you could do a wedding cake instead, couldn't you, Mum? We only want a simple one, not masses of tiers and pillars and everything, please Mum?' Laura begged the last time she'd seen her. She had, of course, agreed, though there was not nearly enough time for the mixture to marinate properly.

She'd soaked the fruit in brandy for three days and then baked it and it stood on top of the microwave being fed from time to time when she remembered. She realised she should have made a Christmas cake at the same time, after all Christmas was just after the wedding. Who would be with her, or would she be alone?

News must have got round that she was coming to Suffolk because just before she left London she had a call from Freya asking if she'd mind coming over for a drink; Nick was away and she wanted to talk about the wedding.

'OK, see you about seven, then,' Alice said, anxiety clutching at her. It was so annoying, tactless even, of Laura inviting them, well Nick anyway. She could imagine him schmoozing round, chatting up any pretty women and perhaps even boasting about his sexual prowess by showing off Raffi, adding to the embarrassment of having to explain about Evie's new role as a single mother. With any luck, Freya, wanting to see her on her own, was going to refuse the invitation.

She told Evie she was going to meet up with Freya, Evie just shrugged and asked if she'd mind keeping an eye on Raffi while she worked. Raffi was beautiful, round and plump and very smiley. She sat with him on the sofa as Evie scuttled back to her drawing, planning out a new set of illustrations for the next book. Watching him looking round chortling to himself, Alice felt bathed with a feeling of completeness of the continuity of life, though for the scene to be perfect, Julian, the man she thought he was, should be here too, basking in the joy of their grandchild. Raffi chuckled waving his fists at her; it was a bittersweet moment.

Sitting with him on her lap while Evie worked, she thought of her youngest daughter. She seemed different; she'd noticed it the moment she'd arrived about an hour ago. She was blooming and she hadn't once mentioned Nick. She'd been so pleased to see her too, not in a relieved way as if now she was here she could take over the baby, cook a decent meal, tidy the place up a bit, but just pleased to see her as if she wanted to share her happiness with her. Could it be motherhood giving her a sort of peace, someone to love of her own, or more likely someone else to love? Unless... and the thought worried her, Nick had decided to leave Freya and come to Evie. Was that why Evie seemed so upbeat? Why Freya wanted to talk to her?

The thought now became a reality and she almost jumped up to go and confront Evie, tell her in no uncertain terms that having a child with a married man was bad enough but him leaving his wife and family for her was much worse. But what if Freya had chucked him out and he'd come here? If that were the case, how long would he stay, until he took up with the next woman? She glanced round the room as if expecting to see some evidence of him, a discarded jacket, the battered, once expensive, briefcase he carried with the papers concerned with his work, but untidy though the room was, there seemed to be only Evie's shoes flung in a corner, her coat over the back of a chair and Raffi's things strewn around.

She heard Evie coming out of the study and she came into the room interrupting her panic.

'It's so dreadful about Glen,' Evie said, scooping Raffi from her arms and sitting down on the floor, putting him between her legs, propping him against her now flat stomach. 'Don't you remember how Dad always wondered how they'd managed to buy that house. Buying a derelict house and doing it up and selling it on for a profit is one thing, but they didn't sell it did they, they kept it and lived in it.'

Alice thought the same thing and they'd filled the house with expensive things, but she didn't want to say too much in front of her children who might inadvertently pass it on to Margot and ruin their friendship. 'I don't know exactly what happened. Glen had shares and things and the value of the Fulham house had gone up,' she said vaguely, her mind more concentrated on Nick and his whereabouts than Glen's troubles. How could she broach the subject of the state of play with him without antagonising her? 'Have you got something nice to wear for the wedding?' she asked to gain time.

'I'll find something, I'll come to London a few days before and... Mum...' Evie didn't look at her but kept her eyes on Raffi. 'Would it be all right if I asked someone, just one person, to the wedding?'

Alice looked at her sharply. Here it was... but Nick had been asked to the wedding already, with his wife and Lexie who was to be one of the bridesmaids. But it was obvious from Evie's manner that this was not some random friend. Evie was rather self-consciously playing with Raffi, tickling his fat little feet.

'We're pretty much full up,' Alice said. 'Is it someone we know?'

Evie looked at her, her face defiant, the face she always put on when she had done something, or was about to do something, she suspected her parents would disapprove of. 'It's just someone I've met, and we've got quite close.' She threw it out as if it was not important, though it was obvious from the light in her eyes that it was very important indeed.

Alice's heart lurched; it wasn't Nick. But if not him then

who? Oh, not another married man drawn in by Evie's beauty and vulnerability? She couldn't bear it. 'His name?' she asked weakly, it was bound to be a man.

'Luke, he's a sculptor. We met in the pub, he's...' she didn't look at her mother, 'we've become quite close,' she repeated.

'Is he single and does he know about Raffi?' Alice asked. She was definitely going to take a gap year, escape from her family... and Frank and all the problems they kept throwing at her, expecting her to accept them without question and share the responsibility of them.

Evie scowled, 'Yes to both, he loves Raffi, wants to sculpt him, says his rounded squidgy limbs are perfect for something he's working on.'

Was that the only reason this Luke was close to her? When he'd finished his work, would he leave her or was this a more hopeful chapter in Evie's love life? 'So is that the end of Nick?' she asked.

'He doesn't want to know, does he?' Evie burst out as if she was somehow at fault for finding someone else. 'He hasn't been near us since Raffi was born, he pays money for him but that's all. I suppose Freya won't let him out of the house.'

'That's hardly fair, darling, but I'm glad you've found someone else, someone who is not attached,' she finished lamely, hoping that was true.

'So it's all right if he comes then?' Evie demanded.

'I suppose so. Will he pop in while I'm here? You know I've got to go back early the day after tomorrow. Laura's coming down for the last fitting and we'll go back together.'

'He might, he's working very hard,' Evie said, 'but you'll meet him at the wedding.'

285

'Does Laura know him, have you asked her if he can come?'

'No... I'll ask her when I see her tomorrow. He won't take up much room and it's only one more person.'

Alice refrained from asking if he was a midget or a ghost. 'Laura and Douglas know the numbers, square it with her when you see her,' she said.

Evie showed no interest when Alice told her Freya had asked her to pop over for a drink.

'Perhaps she's going to say she doesn't want to come to the wedding.' She watched Evie for her reaction.

Evie shrugged, pushed a strand of hair from her face. 'Don't know, I haven't seen her or Nick for ages. Don't know why Laura asked them anyway, they're not exactly family.'

'They are old friends and now sort of family,' Alice said. 'And apparently Lexie begged to be a bridesmaid and Laura found it difficult to refuse her.'

'There's lots of friends we haven't asked, and anyway there'll be more champagne for Luke if they don't come,' Evie said, handing Raffi to her to kiss goodnight before taking him upstairs to bed.

Alice drove over to Freya, wishing she didn't have to go out again, especially as it was dark now with winter setting in. She felt apprehensive about the meeting. She'd driven down from London that morning and gone over to Edith and Amy with all the fabrics, trimmings and such for the baskets this afternoon and now here she was, just when she'd like to curl up with a glass of wine and a gossip with Evie, driving the five miles or so over to Freya.

The house was in turmoil. As Freya led her through to the living room, she heard sounds of squabbling coming from the back of the house and a voice saying, 'Oh Lexie, stop being such a brat.'

They had just sat down together when there was the sound of small stomping feet coming down the passage and the door was flung open dramatically and Lexie, in a purple feather boa, one hand hitching up her pyjama bottoms, wailed, 'Jonty won't let me have the cherry on the top and I'm the littlest and I should have it.'

'Lexie, it's very rude to disturb people like this, say hello to Alice nicely and stop being silly. If you can't behave you can go to bed, it's time anyway,' Freya said wearily. 'Tell Jonty to come here now, please.'

Pouting theatrically, Lexie stomped off again chanting, 'Jonty, Mum wants you and she's very cross.'

Freya raised her eyes heavenwards. 'Sorry, she's such a drama queen, like her father really, though not the queen bit.' Her smile was bitter.

Alice smiled weakly back, wondering what it was Freya wanted to talk to her about. It was going to be difficult if her children were going to disrupt them all the time. She wondered if Raffi would have inherited some of his father's traits, though Evie was a drama queen too, so, poor baby, he might have inherited a double dose.

Jonty, a tall slim boy, looking like a mini Nick came in, his expression defiant. 'She's such a pain, Mum. Rowan has eaten the cherry anyway.' There was a howl as Lexie had obviously just discovered this. Jonty smiled at Alice, 'Hello.'

She smiled back, wondering if he knew that she was the grandmother of his newest brother?

'Alice and I want a bit of peace,' Freya said firmly, 'see that we get it please.'

'I'll try,' Jonty said darkly, leaving the room and shutting the door carefully behind him.

'Lovely boy,' Alice said.

'He is and very artistic. I don't want to push him but he's great at painting.'

Alice was about to tell her about Evie's painting, how as a child she drew everywhere, the margins of newspapers and magazine, school books, even the blank flyleaves of books, but she stopped herself in time. It would be tactless in the circumstances. Oh, these complicated relationships.

'I wanted to discuss the wedding invitation with you,' Freya said, ploughing in before they were disturbed again. 'It was very kind of Laura to ask us and ask Lexie to be bridesmaid but I wondered if you really wanted us there... well Nick really. I mean, Evie and the baby are sure to be there or is the baby being left behind?'

Now was the time to say that Nick's presence might be embarrassing. Freya looked as if she expected it, even hoped for it. Alice admired her even more for asking her opinion, though she knew it would probably be a worse embarrassment for Freya than for them, and who could blame her for wanting to stay clear of it? But Alice found herself floundering, saying that Laura and Douglas had the guest list and as Laura was coming to Suffolk tomorrow perhaps she'd like to talk to her.

'No, it's you I want to discuss it with. I saw Laura in the street and made some remark about her wedding and Lexie pushed herself forward. You know how the bride hardly notices the day, it goes by like a blur, my wedding day did anyway, but I want to know what you feel, Alice.' She leant forward a little in her chair as if she were a doctor enquiring about her health.

'I probably won't notice either,' Alice said, 'but I'll discuss it with Laura tomorrow, but it's you I worry about, Freya, I don't want to cause you any more pain over this. Evie tells me...' She paused, wondering how much to tell Freya and if it would be some comfort to her, 'She's met someone else. I haven't met him yet, Luke his name is, a sculptor. Do you know him?'

'Luke Morgan, I expect. I know who he is. Oh...' She looked surprised, filling Alice with more anxiety, was he some weirdo, someone else likely to cause yet more drama and disruption? 'He's young and, as far as I know, not in a relationship. He's a bit here today and gone tomorrow, doesn't really settle down enough to his work to show how talented he really is, but perhaps with a steady relationship he might improve. Evie might make him more committed.' She threw her a pitying smile. 'These relationships are the devil, aren't they? I've got them all still to come with my brood, though their father has led the way spectacularly.' She sighed. 'Still, Laura seems happy; do you like the man she's chosen?'

Her eyes were sharp on her face and Alice had the unwelcome feeling that Freya was a little jealous of Laura, though why, she couldn't think, unless it was because she seemed to be on track for a happy, uncomplicated life.

'Douglas is very nice, divorced with two children – I suppose that's pretty common these days. His ex-wife is high-powered and was head-hunted to Hong Kong.' Even as she said it, Alice realised that Freya knew it was not what she wanted to hear. She went on, 'Julian's death seems to have caused such extreme reactions in the girls, Evie with Nick and Laura rushing into marriage with Douglas.'

'So you don't approve of him?' Freya asked.

'He is nice...' She was not going to admit she found him dull. 'But I just wish she'd wait awhile before she commits herself to him and his children. It's a lot to take on and she's no experience of children. They are quite sensitive, well the boy is, he needs a lot of care with his mother gone, though she does come back and see them, loves them I'm sure, only her work comes first.'

'You wouldn't say that if their father's work came first,' Freya said. 'Even today, in these enlightened times, women, even if they are more successful than their husbands, are criticised for putting their work before their children. Most of these jobs only have a small window of opportunity and they must grab it or lose it forever.'

'I know, it is difficult.'

'If I hadn't grabbed that chance with the V and A, I'd have lost it. There are so many talented people in the creative world and someone else would have jumped eagerly into my place. I worked very hard to get there but perhaps I should have kept more of an eye on Nick.'

'Don't blame yourself, Freya. Evie is old enough to know better than to go after a married man,' Alice said.

'Maybe, but I know how persuasive Nick can be,' Freya said darkly. 'I want my pottery to take off. I've put a lot of effort and time into it, and I suppose I knew deep down that if I gave too much attention to it, it would mean I'd have less time for the family. Nick is only supportive up to a point and the children are still young and I feel he should help out, it's not as if he is tied to an important office job. He can fit his garden jobs round them sometimes and even take them with him to help dig and prepare the ground, Rowan is good at planting.'

Perhaps Freya hoped by encouraging Nick to take his

children on site he might be dissuaded from scattering his own seeds around, Alice thought acidly.

'I felt the children's needs were a priority and Nick felt left out and...' she shrugged, 'you know the rest, after all you're a grandmother now, not, I assume, in the way you hoped it to happen.'

'You're right, but is it so strange to want one's children to conform, settle down with lovely, uncomplicated and un-attached people and have children with them?' Alice said with a sigh.

'Of course not. And in your case, you had the perfect marriage to such a special man. You must miss him dread-fully, especially with all this going on,' Freya said with sympathy. 'All the women round here envied you for having him, and he loved you so.'

Before Alice could answer, the door burst open and Lexie stood there, hands on her non-existent hips. 'Jonty says I'm not going to be a bridesmaid at Laura's wedding but I am aren't I, Mum? He says I'm too brattish, but I'm not am I? Am I, Alice? Laura said I could be, so I am?'

Alice, confronted with this resolute little person knew, like Laura before her, she could not refuse her.

Chapter 41

It was two weeks before the wedding. Laura's beautiful wedding dress waited for the big day in her wardrobe, the menus were decided, the venue booked and the cake baked and ready to decorate and it was full steam ahead. As the day crept forward, Alice kept her misgivings to herself. Laura, who'd moved back home, seemed happy enough, but she was not shining with passion and excitement, but then that wasn't really her style, and how could she tell if Laura's nerves were not dampening down passionate feelings of love for this kind, but to her mind dull, man?

As the days slipped by, Alice could not help but compare the two of them to her and Julian in their early days together, their love and passion for each other all consuming, but then the sick feeling gripped her. It was not quite as rosy as she thought. She must give Laura more credit for her choices. She was going into this union with her eyes open, coping with an ex-wife, a difficult mother-in-law and two children, one, if not both, needing extra support. Laura was not some naïve adolescent; both of the girls had been encouraged to choose their own friends and Laura had chosen Douglas and wanted to marry him, and she must accept him into the family with open arms and do all she could to support her daughter, instead of wasting her energies on wishing it wasn't happening.

Petra came round to help her decorate the cake; she'd done a course in cake decoration and was brilliant at it. As they grappled with mounds of white icing sugar – the kitchen seeming to be powdered with sweet-scented snow – they gossiped, mainly about Margot and Glen.

'How do we know what these men are up to in their offices all day?' Petra started. 'We have to trust them to be doing what they say they are doing, and anyway how could Margot know if Glen was on the fiddle unless...' She paused, a worried expression creasing her face, 'I mean, she might have wondered why she could suddenly buy those ridiculously expensive handbags or be given new jewellery and fly first class to exotic places. I certainly would, when before, though money was good, it didn't stretch to such luxuries.'

'I'm sure he wasn't fiddling, I mean some of these people in these financial firms do earn zillions these days with all those shares and bonuses and what not.' Alice was concerned about them too, but she didn't want to condemn Glen until it was proved he had done something wrong, though she remembered how he never talked about his job, saying he'd rather leave his work in his office. 'But there are so many rules and regulations these days, I suppose one could get caught out,' she finished.

'Yes there are, but presumably you have to keep abreast of them,' Petra said. 'It's amazing when there's trouble in a company how many extremely well paid and senior people profess not to know anything about it. When Hugo was seducing every passable woman, no one seemed to have noticed at all,' she sighed, thinking of the treachery of her ex-husband.

'True,' Alice smiled at her sympathetically. The fallout of Petra and Hugo's marriage had been spectacular and very painful. Their daughter, then in her early teens, bearing the brunt of it, while Petra retaliated by indulging herself in a series of love affairs, surely to prove that she was a woman worth loving.

'I wish Frank would tell us what's going on, he's reporting on the scandal, isn't he?' Petra regarded her intently. 'You'd think he'd drop a few hints.'

'I don't expect him to, until his report is finished,' Alice said.

Frank had come round a couple of evenings ago looking pale and tired and Laura had asked him about the case.

'Can't say anything,' he'd said with a weary smile. 'It's highly complicated, as these things often are, so I'm going to be hard at it for the next few weeks.'

'But you can still come to the wedding, give me away?' Laura sounded anguished.

'Of course, wouldn't miss that for the world, but I'd have liked to spend more time with you all.' His eyes skimmed over Alice and she'd felt a jolt of anxiety. Had he other secrets to tell her about Julian? 'When are Evie and the baby arriving?' he asked.

'Next week, Tuesday,' Alice told him.

'She's got a new boyfriend,' Laura said.

'Oh, is he nice?' Frank turned to Alice to see her reaction.

'We don't know, we haven't met him yet, but he's her age and not married, or got any children,' Laura said, getting up to fetch the wine bottle to pour them more wine.

'That's a relief,' Frank said.

'You don't know with Evie, he's bound to have some complication in his life. Talking of complications, Frank, I can't believe Dad had a son all the time. I wish he'd told us; I always wanted an older brother,' Laura said. 'Tell us all about him, Dad should have told us, but as he didn't, you've got to.' She eyed him fiercely.

'Don't bully Frank, he's had a long day and it's not really up to him.' Alice didn't want to hear any more about it.

'She's right; you should know everything,' Frank said, 'though there's not much to say. Your father, long before he met your mother, had a brief fling with my sister, Sarah, and Ned was born in the US where she went to study. She met someone else and married him and Greg accepted Ned, brought him up with the other children they had later, though Ned always knew who his father was.'

'But we didn't, why didn't he tell us? It's not like he had a baby with some dreadful woman... Like a...' she searched for a word.

Frank jumped in, 'No, it's not, and I don't know why he didn't tell you. Ned was brought up in America until he grew up and came here occasionally to study and perhaps then it was too late to tell you. When your father married your mother, I assumed he'd tell her about him, and perhaps there never seemed to be the right time. I don't know.' He studied his wine glass as if he didn't want to face Alice.

'Does he... Ned know about us?' Laura went on as if she were interrogating him.

'I think his mother told him, but to be honest I don't know how or when he was told. I didn't see an awful lot of him when he was little, but when he came to London to do an internship I lent him the flat. I didn't see much of him then either as I was working all over the world, but you'll all like him and we must arrange a meeting when he's next over.' He smiled as if they were talking about the son of a friend not the illegitimate son of her husband. Alice stayed silent, afraid she might say something she regretted in front of Laura. She felt she no longer knew the man she'd loved and trusted all these years.

'So Dad never talked about us to him?' Laura asked sadly.

'I just don't know, Laura, I'm sorry. The few times I saw Ned when he was an adult we seemed to talk about the things he was studying, as I'm in the same field, or he'd tell me about some girl he'd met, film he'd seen. We didn't see a lot of each other, but I'll arrange for you all to meet up next time he is here.' He finished his drink and got up. 'Sorry, but I've got to get back to my work. Ring me if you need anything and I'll pop round when I can.' Frank kissed them both quickly on the cheek and made reluctantly for the door as if he found it hard to leave the comfortable room with its pretty furnishings and the company of the two women.

'Are you here for Christmas?' he asked Alice as she followed him into the hall.

'We thought we'd go to the cottage. I've ordered everything from the butcher down there. He makes the stuffing, puts bacon round prunes and sausages, all the fiddly bits. It costs a bit more but it's worth it this time with the wedding. Laura and Douglas are coming as his ex-wife is over and she's taking the children to her parents,' Alice said, relieved that the plans had been made for her and she would not be alone.

'And Evie and Raffi?' he asked as he made for the door.

'They'll be there,' she said, not knowing if Luke would be with them too. Everything she used to count on was changing and she must change with it.

'And you, Frank, where will you spend it?'

'Skiing with my children,' he said. 'I'd ask you to join us but you seem to be tied up already.' He smiled, 'We'll go another time,' and he kissed her quickly on her cheek and left.

Alice watched Petra now with admiration as she skilfully piped a latticework pattern over the sides of the cake, in each square she stuck a delicately painted sugar flower, the effect was simple but stunning.

Petra's work took so much concentration that their discussion of Frank's part in Margot and Glen's drama was put aside, and then Laura appeared and exclaimed with wonder at the beautiful cake, showing far more excitement than Alice had ever seen her show with Douglas.

Chapter 42

'Time we went, Mum,' Evie said, hauling up Raffi asleep in his baby carrier. Frank wondered if it was a good idea to bring such a small baby to the wedding, though he understood that a friend of Evie's was coming to collect him during the reception so she could stay on as long as she wanted.

It was almost time they left for the church and he felt the longer Alice hovered around Laura, the more she'd feel Julian's loss on such an important day.

He'd arrived just before lunchtime with a ready-made lunch he'd picked up from Fortnum's with tiny sandwiches, gulls eggs, little squares of cheese, and large, luscious grapes and a chilled bottle of champagne.

'Oh, Frank, how perfect, you are a star,' Evie exclaimed. 'I'm starving and we've nothing here.'

'Thanks so much, Frank, but I don't dare eat much in case I can't fit into my dress,' Laura said.

'You won't put weight on at once and you need to eat something, we don't want you fainting at the altar,' Alice joked, but Frank could see how much of an ordeal she was finding this. It would surely be better when she had left the house, was somewhere away from Julian's shadow.

'We won't be far behind you, but you want to be in your place,' he said, gently steering Alice towards the front door, wishing he could hold her close, soothe away her pain at missing Julian on this special day. All he could do was to carry out his duties as 'giver away' of the bride, though it made him feel a little like the spectre at the feast.

'Yes, we must go,' Alice said, taking a deep breath, and with one last look at Laura standing in the middle of the living room the beautiful bride, her veil like a soft cloud around her, she blew her a kiss and turned towards the door and left the room, with Evie fussing round, collecting up all Raffi's paraphernalia.

Frank hustled them out to the waiting car and helped them in. The car to take him and Laura glided up to take their place as they left. There was plenty of time to get to the church but they should leave fairly soon. He went back inside to Laura; she was his priority now.

She looked wonderful, her brown hair shone like silk, softly framing her face, the veil held by a band of white and the palest pink flowers. She smiled nervously at him. In the bustle to get ready, snacking on the lunch, having a bath and changing into her dress had taken on a rhythm of its own and now all was done, her mother and sister gone and the two of them were alone in the house waiting to leave, seeing out the last minutes of her old life before starting a new one as Douglas's wife and stepmother to his children.

'You look beautiful. Your father would be very proud of you.' He took her hand and squeezed it.

'Do you think he would be?' she asked, not moving from the middle of the living room where she stood to make space for her dress which skimmed over her figure, the skirt swirling out by her feet.

'Yes, I'm sure of it.' He didn't add that he wished he were here. His absence loomed so large, cast a shadow over all of them and he wondered how many times others would remark on it today.

'It seems so odd, unreal, me in this dress waiting to get married, must be worse though for Mum, thinking of her wedding day and Dad not here. Did you go to their wedding, Frank, what was it like?'

Of all the many weddings he'd been to over the years he'd never forgotten Alice and Julian's, the day he'd known for sure that Alice would never be his.

'Yes,' he said, 'I did go. I was Julian's best man. Your mother was so young, younger than you even, and your father... Well, he looked very distinguished, so proud of her, both so in love.' He smiled at Laura though his heart ached. He had been in love with Alice himself but seeing her with Julian he'd known he didn't stand a chance, and the last thing he wanted was to spoil their relationship, so he'd stayed away, made his life in France.

'What was she like then, my mother?' Laura asked. 'I can't imagine her younger than me, did she do mad things, like she says she's going to do now?'

'I'm sure she did, but I didn't meet her until she was almost engaged to your father and he had tamed her a bit, but she's as she is now, a bit older of course and a mother, but she still has the same magic.' If only he hadn't lost her trust by destroying her image of a man she thought was a perfect husband.

'Oh, Frank, you sound as if you're a little in love with her yourself,' Laura teased him.

He smiled back, 'Do I? Well, you're the one in love today and we better get you to the church.'

She took a deep breath, 'Yes, I'm ready.' She let go of his hand and walked to the door. She glanced at herself in the

300

hall mirror. 'I hardly recognise myself,' she said, staring at the vision in white in the mirror.

'It's you all right, a stunning woman. Douglas is a very lucky man,' he said, picking up her bouquet, also of white and pale pink flowers, that lay on the table by the door and handing it to her.

She watched him in the mirror. 'Do you think I'm doing the right thing? I don't think Mum does. She thinks I'm using Douglas as a father figure, a sort of replacement for Dad. Do you think that, Frank?'

It was too late now to say perhaps she was, and perhaps it would have been more prudent to have waited a little longer to see if marriage to Douglas and being stepmother to two young children was what she really wanted, but how did anyone ever know if a marriage, however well thought through, would last? He'd loved Simone, or thought he had, and she him, but after a few years together both admitted that they were acting out the part of a married couple, and apart from the children there was no depth to their union. He was away often on business, so that didn't help, though she could have come with him sometimes but chose not to.

'No one can predict how a marriage or a relationship will pan out,' he said gently, 'but Douglas is a good man and loves you, so I'd say you have more than a fair chance it will work.'

'Mum and Dad loved each other but then we found out that all the time he had a son with someone else... your sister,' she added hurriedly as if she was warning herself not to say anything unpleasant about it. 'He should have told her, told us...'

'I don't know why he didn't tell your mother, but remember he was much older than she was, had lived a life before he'd met her, and perhaps he thought it better to keep quiet, or even meant to tell her but there never seemed the time and then it was too late, we'll never know. But forget that all now, Laura. This is your day and though a bride is meant to be late we mustn't overdo it.'

He helped her into the waiting car; the bridesmaids, Lexie and Zara, were meeting them at the church. Johnny had refused to walk with her up the aisle, wanting to be with his father until the last minute.

Alice, Evie and Raffi should be there by now. He wished he'd been able to take Alice in his arms and hold her to try and soothe her fears and battered feelings. He understood how she felt betrayed by Julian though, wishing he were with her to share this special day.

Perhaps he'd been wrong to tell Alice about Henry and Ned, it was not really his story to tell.

But he couldn't think like this today, on Laura's wedding day. He must keep her nerves at bay as the car edged forward over Putney Bridge towards the church.

Chapter 43

Alice felt spaced out as if she were acting a role in a film. Here she was, mother-of-the-bride, grandmother of her second daughter's child, and she didn't feel like either. It was as if these roles had been foisted upon her when she wasn't looking.

It was a relief that some of her old friends were here. They greeted her warmly, and though no one actually voiced it, the words hung heavy between them, mourning Julian's absence. Friends hugged her tighter, laid a hand on her arm, their eyes eloquent in their understanding, and for that she was grateful. If anyone had elaborated on the tragedy of his absence she would have burst into tears.

Cecily, who'd arrived with Kalinda, made the only reference to his loss. 'Even if you can no longer see them, they never leave us,' she said, squeezing her hand. 'You look wonderful and so do your girls, especially the bride. It will work out, you'll see.'

'It better,' she smiled at her, pleased she had come.

Frank was never far from her side during the day. She sensed that he was keeping an eye on her, making sure she was not alone, though her friends kept close to her too, especially Margot and Petra. Glen hovered between them awkwardly, drinking a little too much and shooting looks from time to time in Frank's direction as if he were wondering if he could approach him and ask about the case against his company. All the directors had been suspended while the various matters were being investigated.

Douglas seemed relaxed and happy; he introduced Alice to some more of his relatives and some friends from his chambers. Elspeth, safe in navy, and her sister, Margaret, a far more amusing woman, with a round and jolly husband, kept watch over the children. Freya and Nick beamed proudly at Lexie who looked adorable in her dress. She and Zara had taken their role very seriously, though there'd been a slight tussle over who would hold Laura's bouquet during the short marriage service. Johnny, with encouragement from Frank, had walked up the aisle with them. He was dressed in a smart jacket and long trousers, but he refused to do any more and sat happily in the pew next to Frank when he'd done his bit, and asked him in a loud whisper when he would take him paragliding.

Their 'other grandparents' had not been invited, as, Laura told her, although they were the children's grandparents, they were also the parents of Douglas's first wife, and though he got on well enough with them it would be awkward to have them there.

'I suppose so, but families come in so many different shapes and sizes today, I wouldn't have been surprised to see them here,' Alice said.

They'd had the speeches before the dinner and Frank's touched her deeply, saying how he felt so honoured to be taking Julian's place, though he could never hope to fill it. The stunning cake was cut after supper, so now all that was left was the dancing. Alice rather wished she could go home, be alone to absorb it all.

Cecily, who'd stayed until after supper, came to say goodbye. 'Your girls are now settled one way or another, so your life is your own, Alice, some of it anyway, so seize it and enjoy it.' Her glance flickered over to Frank for a second before she turned back to her and kissed her goodbye, leaving Alice feeling perplexed. What did Cecily mean? Join the queue of her besotted women friends to worship Frank, or live free like Frank, travelling all over the place?

Elspeth, leaving with Zara and Johnny, interrupted her thoughts. She made a great display of them saying goodbye to their father as if he were leaving for a war zone instead of his honeymoon early the next day.

The music for the dancing began, and one or two of her old friends – contemporaries of Julian's – got up to dance with her, but it was Frank who insisted on the first dance.

He held her close, but not too close. 'You're doing wonderfully and I know how hard you find it,' he smiled down at her.

'I can't think. It doesn't seem real,' she said, conscious of the others watching them; Margot and especially Petra's sharp eyes ready to pick up the slightest spark between them. 'And thank you for your speech,' her eyes filled with tears and she couldn't go on.

He held her closer and they danced in silence a moment before he said, 'It is all real enough, and now the girls have their own families, I... wondered,' he paused and she had to lean closer to him to hear. 'You said you wanted to ski the four valleys. How about it after Christmas?'

She frowned; did he mean with him or that she should just go and do it?

He took her frown as disapproval with him and a shadow of despondency crossed his face. 'Think about it anyway.'

The music ended and he took her back to the table, and Petra jumped up as eager as an adolescent faced with a rock star and grabbed him.

'My turn, please Frank. You dance so beautifully,' and he laughed and took her outstretched hand and led her to the floor.

After a few more dances with friends, Alice got up to go to the loo and check on her make-up. The house, where they were having the reception, had large rooms downstairs and a front lawn overlooking the Thames where they had the marquee, where the dinner had been served and they now danced. She went up the stairs; the wood surrounds darkened over the years made it seem full of shadows. A mishmash of pictures hung on the walls of the narrow, dimly lit passages, with various rooms, all the doors closed leading off them. The Ladies on the first floor was quite crowded, mostly with young women jostling for the mirror to touch up their make-up, and Alice, feeling the need for a moment's peace from it all, knowing that there was another loo on the top floor, went on up to it.

She had the room to herself and when she was ready she came out and, deep in thought about the event and Frank's suggestion of skiing, she turned the wrong way. It was dustier here and realising her mistake she turned back. She heard a noise, whispering, a giggle, then silence. The passage took a turn, curving down towards the back of the house and instinctively she turned towards it. In the murky light she saw two people close together and in a moment they went into one of the rooms and closed the door but not before she had seen the back of Laura's long white dress. Alice smiled; no doubt she and Douglas were snatching a

306

few moments alone, and who could blame them?

She turned and went down stairs to the hall and the first person she saw was Douglas. Her heart stopped.

He smiled, 'Alice. Have you see Laura?'

'No, I haven't.' She couldn't look him in the eye but she had to steer him away from upstairs. What if Laura came down with... with who? Had she invited some ex-boyfriend and they were sharing one last embrace? But which boyfriend, she hadn't had that many and no one particularly special.

'Must be in the Ladies,' Douglas said. 'You didn't see her up there?'

'There're are a couple of loos up there and one was occupied with lots of girls, so perhaps that is where she is,' Alice said quickly.

'If she doesn't come soon, I'll send out a search party. In the meantime, how about a dance.' He smiled.

'I... I'd love one later... my shoes are a bit tight. But thanks, Douglas... Later would be lovely.'

'I'll come and find you then,' he said and left her to go back to his friends.

Hastily, in panic mode, Alice examined everyone in the room, wondering who on earth Laura could be with. It was difficult to know; some people had already left, others could be outside in the small front garden getting some fresh air, or smoking. She saw Frank and went towards him.

Freya was sitting with a sleepy Lexie in her arms, and she said as Alice passed, 'Have you seen Nick anywhere, Alice, I think it's time we took this one home.'

Then she knew, knew without doubt that it was Nick who had pulled Laura into that room. She felt sick. She mumbled something about looking for him and saw Freya glance with relief at Evie who'd come onto the dance floor with Luke. 'I'll ask Frank,' Alice said. 'Get him to go to the Gents, see if he's there.'

Frank was talking to some of Julian's friends when she came up to him. He turned to smile at her but saw by her expression that something had happened and came at once to her. 'What is it, come and sit down,' he took her arm.

'No,' she said. Standing firm and leaning close to him, she whispered, 'I was upstairs at the top floor loo and I saw Laura... and I'm certain, as he's missing and his wife wants to go home, that Nick is with her, they went into a room up there together.'

'Oh God,' he said. 'Can that man never keep himself under control. I'll go and find them, sort it out if I can.'

'Oh... thank you Frank. Do you think Laura's now regretting this? I mean, going off with another man on her wedding day... it's...' Alice felt faint; surely Laura's marriage couldn't end on the day it began?

He pressed her arm, 'Let me deal with it. You say they are at the top of the house.'

She nodded, explained the layout by the passage and the room she'd seen them enter. He squeezed her arm and left her, and Petra, who'd been watching, said, 'What's up, Alice, is everything all right?'

She forced a smile and joined her at her table. 'Fine, are you enjoying it, the band's great isn't it?'

'It's all right.' Petra studied her face. 'I just wondered if something had happened about Glen, you looked so solemn talking to Frank and now he's hurried off somewhere. There aren't police at the door wanting to arrest him, are there?'

'Of course not, Petra, it's just something about... the staff. It's easier for Frank to deal with it than me.' Alice was relieved when Keith, one of the men at the table, got up to claim Petra for the dance she'd promised him, and for a moment she was left in peace.

She saw Nick appear, he couldn't help but see her as she was in his line of vision. He pointedly ignored her and going up to Freya he announced loudly that he'd been looking all over for her. 'We must have kept missing each other, you going out of one door while I came in, pantomime style,' he said.

'I've been sitting here with Lexie, so you can't have been looking that hard,' Freya eyed him sharply.

'I didn't see you,' he said lamely, picking up the sleeping child and making for the exit, leaving Freya to say goodbye.

Alice went to her, praying Freya didn't know about Nick and Laura. 'You're not going all the way to Suffolk tonight, are you?'

'No, we're staying with my sister who lives in Clapham,' she hugged her. 'Thank you so much, Alice, it was wonderful. I expect Nick will come back to say goodbye when he's put Lexie in the car.'

'Don't worry, you'll want to be on your way,' Alice said, certain that Nick would not return.

Frank appeared back in the room, he came over to her and took her in his arms to dance. 'I've dealt with it,' he said in her ear. 'Sent him packing. I don't know how far it would have gone if I hadn't arrived, but I don't think it was much more than a few kisses.'

Before she could answer she saw Laura come into the room. She looked pale but calm as if she had settled something in her mind. Douglas appeared smiling and she hugged him and he swept her up in a dance.

The party broke up soon after, Laura and Douglas had an early flight and left for an airport hotel. Evie and Luke, who was a charming but rather fey young man who obviously adored Evie, went off somewhere else together. A friend had collected Raffi much earlier in the evening and Frank drove Alice home.

'What did Laura say when you caught them?' she asked as they drove over Putney Bridge, the river like black oil gleaming in the moonlight.

'She didn't see me, the door was slightly ajar and I pushed it open. She had her back to me but Nick saw me, that was enough.'

'He ruins everything. Laura's had a crush on him forever and I suppose he knew it and played on it, though she shouldn't have gone off alone with him. But seeing her with Douglas at the end, I think in a way it settled things for her. She looked very happy to be with Douglas. Laura needs to depend on people and I think she realised that Nick can never be depended upon, but Douglas can.' Alice said, wondering how far Laura would have gone if Frank had not caught them?

'That's a relief, it would be dreadful for a marriage to end on the day it started.' He turned to her. 'Think about what I said about skiing, there's a chalet in Switzerland that I can borrow, belongs to my cousin, we could go there, and ski the four valleys, would you like that, Alice?'

His voice was gentle and she felt he was asking her something very important. She was free now to choose her own life with both her daughters in their own relationships. She didn't know what to say to him.

As she didn't speak, Frank said, 'I know you're angry with me for telling you about Ned, souring your picture of Julian, but he, like the rest of us, made mistakes. Let it go, Alice, before it eats you alive.'

'I can't think about it now,' she said, wishing they could

go back to how it was before she'd known about it.

They'd reached her front door now and he stopped the car. 'Will you be all right? I'll come in if you don't want to be alone.'

His voice was tender, it made her want to cry and cling to him but she was afraid of embarrassing him, being like some of her girl friends who flirted so outrageously with him, hoping for an affair. But she was not like that, she had never had a love affair apart from with Julian, and she had married him. She felt shy about it all, knowing she could not embark on an affair with Frank, it would not be enough. If ever they made love she would want to commit to him forever. She felt very tired and flat and needed be alone to mull over the day.

'I'm fine, thank you Frank. Evie will be back sometime, but I can't thank you enough for everything, it was such a lovely day. We'll meet up soon and I'll think about skiing. It sounds very tempting.' She got of the car, taking her house key out of her bag and he took it from her and unlocked her front door.

'Sure you're OK?' His hand was on her arm.

'I'm sure,' she hugged him hard and felt his lips against her cheek. 'Thanks so much again for everything,' she said and shot inside before she lost control and dragged him into the house with her.

Chapter 44

The tumultuous year had ended. Christmas had come and gone. Alice with her daughters and Douglas, spent it in the cottage in Suffolk; Laura wanted Douglas to see it and his children were with their mother. Evie wanted to be close to Luke, who spent part of the holiday with them and the rest with his parents who lived in Cambridge. Frank was in France with his children.

It was Raffi who made it such a success. His fascination with the coloured lights and the sparkling decorations on the tree, bringing his own magic to the occasion.

Alice greeted the New Year with a mixture of relief and trepidation. Surely it couldn't throw up any worse changes than had occurred already, could it? She was a grandmother in circumstances she wouldn't have wished for, though Raffi had stolen her heart and Johnny too, and she couldn't imagine a life now without them.

Raffi and Evie were about to move to Norfolk to live with Luke in a large, rather ramshackle house that once belonged to his grandparents. It would give him room to do his sculpture and there was a studio with good light for Evie to continue her illustrations and, as Alice remarked to Cecily, they suited each other well, both driven by their creative personalities, spurring each other on to produce their best work, and both adoring Raffi.

Alice saw how content Laura now seemed with Douglas. He had come out of himself since the day she'd first met him, and she realised now how perfect they were for each other. Perhaps his first wife had been too domineering, squashing him into the dull man Alice had first thought him to be. Nick was never spoken of. They'd glimpsed him briefly in church at Christmas but neither girl remarked on it.

As January slipped by, Alice saw more of Johnny, sometimes collecting him from school and keeping him until Douglas or Laura got home. Zara was at a different school and always seemed to be busy with friends or activities, and for that she was relieved, finding her rather bossy and spoilt, though she accepted that that was probably her way of coping with the difficult changes in her life. Johnny was slowly emerging from his shell and he kept asking when Frank would take him paragliding.

'He's very busy, but if your father lets you go to watch, I know he'll take you. It's too cold and grey now, wait until the spring,' she told him, wondering when, if ever, she'd see Frank again.

She had barely seen him since the wedding. He'd come round the following day to see how she was but Evie and Luke were there with Raffi. Evie had immediately asked him about Ned and when they could meet him, and Frank, glancing apprehensively at her, had said that Ned was very committed to his job in the US just now but he hoped a meeting would happen some time in the future.

'Well, I must go,' Frank had got up then, 'I've got work to finish here before I leave for France.' He kissed Evie goodbye and Alice followed him to the door.

When they reached it, he had turned to her. 'I've got a couple of assignments to do back home after Christmas but when I've finished them, I want you to come skiing with me,' he said quietly. He was standing so close to her and though they were not touching she imagined that she felt the warmth of him leaching into her and it was all she could do not to reach out and hold him. 'Remember,' he went on with a smile, 'you did say you wanted to ski the four valleys, Alice. And I'm going to hold you to it.'

'But I'm hardly fit enough, I haven't skied for a couple of years,' she said, thinking that that wish must surely stay a dream.

'But you're a good skier I'm sure, you went almost every year, didn't you? You perhaps need to get fit, go to the gym, we'll do it or anyway a part of it, start at Mont Fort. I'll send you the tickets then you'll have to come.' He'd kissed her goodbye, holding her close to him a moment before opening the door to leave.

She remembered Margot wasting away with anxiety, and said, 'Can you tell me if Glen will be all right?'

He frowned, 'There's nothing new about decent people getting caught up in various dodgy practices, especially when those in charge do it too or don't keep a strict enough eye on things. I don't know. I'll be in touch when I get back.' He kissed her again on her cheek. 'Get your skiing things out,' he said and was gone.

Frank's words about Glen and his firm did not comfort her but Margot would cope; hard though it might be, she would come through. She thought of the shattering changes in her own life, things never stayed the same forever and the only way to survive the difficult bits was to keep going.

Their nursery basket business was going well and the two of them concentrated on that. They worked from Alice's house as Margot felt intimidated in hers, the luxurious home she'd adored now felt tainted after the heavy-footed raid on it and also, though she didn't say but Alice guessed, relations between her and Glen were strained, but Margot was a stayer and she was pretty sure she wouldn't leave him over this.

While they worked together, one dark and gloomy afternoon in February, Petra had come over to see them, the three old friends together, Alice told them about Ned.

'I don't believe it? Julian? He always seemed so straight-forward. What you saw was what you got, a dear, dependable man with no secrets.' Margot and Petra were both amazed.

'How did you find out?' Petra asked. 'Did he turn up?'

'No... Frank told me.' She then told them about that afternoon when she'd glimpsed Ned and thought he was Julian. 'Ned is Frank's sister's child, but it all happened before Julian and I met, and his sister is happily married to someone else and lives in New Jersey,' she finished with a rush.

'Who'd have thought it? So no wonder they were such friends, they shared a family... and a secret,' Petra said in surprise.

Alice said no more, Petra was fascinated but Margot was quiet, her face pensive, then she said, 'It's not as bad a secret as Glen's... I don't know how much he is involved in this financial business. We don't talk about it but... well I'm so frightened.' She burst into tears and Alice held her, trying to comfort her.

Petra, stroking Margot's back, asked, 'What does Frank say about it?'

Margot blew her nose and faced them. 'He can't say

anything while he's working on it and he must keep away from us, be impartial.'

'He needn't be impartial with me,' Petra said. 'I'll arrange for drinks, have him round.' She smiled at them all, fired up with her idea. 'It's such a dreary time of year, we need to keep cheerful.'

'He'll hardly tell you anything at a party, at least I hope he won't.' Margot was rather irritated with Petra for seeing their disaster as a topic for party gossip.

Alice had not heard from Frank since Christmas and she assumed he was in France. He'd told her he had work to do there. Then one evening he rang and asked her out to supper.

'I've finished my part in reporting on Glen's firm,' he said when they were settled in a quiet corner of a cosy restaurant in Kensington.

'So it's all over?' Alice tensed herself for what he was going to say.

'No, but I've finished for the moment. I'm afraid there will probably be a court case, well bound to be, there's been some highly corrupt practices going on. The management seemed to have lost all sense of their responsibility. There are some big names involved but I think Glen is safe, safe from jail anyway. He's made a few bad decisions, but I don't think he'll be prosecuted, though they'll all lose their jobs and the perks that came with it.'

'That's a sort of relief, but will they lose the house?' She felt sympathy for Margot who'd spent so much time and energy doing up her house, but then she no longer felt happy there now so she might not find it so hard to move.

He nodded. 'It's not going to be easy for them, but when the fuss has died down Glen will probably get another job but...' He reached across the table and took her hand. 'Perhaps everyone has a secret, and it doesn't always mean the end of everything.'

'Yes, I've been thinking that,' she said. 'I'm sorry if I was...'

'I understand,' he interrupted her, 'we all carry secrets and sometimes we don't tell them because we're afraid it will damage the relationship. We don't quite trust it to be strong enough to survive any difficult news. Julian might have felt that with you, after all you are so much younger and so beautiful, and at the back of his mind he might have been afraid that you would leave him for someone else.'

'Surely not, he was so strong, so dependable,' she protested.

'Outwardly yes, but who knows the insecurities that lurk inside us all. I don't know why he didn't tell you but it wouldn't surprise me if it didn't have something to do with that.' His eyes were bright on her face and she felt closer to him than she ever had, he went on quietly, 'You have to be sure of a relationship before you bare your soul, Alice.'

'I suppose so,' she said, puzzled by his words.

Frank let go her hand and picked up the menu, 'Sorry, let's not get too heavy now, I hope you're hungry.'

After dinner, he dropped her home and they sat in the dark of the car a moment before she got out. 'I'm going back to France tomorrow but I want to take you skiing as I said I would, take us both out of the life we know into something else. Early March, we'll meet at Geneva airport, you will come, won't you?' He turned to her and for a moment she thought she would refuse, afraid that she wouldn't match up to him, afraid of the feeling that he was offering her something more than just a skiing holiday.

'Remember you wanted to break out, do exciting things, you've test-driven a sports car, paraglided and now only skiing remains on your list and the time for that will run out as the season changes.'

It was four weeks away; she wasn't busy, not really. Her daughters were settled for the moment, and Margot was grateful to immerse herself in their small business. Alice had said she wanted excitement and now here it was being offered to her, was she going to be coward enough to turn it down, just continue on as she always had?

'I will come,' she said though she felt fearful.

'Good, I'll book it all and send you the tickets.' They got out of the car and stood in front of her house that was in darkness and empty of children. She wondered for a moment if he would come in, but he kissed her, gently on her cheek. 'Until then,' he said. 'I'll be waiting there for you.'

She smiled and went inside, snapping on the lights to give life to the empty house. What was she thinking? No doubt he had a girlfriend waiting for him in France, she might join them and perhaps there'd be a group of his friends.

The tickets arrived a fortnight before they were meeting. She felt excited, yet nervous too. It would be the first proper holiday she'd had since Julian's death. She looked out her ski clothes. She'd hire boots and skis out there.

It was strange yet exciting arriving at Geneva airport alone. She'd told everyone she was going skiing with Frank, and they'd been pleased for her. Cecily had smiled, taken her hand, 'I'm so glad, Alice. Love's quite elastic, you know.' She glanced at the photographs of her two dead lovers; 'There's always plenty to share with others.'

Frank was waiting for her, her spirits lifted when she saw him. He came joyfully towards her and kissed her, holding her close. 'It's so good to see you, Alice,' he said, taking her case and with his other hand, took hers and led her out towards his car.

He had a different Bristol with him to the dark blue one she remembered from so long ago. It was sleek and silver grey and they drove on up the valley to the resort perched high in the mountains, the small houses and villages scattered below them. She reminded him of the last time she'd driven with him when she was young and the children had not been born.

'I remember,' he said, smiling at her, 'we went quite fast, I won't try it here we might go over the edge.'

'Please don't,' she said watching the narrow road in front of them

The chalet was small, overlooking the valley. 'There's a chalet girl, or I think a boy this time, who'll come in and clean and everything, get us breakfast if you want,' he said as he took her case and put it into one of the rooms and his own luggage in another.

There seemed to be no one else there though she saw another bedroom. She felt a little relieved but also regretful. He was taking her skiing, helping her achieve her wish, she reminded herself firmly. She must not be like Petra and expect a more intimate relationship. Frank was Julian's great friend, Laura's godfather, a close family friend, which perhaps was a more lasting relationship than that of a lover.

She had little time to reflect on their relationship as they rushed down to the village to rent her skies and boots and then had supper with Frank's friends. He seemed to know a lot of people out here. They got back late to the chalet and both were only too glad to sink into their own beds and sleep.

For three days, their life was the same, skiing all day, sometimes just the two of them, sometimes with friends, and every evening pleasantly tired. With all their exercise they slept well… alone. Frank was friendly and kind but there was no hint of a romance.

The day came when they were to ski part of the four valleys.

They reached the hut at Mont Four at the end of the afternoon, straggling up the steep path to reach it perched in the mountains. The day-skiers were setting off on their last run home, leaving those skiers who were spending the night here to the majesty of the sky, the snow and the ring of mountains all around them. Frank and Alice took off their skies, leaving them in the entrance before going into the warm, wood-lined hut, the welcoming smell of hot soup waiting for them. There were rooms off the main living area, each holding four narrow beds where the skiers snatched a few hours of sleep before getting up at first light to set off on the first run. It was important to catch the snow at each place at the right time when it was cold and crisp enough not to give way.

'I've been here for lunch in the day but I never really took it in,' Alice said to Frank. 'Now at the end of the day it feels different, wonderful, just us few in the world.' She turned to him, her eyes shining, an energy driving through her, lifting her spirits.

'Wait until the sun goes down,' he said smiling at her, 'it is magic.'

They stood a little apart from the others, looking out over the sea of mountain peaks. The sun was slipping down the sky, drenching the mountains in pink and gold in one last flourish before it sank. The silence was extraordinary, deep and meaningful, and even the hardened skiers were awed by it all.

Frank put his arm round her and pulled her close to him. 'I am so happy to be here with you, Alice, to share this.' He turned to her and she saw his love for her in his eyes. She leant towards him and he kissed her. After a while he drew away, his arms looped round her waist. 'I've been in love with you for so long.' His face was close to hers. She could feel the warmth of his breath on her cheek. 'I loved you from that first time I met you with Julian, but I saw how much you loved each other so I wasn't going to hang around, get in the way, so I went to live in France. I thought my feelings would fade over time, but when I saw you again I knew my love was as strong as ever.' He smiled, stroked her face with the tip of his fingers. 'I'm telling you the secret I've held close with me all these years and you can do with it what you want.'

'I didn't know that, Frank.' She was surprised at his confession. 'I loved Julian, only had eyes for him, but when you came back after he'd died, that time you found me pruning that tree, I felt...' She paused, 'Well, I just knew I wanted to be with you, but I didn't know if you had a wife, a girlfriend... If you were free, or,' she laughed, a little self consciously, 'would be the slightest bit interested... romantically I mean, in me.'

The sky was getting darker as the glow of the sun slipped away into the velvet darkness behind the mountains that surrounded them. The moon, like a great silver ball, hung above. Alice, safe in Frank's arms, felt that they were enclosed in the power of nature.

'There is no one in my life, but I hope there is you,' he said. 'I have waited for you for so long.'

'I love you,' she said, the joy of it rising in her as they kissed again.

Then she remembered outside that car showroom when

she'd asked Julian for help to cope with their girls and the bombshells they'd dropped on her. Frank had suddenly come into her mind. It was a foolish thought perhaps, but had it come from him? Now it was time to let Julian go and love again.